Praise for the *Irregular* series

'A rip-roaring and action-packed derr...
tongue-in-cheek fun at modern thriller tu...
Irish Independe...

'Engaging series of historical thrillers . . .
at pace, the characters are engaging an... ...burst
with action. But Lyle's great strength is in his depiction of
time and place; from its stinking tenements, where babies cry
from hunger, to its sinister docks and upmarket brothels, the
Edwardian city - then still part of Britain - is brought to life in all
its squalid, magnificent glory'
Financial Times

'Full throttle . . . delivering entertainment in spades'
Myles McWeeney

'What HB Lyle has done . . . is nothing short of inspirational.
There are echoes of John Buchan in these books, and enough
hard-core spy stuff to keep aficionados happy. The story ends
with a promise there could be more adventures with Wiggins
should the author choose to record them. We can but hope'
Spybrary

'Thoroughly entertaining'
Mail on Sunday

'Cracking pace, tension, twists and humour. It mixes a hot plot
and historical events with real and fictional characters'
Sun

'Lyle truly captures the spirit of Conan Doyle in these playful,
gripping yarns'
Daily Mirror

'Ripping fun for fans'
Peterborough Telegraph

Also by H.B. Lyle

H.B. LYLE

Spy Hunter

**HODDER &
STOUGHTON**

First published in Great Britain in 2023 by Hodder & Stoughton Limited
An Hachette UK company

This paperback edition published in 2024

2

A CIP catalogue record for this title is available from the British Library

Paperback ISBN 978 1 399 70262 1
ebook ISBN 978 1 399 70263 8

Typeset in Plantin Light by Manipal Technologies Limited.

Printed and bound in Great Britain by Clays Ltd, Elcograf S.p.A.

Hodder & Stoughton policy is to use papers that are natural, renewable
and recyclable products and made from wood grown in sustainable forests.
The logging and manufacturing processes are expected to conform to the
environmental regulations of the country of origin.

Hodder & Stoughton Ltd
Carmelite House
50 Victoria Embankment
London EC4Y 0DZ

www.hodder.co.uk

For Annalise, R and E

Sunday 28 June 1914

Magnificence on wheels. The most wonderful thing he'd ever seen. A line of them, catching the sunshine in metallic bursts. A motorcade of power. Mehmed Mehmedbasic watches as the glorious cars go past and onwards down the Appel Quay. His hand closes around the pistol in his pocket but he does not draw it, does not do what he promised.

Nedeljko Cabrinovic did not care so much for cars. He stood on the thin riverside pavement, pressed between idiots waving imperial flags. The approaching cars winked and glared in the flitting sunshine. Heat crinkled the dusty quay. Faint cheers rolled towards the nineteen-year-old Serb. Young girls crowded the upper windows of the school opposite.

He could see the Archduke, now, fifty yards and closing. The purpled plumes of his ridiculous hat bent and fluttered in the wind. Twenty yards now. The third car in the line. Light blue, like the clear Bosnian sky, his country's sky, not Austria-Hungary's.

Cabrinovic ripped the cap from his grenade and stepped forward. He flung it at the car. But the speed of the magnificent motorcar surprised him. He threw too late. The grenade bounced off the rolled-down roof at the back and trickled along the road.

Kaboom! The grenade detonated under the car behind, blowing it over. The explosion shocked even Cabrinovic. His ears rang. Women screamed. Men roared out in pain. The Archduke's car burst forward, a smacked horse.

Cabrinovic cursed. Across the road a man stared at him, pointed, shouted. Then another. Then a gendarme came running. Whistles blew. More police now, and other men, shouting, running, screaming. Cabrinovic turned, vaulted over the wall and dropped fifteen feet into the Miljacka river.

The water only came up to his knees and for a moment the shock stalled him. But gendarmes streamed over the wall after him, and he began to stumble across the stones out into the river. He fumbled the cyanide pill from his pocket. He had no idea if the dose would be enough. None of the Black Hand did, but they'd all vowed to go down in glory. Death and glory and the Empire would never be the same again.

He jammed the pill into his mouth just as the gendarmes closed. The public too, each to get a boot or fist in where they could, before Cabrinovic was hauled away. The cyanide had failed to kill, just like he had.

Further up the Appel Quay, the Archduke's car sped on. It passed Trifko Grabez, Cvjetko Popovic, Vaso Cubrilovic and Gavrilo Princip. The men, teenagers, students, each alone in the crowd at points along the route, each armed with pistol, grenade and cyanide, could only watch on as the limousine raced by.

Once they realised that the Archduke had survived the blast – his speeding car, his ridiculous plumage signalling to all that he lived – Grabez, Popovic and Cubrilovic presumed their deadly game was up. Their chance had gone, and so they slunk away. News of the bombing rippled along the crowd, but they had seen Franz Ferdinand motor by at pace. He was alive. They had failed.

Princip, nineteen, did not make that decision. He had smuggled into Bosnia from Belgrade, hiding in his own country, a Slav, and he would not give up so easily. He felt the FN10 Browning semi-automatic pistol in his pocket. Cold comfort, but comfort all the same. The flag-waving disciples dispersed around him. Some complained about the Archduke's rudeness, the speed of his car, while others speculated about the commotion further along the river. Princip too wondered about this and he set off towards the site of the first bomb, to see what damage had been wrought. But then he stopped, and turned back. He remembered the Archduke's itinerary.

The bombing will have thrown those plans awry but he looked up at the street sign on the wall. Franz Joseph Street. On his left, the Latin Bridge over the Miljacka. Behind him, the smell of dark, thick coffee caught in his throat. Schiller's, a German cafe. No, Austrian. Here on Slav soil. A reminder he needed. For if the Archduke did stay on schedule, he would come back down the Appel Quay and turn right here, into this street towards the old town. Princip decided to wait.

Archduke Franz Ferdinand, together with his wife Sophie, did indeed change his plans. He spoke at the town hall, he joked about the 'warm' welcome the city had given him, and then he resolved to skip the tour of the old town and head straight to the hospital to look in on those injured by Cabrinovic's grenade. Unfortunately, no one told his driver.

The magnificent motorcar trundled back down the Appel Quay, this time with the river on its left. The crowds had thinned, especially on the river side of the road, for the sun burned fearfully hot, despite the early hour.

Princip sensed the car's approach before he saw it. A throaty roar, a ripple among those watching on. He stepped back, around the corner into Franz Joseph Street, out of the glare of the sun and the oppression of the blue, blue sky. He waited. Hoped, hand on the FN10 Browning in his pocket.

The motorcar did indeed slow when it came to the bridge, and turned right into Franz Joseph Street. An army officer riding the tailboard shouted out. Someone cried. The car screeched to a halt. Another shout, then the engine stalled. Finally, the magnificent Graf and Stift PS 28/32 Double Phaeton failed.

Gavrilo Princip saw this all happen, right in front of him. He stepped forward and discharged two bullets at the passengers in the car. The first bullet lodged deep in Sophie's stomach. The second nicked the jugular vein in the Archduke's neck.

Gendarmes scragged Princip in seconds. He stood as they engulfed him, shocked and stilled by what he had just done. He did not feel the blows, nor hear the shouts and screams.

Nor did he hear the man, Archduke Franz Ferdinand, utter the words which turned out to be his last. 'It's nothing, it's nothing, it's nothing.'

I

'Wiggins,' a faint cry went up.

'Wiggins!' Another voice, louder now.

'WIGGINS,' cried a third, closer still.

'Wot?'

'I don't know wot fucking wot. Get your arse down here!'

Wiggins sighed. The best thing about his job was the inaccessibility of it, the sheer impossibility of being reached by mere mortals, those who could not climb the towering cranes and traverse from iron beam to iron beam, carefree of the drop. He leaned out, over the side of the criss-crossed iron structure, and glanced down to the distant ground. 'Give us a mo,' he said to the red-faced bellower below.

He knew what they wanted. He'd watched from his vantage point on top of the crane. He'd been sent up, with ropes slung over his shoulder, to rig, up in the sky, where the gulls cawked and swooped. The Thames, a river of work and history, bending below past the Houses of Parliament in one direction and along underneath the bands of bridges, twisting out through the heart of an empire, where nations are traded and fortunes lost, to the busiest port in the world, wreathed in industrial smoke. Stood atop this, Wiggins could see the shimmering heat haze of the hills in the distance, and sighed once more.

He knew why they called his name. He'd seen the reason, pigeon-toeing his way across Westminster Bridge twenty minutes earlier, the high sheen of his top hat catching the sun even from a distance. A man, even at two hundred paces, dressed so perfectly, so just so, that the very idea of him turning into a building site – even one so vast and grand as County Hall – was an anathema to common sense. No one on Westminster Bridge, as it reluctantly approached more down-at-heel Lambeth, would fail to be surprised to see such a well turned-out gent picking his way off the main road and through the ruts, shouts and dust of the big dig.

Wiggins clambered expertly down. He had been half-way up one of the tendrils of the great crane. There were fifteen or so cranes arrayed across the site, and each had a long bending shaft that rose up into the sky. At the base of these shafts stood a platform, raised off the ground by three iron 'legs' each criss-crossed with iron supports. These platforms themselves were enormous, monuments of industry. Those without a head for heights would sway and wobble, clinging to the central shaft. The angled spindles that rose above, tapering into the sky, were the domain only of the 'spidermen', men and boys like Wiggins, who had a stomach for the height and the balance to stay alive. They didn't let women onto the site at all, and so no one knew if women had the chops for it – other than, of course, the tightrope walkers and trapeze artists who swung and sparkled in the vast big tops of Blackheath, or the cavern of Alexandra Palace.

Wiggins slid down the last ladder from the platform and went to meet his one-time boss, Captain Vernon Kell, head of the domestic arm of the British secret service.

Kell stood not to attention as such, but so straight and solitary, as if he were a toy soldier placed there by those giant cranes. Wiggins walked towards him with a slow, considered tread – it's never a good idea to show the quality you're keen. Wiggins hadn't seen Kell in a long time, and him showing up never meant good news. Still, he treated Wiggins better than most toffs did.

'Big show's coming, is it then?' Wiggins said, without preamble.

'How did you? Have you read the papers, I mean, what?' Kell spluttered. 'I didn't think . . .'

Wiggins grinned. 'I ain't read nothing, except your face. Your eyes, even. You're on. They're blazing.'

Kell coloured slightly. 'Right, yes well,' he said at last. 'I resent the implication that I'm excited about the prospect of war.'

'Resent away, I've got work to do.'

'You'll come back?'

'Nah, up there.' Wiggins gestured skyward with a thumb.

'But you must,' Kell insisted. He glanced around at the builders traipsing to and fro, the constant clouds of dust rising from their boots, and drew Wiggins to the side. 'The spring is wound too tight. This assassination, in Bosnia.' He tapped the paper in his hand. 'It's the trigger, I'm sure of it.'

'No ta.'

'You gave me your word. If it ever comes to war, you'll come back. Your word, man.'

'I ain't no gentleman though, am I?' Wiggins gave a half-smile. 'Besides. War's a rich man's game, scored in the lives of poor men.'

'Bolshevism?' Kell looked questioningly, disgusted.

'Ere, did you come straight from the office? Were you followed?'

'No one cares about you,' Kell said bluntly. He had forgotten how insubordinate Wiggins could be, how seemingly unaware he was of their difference in status. He wanted to remind him.

Wiggins looked away, beyond the great cranes out to the river, prickled sweat on his neck, unsurprised Kell had missed his point. Instead, he imagined the taste of the first beer in his mouth later that day. 'I'm alright here.' Wiggins gestured around him. 'Another Monday morning, building a temple of democracy.'

'County Hall?' Kell scoffed. 'Look across there. The mother of all parliaments. That's your temple. That's what we'll fight to save.'

'That knocking shop? Do me a favour. I don't get no vote for that. Not Constance neither.'

'Mrs Kell, to you!' Kell said indignantly.

Wiggins grinned. 'She'd do a better job than half the drunks in there. She should be running the place. I bet you wouldn't be coming round to the likes of me with ya begging bowl if she was in charge.'

Kell scowled. He still had no idea how Wiggins could be so right, so often. He'd spent the first part of the morning pacing the corridors of Whitehall trying to find anyone to agree with him about the importance of the Franz Ferdinand assassination. He had found that no one, not one official, minister or War Office functionary, thought anything of it. Even his friend Soapy in the Cabinet Office was blithe: 'Let them squabble amongst themselves. Have you heard the news from Larne?'

'Yes, well,' he said to Wiggins and dusted away a patch of clay dust from his pinstripes. 'I'm at Watergate House, as I'm sure you know.' He gestured down river. 'If you deign to reconsider, we'll be waiting.'

'There's not going to be a war!' Mansfield Cumming blasted. 'At least, not for a year or two.'

Kell clicked his tongue. His counterpart at the foreign branch of the secret service, Sir Mansfield Cumming, stood up at his desk and waved his hand across the room, as if surveying the globe itself. 'Unless you mean the bloody Irish.'

'I didn't mean the Irish.'

'They're going to rip each other apart if we let them.'

'In Europe,' Kell said, trying not to rise to the older man, who now paced up and down, pointing his pipe.

'None of my agents have reported anything amiss.'

Why would they? thought Kell. Cumming – the foreign service chief – had a rash of incredibly unreliable 'agents' across Europe, most of whom were worthless. They were amateurs, with names like Ruffian, Counterscarp and H2O, who drained Cumming of his budget while providing almost no intelligence at all. It was a racket. At least Kell could rely on the British police to act when he called anything in. That and Wiggins, if he could be persuaded.

Wiggins. The impudence of the man. That Wiggins could refuse his country was one thing, but taking Kell's wife's name in vain was beyond the pale. It made him angry still. Kell had left him an hour earlier, extracting himself from the vast and filthy building site as quickly as possible. He hadn't gone back to Watergate House. Instead, he'd crossed back over Westminster Bridge and made his way to Cumming.

Kell was unsurprised at the older man's reaction. He'd already tried every other door in Whitehall, and it was perhaps too much to hope that Cumming might buck the trend of bureaucratic complacency and indifference. In his view, it was the job of the secret service to jump at every shadow, to fear death and destruction at every turn; it was for them to live the fears no one else dared speak.

'We should let them fight it out,' Cumming broke back in on his thoughts. 'The micks I mean. I'm more worried about these blasted women.'

Kell's ears pricked up at that. 'What do you mean?'

'Haven't you been following the news, man? These bloody suffragettes.'

'I see,' Kell said slowly. It was a difficult subject. Kell's wife, Constance, had been an active suffragist years earlier – an activism that had sent her into a riot on Parliament Square. She'd actually saved *his* life that day. The Metropolitan police had succumbed to a kind of madness, beating and hitting women protesters – one woman even died, although officials managed to suppress that story. Kell had stepped in to help, and was truncheoned by a huge sergeant. He escaped further injury only thanks to Constance's newfound skill at ju-jitsu.

Subsequently, she'd promised to step back from the movement, to avoid any embarrassment. But he suspected her interest had been reignited. How could it not be, if you believed in a cause so stark? When hunger-striking women were being routinely force-fed in prison, so brutally as to amount to torture?

He could only hope that she had the sense to keep herself out of prison. For the moment, she'd stopped telling him where she went in the day, and he'd stopped asking. That's how they protected each other.

In any event, Kell silently recused himself from the subject of suffragism whenever it came up in government. He left Cumming fulminating and went back to Watergate House, just south of the Strand by Charing Cross. He took a cab this time, eager to escape the complacency and ignorance of Cumming, the blindness.

His branch of the secret service – the home section – would not be so stupid, he vowed. Immediately on his return, Kell went upstairs to the roof. He disliked smoking in front of the staff if he could help it. He didn't want them to see his agitation, either. For while the assassination was far off in the Balkans, he knew it meant war. A modern war the likes of which the world had never seen. And he knew Britain was unprepared, in warships, in arms, in training; and most of all (as far as he was concerned) in intelligence. A whole network of German spies was surely at work in the country, had been for years, and their time was coming. He'd barely scratched the surface of this network, he knew, and his ignorance of the rest burned him like a fresh scald. He knew enough to know he knew nothing.

He smoked two cigarettes alone, as a pleasing coolness finally began to settle on the day. He gazed out along the river now, at those great cranes that dotted the vast building site on the southern bank of the Thames. A gigantic grid. It was another thing that troubled Kell, this palace of local democracy, facing Parliament. He saw it as an affront. What right did the people of London have to challenge the government? It would not end well.

Was Wiggins still there, stepping from bar to bar, with the elegance of a dancer? Was there nothing he could not do? Certainly, he had no other agents like him and now he was needed more than ever.

Kell peered at the far-off cranes, but could not see him. Off to drink, no doubt. *He* didn't need any convincing about the coming war. He'd read the truth in his face, damn the man. Like his teacher, too clever to be with, too clever to be without.

'Sir?' The voice of Simpkins, his long-standing secretary, carried across the empty roof.

Kell tossed away his half-smoked cigarette and nodded. 'Coming,' he said, as he watched the tobacco burn and fizzle in the dust.

'Get out of it, you stinking diddycoy fuck.'

A man flew out of the Kings Arms and sprawled onto the street at Wiggins's feet. The pub's door slammed shut and the owner of the voice disappeared back inside.

'Tosher?' Wiggins said. 'What's the matter?'

'Big Ed's in.'

'Not for fucking long,' Wiggins said. He grabbed Tosher by the arm and pulled him back into the pub.

'God's sake,' someone muttered as they came through the doors. 'He facking stinks something rotten, worse than rotten.'

This was true. Tosher, a man in his thirties, was named after his profession. His real name had long been lost and all the folk round Waterloo knew him as Tosher. A tosher was someone who earned their living by scavenging in the sewers, mostly for copper but anything of value. There weren't many left, but Tosher didn't know what else to do. His old man had been a tosher, and his old man before him too, in the golden age of toshing. It was a dying art. He lived in a shed in the backyard of the boarding house where Wiggins lodged, a few streets away.

Wiggins ignored the snide remarks of the others packed into the pub and fixed his eyes on Big Ed. Big Ed worked on the railway engines at Waterloo station and every evening he'd come into one pub or another in the area, stand at the bar and drink his first pint of bitter in a very peculiar way. Wiggins waited and watched, as Big Ed took his red, spotted handkerchief out of his pocket and twisted it into a cord. Then he held each end, reached behind him and drew it tight across the back of his neck. He then leaned down, picked up the pint pot in front of him with his teeth, and slowly tipped his head back. Big Ed drank the entire pint this way, with the glass clamped between his teeth and the beer dribbling around his mouth. Everyone in the pub watched on, conversation stilled, as they did each day he came in. Children would sometimes poke their heads in to watch the sight too, to giggle and cheer this mountainous engineer and his party trick.

Big Ed finished the pint, placed the glass down and held his hands up in triumph. As he did so, Wiggins stepped towards him. 'Aht of it, Ed. Piss off, you're not wanted here.'

Ed glanced sideways but otherwise said nothing. He pointed to the ale pump for another and spoke out of the corner of his mouth. '*He's* not wanted here, the stinking diddy—'

SLAM!

Wiggins smashed Ed's face into the bar.

'Oi!' the landlord cried. 'No fighting.'

'I ain't fighting.' Wiggins glared at him. 'I'm just keeping a good and orderly house cos you don't seem able. And two pints of half and half.'

Big Ed grasped his face and groaned in shock. Wiggins took hold of his collar and dragged him out into the street.

He flung him to the ground. 'I said, piss off.' With that, he turned and went back into the pub.

Tosher stood alone at the bar. Wiggins could hear a couple of comments too, for Tosher did smell a bit. But then, everyone smelled. That was why they were in the pub. That was why most of them smoked. 'He's got a point,' someone muttered. 'The bloke's rank.'

'Cos he's a tosher, not cos he's a diddycoy,' Wiggins snapped back. Then he turned and looked around at everyone in the now silent pub. The two women, sat close by the door, nursing their gin and water. The lined-up pints on the bar in front of the builders from the site, most of whom he recognised. A cabby, his cap resting on a weary shoulder. A knot of young lads, who joked and drank and spent some windfall on the lash. And the old, broken men, scanning the tables for spare booze. Wiggins glanced around at them all.

'This is London,' he slammed his chest. 'Not some shite pile in the sticks. We are everyone. This is who we are.'

The silence went on, a curious sound in such a place. Until finally one of the builders leaning against the bar straightened, picked up his glass, and said, 'I thought drunks is wot we are?'

Wiggins softened. 'Well, if you're buying?'

'Nah, just drinking.'

Wiggins picked up his glass and nodded. The pub breathed again, and turned back to the business of relaxing and drinking. The two women by the door fell back into conversation, and Wiggins heard the gist of it. 'I ain't been the same since those pills the doc gave me, to bring it off.'

There was nowhere like a pub. Wiggins soaked it in, the smell of burning tobacco, stale beer and fresh piss.

Toffs had their drawing rooms, their dining rooms, galleries, even a fucking room for billiards. He had this. The women by the door. 'You should be ashamed, looking so antique.' The professor in the corner, reading the *Daily Sketch*. (They called him the professor because he was a numbers clerk at Legal and General, and could tell you the chances of getting run over by a train at the drop of a hat.) Little Ronnie who ran bets for the bookie down The Cut, who refused to wear a hat cos he said it'd make him go bald, snicking a half of mild before he was off again. Even the mugshots on the wall made Wiggins feel at home. The police insisted all the local prostitutes had their photographs pinned to the wall, as the landlord had to bar them. To protect the morals of this lot, Wiggins smiled. The women didn't mind. The punters used to come in and use it like a menu. It was good for business.

Tosher touched Wiggins's elbow gently, and took his pint. 'I'll be outside,' he said quietly.

'Alright, Tosh, I'll join you,' he replied. 'And remember, always keep your mouth shut when you're under.'

'Always keep it shut,' Tosh smiled sadly. The gypsy, a settled gypsy hence the diddycoy jibe, picked his way through the press to the exit.

'Oi, Judge Jeffries,' the landlord called to Wiggins. 'Got a message for you. Near forgot, what with your sermonising and all. A cabby came in.'

'Which cabby?'

'I don't bloody know. He just said, "Tell Wiggins she's in again. Bow Street, the morro."'

And so Monday 29 June 1914 began to close, with Wiggins drinking on one side of the river and Captain Vernon Kell fretting on the other. The huge

shops of Oxford Street – John Lewis, Selfridges –
and the great titan of Knightsbridge, Harrods,
tried vainly to close their doors, to shut out the
arguing, twittering, voracious hoards that had
jostled and fought through their aisles, search-
ing – fighting – for bargains, for Monday 29 June
1914 was the start of the 'sales', the bargain sea-
son, that no self-respecting shopper could deign
to resist. It was news that made all the papers.

* * *

'Ere mister. Gis a tanner.'

Wiggins stopped. Men streamed around him onto the
building site off Belvedere Road. He turned and peered
again at the pile of rags beside the road. A beggar.

The aging man pinned him with a stare. 'A tanner, sir?'

Wiggins stared back. The last of the men jostled past him
onto the site. A foreman shouted. 'Wiggins! Get your arse
in, it's time.'

The beggar stood up and then stumbled, clutching his
heart. 'Ah, gawd,' he cried and tumbled to the floor.

Wiggins crouched down beside the man. 'I'm do-good-
ing,' Wiggins shouted back.

'Aht your pay,' the foreman replied sourly.

The beggar, flat on the floor, gasped and groaned and
waited for the foreman to step out of view. 'I'm sorry, Wiggins,' Sherlock Holmes said. 'I may have cost you a day's pay.'

'Don't worry about it, sir,' Wiggins whispered. 'It's worth
it to see his face.' He helped his old mentor up, so that he
leaned against the wall, and crouched down still, as if min-
istering to the afflicted. Holmes, of course, was perfectly
well, as Wiggins could tell by the clear dancing eyes that
bore out of the ragged beggar disguise.

'A shilling a day, eh Wiggins?' Holmes said. 'And a guinea for the boy who finds the steam launch!'

Wiggins grinned, despite his hangover. 'Rates have gone up, Mister Holmes.'

'But you're still up for the game?' Holmes asked. 'We need you.'

They were the first words Holmes and he ever shared. 'Ere mister, gis a tanner.' Wiggins had never forgotten that day, as a seven-year-old, running from the orphanage, ending up in Baker Street and coming under the glare of those extraordinary eyes.

Holmes had given him some money, too (though not as much as a tanner) and had eventually enlisted Wiggins – and his friends – as his eyes and ears in the dirty, dangerous backways of the world's greatest city. A gang of street kids, invisible to the adult world, scrapping a living – scrapping an existence – on their own. Wiggins had become their leader, with Sal's help, and part of him had been bearing that weight ever since.

Sal was his oldest friend. She'd helped him bust out of the orphanage when they were seven, and he'd returned the favour. She was like a sister to him now, a sister he didn't see often because it reminded him too much of the past, but a sister nevertheless. She ran a cabbies' caff just south of Waterloo, and was as much a part of him as the city itself.

Other than Sal, he hadn't seen any of the Irregulars for a couple of years and he didn't want to. A futile need to escape a past that would be with him forever. A saying he'd heard somewhere, *give me the child until he's seven and he's mine for life*. London, the streets, a gang of kids long scattered to the wind. That was who he'd always be.

Sherlock Holmes and Doctor Watson were the first toffs he'd ever known. They were the only toffs he'd known until he joined the army, and even then the nobs up the chain of command barely tossed a word his way. Even dying in the dirt of South Africa, they kept up the social barriers – better to die alone and intact, rather than let the standards drop old boy, rather than embrace one of the men. Holmes at least had the common touch, he spoke to him even then as an adult. He was, Wiggins realised suddenly as he crouched down, the only *man* Wiggins had known in his youth who was worthy of the name. And here he was, asking him for help.

'I can't do it,' Wiggins said at last.

'But Wiggins,' Holmes pressed. 'I'm so close. To Von Bork.' Wiggins couldn't hide his surprise. Kell had been after Von Bork – the Germans' master spy – for years. They'd almost got him, but he'd squeezed out of their grasp each time.

Wiggins had seen Holmes last in New York, back in '12. Holmes had been setting up a deep cover story, working with Kell, but Wiggins had thought it far-fetched and unlikely. Yet now, two years later, the great detective was there in front of him, detailing the latest chapter of that two-year pursuit.

'He is a man of aliases, Wiggins,' Holmes went on. 'He is Hosmer Angel. He is Neville St Claire. He speaks five languages like a native. He is many men. But at bottom he is a German, he is Von Bork to his bones. And I nearly have him. One, two more meetings and I'll have his little black book to boot.'

'What little black book?' Wiggins asked.

'His spy network in England.' Holmes's eyes burned brightly, for all the age showed on his face; the creeping lines about his brow and forehead, the papery skin around his neck, and the slight tremble in his right hand. This was an old man, but as alive as any youth. 'I'm *this* close,' he went on. 'That book details every German agent living in this country. In cipher, of course, but once we have it we will decode it.'

'And round up every German snout in England.'

'Precisely! So what do you say, Wiggins, one last time? It's the biggest show of all.'

Wiggins didn't respond straight away. Instead, he helped the old detective to his feet, and loudly enquired after the old man's health, for the benefit of passers-by. Then he whispered, 'I'm tired, Mr Holmes.'

'Nonsense! For all that beer you drink, you must be the finest specimen since Blondin. I've seen you up there, on those cranes, a veritable spiderman.'

Wiggins smiled. Mr Holmes might be a toff, but trust him to know the lingo. What he didn't know, mind you, was what made Wiggins tired. It wasn't the climbing up those cranes all day, the shifts on the site. It was being told what to do by his 'betters' – ordered what to do more like. First Holmes, then the army, then his boss Leach at the debt collection and then Vernon bloody Kell, giving orders. And not honest work, neither. Not like building a building. Up there, in the clouds, he felt free.

Them that's always had freedom never knew what it was, not really. You couldn't explain freedom to a man who'd never been in chains. You couldn't explain being poor, not really poor, not so poor that you was hungry and wet and cold and one bad cough from the grave. Holmes was the cleverest man Wiggins had ever met, and yet he couldn't understand the world.

Wiggins smiled sadly. He didn't need to say anything. Holmes nodded. 'I'm alright, guv'nor,' he said loudly. 'Just a turn. Nothing a glass of mother's ruin wouldn't fix.'

'On you go, olden,' Wiggins said, handing Holmes a coin. Holmes pretended to take it, and their hands touched briefly. They'd never shaken hands before, as gentleman and working man never would do. Wiggins felt a tiny jab of comfort in the touch all the same, like touching his youth almost, the good part anyways.

'If you change your mind,' Holmes whispered, 'I am Altamont, lately resident above the Mother Red Cap, Archway. The old protocols, with adjustments for my cover.'

'No fiddle then?'

'No indeed. But you'll know if it's safe, all the same.'

'Oi Wiggins.' The foreman reappeared at the gate. 'If you're not up that bloody crane in two minutes, don't bother coming back.'

'Leave him be, mister,' Holmes cried, in his tramp voice. 'He's the good Samaritan so he is, helping a poor soul down on his luck.'

'Down on his booze more like,' the foreman roared. 'Sling it.'

Holmes threw a wild salute. 'Top of the morn to you, guv'nor!' he cried. 'How about a song?'

'How about a fat lip?' The foreman took an angry stride forward.

Holmes tripped out of reach and burst into song. 'Knees up Mother Brown, knees up Mother Brown.' He danced off, bringing his knees high in music hall parody, sending clouds of brick dust swirling. 'Under the table you must go, ee-aye ee-aye ee-aye OH!'

Wiggins gazed after the remarkable detective for a second, and then turned back to the site. Holmes had let him go, a gift, Wiggins thought as he returned to work. For Holmes had immense power, not only his own personal intelligence and charisma, but the power of the state behind him – it was clear he was working with Kell and had come to do the recruitment job that Kell had failed at the day before. But Holmes had chosen not to push it.

Power. It was another thing taken for granted by those that had it. Wiggins knew every ounce of influence he had, and why, and how quickly it could be taken away. He thought of the message from the cabby in the pub the night before. It had been from Sal. Now running the caff for cabbies, she could get a message to anyone using those cabbies – a telegraph system better than the post office, he reckoned, because she didn't even need to write it down. Half the cabbies couldn't read anyway.

Sal's message had been about her daughter Jax, in trouble with the peelers he guessed. Wiggins had helped out Jax in the past – she'd even helped him on a job for Kell, but that didn't end well (you know it's not going to end well when you're chased through Spitalfields Market at gunpoint). Now he steered clear of Sal and Jax. Sal said he had bad juju, whatever that was, that she loved him still but that an 'air of the fatal' hung about him. He couldn't deny it. Most of the truest relationships in his life had ended in death.

Sal would die for him, of course, as he would for her, and that was part of the problem. But this wasn't about her – it was about her daughter, Jax, a one-time Fleet Street runner (posing as a boy, naturally – no women allowed down that dark street) who had now become an active suffragette.

Which meant regular trips to Bow Street Magistrates Court and the nick.

He hadn't seen Jax for a long time when, earlier that year, he'd bumped into her up Brick Lane way. Or rather, he got swallowed up by a demonstration and it turned out she was involved. He'd been loafing about on his Sunday off in search of a bagel and beer. He much preferred the Jewish areas of town on Sundays. He was less likely to come across people going to and from church and eyeing him up with disdain, for Wiggins categorically did not wear a Sunday best.

That bright spring Sunday, he'd turned a corner near Roman Road to find a stream of women marching down the street. They held banners reading such things as, 'Votes for Women' and, 'Bread for Children'. As they passed, Wiggins could see off to his left behind the column of protesters came a stream of catcalling, screeching, leering, laughing men. Near the back of the line of suffragettes, he spotted Jax.

When he'd last seen her, she'd been doing her best to look like a man. But now she wore a purple cotton dress, and her reddish curly hair hung loose around her shoulders. She looked even more like her mum, except with softer features now, and the freckles that once spattered her face had faded. Despite all the bad juju, it gave him heart to see his young friend, shouting out slogans with the best of them. He tried to call out to her, but the column moved on. He followed, half out of interest, half to say hello.

For the thing was, this march wasn't like the ones he'd been used to seeing. Constance Kell was the only suffragette he knew. Her crowd were posh, well-to-do, women of money and often education even. They were asking for the right to vote, fair enough, but they were only asking for women who owned property – like the men. They weren't asking for everybody, and certainly not for the likes of Jax and Sal (or him for that matter). But this crowd, young Jax's mob, were real people, working people and the wives of working people. He could tell by their clothes and the harsh edges to their accents; and by the fact Jax found herself among them. These weren't the well-to-do.

The march ended at a small community hall on Roman Road, and people squeezed into the hall any which way. Wiggins found himself stuffed down an aisle to one side of the stage, obscured from the audience by a wall of – mostly – men in front of him, who tried to heckle and jeer at every speaker. Jax sat on the far side, and hadn't seen him. It wasn't until she stood up to speak – much to Wiggins's astonishment – that she saw him. She must be nearly twenty, Wiggins thought, yet she took to that stage like a natural. As she rose to the stage, she saw him, and nodded her head. Like a queen.

Her appearance re-energised the hecklers in the crowd, not only because of her youth – they scented an easy kill – but because, Wiggins realised, of her beauty. A young boy at his shoulder whistled with his fingers and then an older, boisterous man with a moustache muscled forward. Wiggins set his shoulders, ready to step in if needed. Just as Jax was about to speak, the man shouted out, 'Don't you wish you were a man?'

Jax looked down at him and shot back, 'Don't you wish *you* were?'

The audience erupted in laughter. The moustached man slunk back, chastened. Her speech went well. Afterwards, once the meeting had broken up onto Roman Road, Wiggins tapped her elbow.

'What's all this then?'

'You sound like a rozzer.' A group of the women were massing, checking their bags, obviously readying themselves for the next stage of the evening.

'I didn't think politics was your cup of cha.'

'Cos I'm a woman?'

'A woman?' Wiggins grinned. 'Last I checked you was running errands down the Street. As a *man*. What happened?'

'I'm an Elf, ain't I?'

'You what?'

'East London Federation of Suffragettes.'

'You lot? I don't see a toff among you. You fighting for the working woman and all?'

Jax adjusted her coat against the evening air. 'Not all suffragettes are toffs,' she said quickly. 'Although we have been chucked out by the others. Cos, get this, we're fighting for more than just the vote. We run milk depots for the kids, soup kitchens and that. It ain't just about the vote, and that's confusing for them posh folk.'

'But what use is the vote when you're hungry?' Wiggins said.

'Zackly. But that trollop Christabel Pankhurst chucked us out. Said we had no value, said the working woman was the weakest part of the sex.'

'Cos you're working for a living, rather than living off some bloke. Sounds weak alright,' Wiggins said in disgust. 'Why'd you bother?'

'What else is there to do, but fight?' She said this simply, and Wiggins had no answer. He was about to ask her if she wanted something to eat – like a father might, or a kindly uncle. She was Sal's kid, and Sal was his oldest friend.

But before he could do so, the group of women by their side had arranged themselves in order and were obviously ready to set off.

'You better go,' Jax said. 'Before the rozzers beat you up.'

'Me?'

'They arrest us, but they'll beat the living shit out of you.'

That was the last he'd heard from Jax until Sal's message the night before. Jax had obviously been arrested again and was up before the Bow Street magistrates. Sal knew about his connections, knew something of his work for Kell, knew that he was Sherlock Holmes's favourite. She knew he had powerful friends. But he couldn't call in that favour now, not after Kell's visit of the day before and Holmes that morning. Calling in a favour now meant rejoining the service.

As the day wore on, and he fixed loose bolts, cleaned wires and the like in the steeplejack height above the river, Wiggins thought more on this gift from Holmes, this release. A sign of weakness, a sign of a man getting old – for he'd barely turned on that tap. As the day wore on, too, Wiggins started to feel a presence watching him. It was odd, because normally up there the roles were reversed. You could look at anyone down below, on the site, out on Westminster Bridge, on the barges chugging past, even across the river to Embankment. You could clock 'em, full on, and they'd never know you were looking. No one looked up.

But now, someone was looking at him. It was late, the sun had dipped beside Big Ben, the orange light bouncing up off the river, the yellow smoke haze of the Battersea factories drifting out over the city, fusing with the gathering clouds to the south, piled up, purple with the malevolent threat of late rain. It was as Wiggins regarded these clouds for a moment, calculating which boozer he might get to before being soaked, when a flash of light caught his eye.

The spectacles of a man glinted. He stood on the platform of a Scotsman two over, staring straight at him. Wiggins shouted. 'Oi!' But the man, Specs, dodged behind a stanchion, hoping to stay unseen. Wiggins caught hold of a trail line and swung, trapeze-style, onto the next crane in a huge arc. He shouted again. 'Oi, Specs. I can see you!'

Specs ducked out from behind the stanchion. He looked around in alarm. Wiggins slipped down the final ladder and ran across the ground to the foot of the next Scotsman. 'Wait,' he cried again.

The man in the glasses panicked. He stepped towards the edge of the platform, saw Wiggins racing towards the foot of the crane, and stumbled back.

Wiggins leaped onto the ladder and began climbing up to the platform. He could see the legs of the man through the wooden slats. The man hesitated, shuffled, and then began to climb.

'Stay there!' Wiggins shouted. 'There's nowhere to go.'

But the man was panicking. He started to climb one of the tendrils of the crane, high up over the site.

The foreman called after Wiggins. 'He'll kill himself.'

Wiggins reached the platform and took a breath, looked up. Specs had gone surprisingly far, surprisingly quickly. But now, out to the side of the platform, and high up, he'd stopped his ascent. Wiggins knew why. For the wind had picked up, those big rolling clouds from the south, the wind before the storm. Even on a still day, once you got up into the sky the wind was enough to chill you to your very bones – the first time, at least. It was windy up there now, and there was nothing like that wind to make you feel alone.

The foreman joined him on the platform. 'Who is it?' he asked.

Wiggins shook his head, eyes trained on the cowering Specs, clinging to the side of the crane like a sailor to wreckage. 'I better go and get him.'

'You'll only make it worse.'

Wiggins shouted up to Specs. 'Stay there, mate. I'll come and get you.'

He leaped up onto the crane and began his speedy rise. Specs looked down aghast, his eyes wild, his mind clearly scrambled. He tried to clamber further on. 'Don't!' Wiggins cried.

It really was windy now. The crane swayed and ducked, and even Wiggins had to check his progress for a moment. Specs missed his footing for a second. He swung out, legs twisted, trousers billowing like a ship's flag in a squall. A strangled cry caught on the swirling gusts. His glasses slipped from his nose and twirled to the distant below.

'Hold on,' Wiggins shouted, trying to keep his voice calm. He scrambled up the last few yards. The man's eyes darted with panic and dismay. 'Don't move,' Wiggins said firmly. 'I ain't going to hurt you.' Specs's legs twisted and writhed as he tried to hold on. Wiggins could see the sweat streaked down his head.

Wiggins braced his leg into a corner of the ironwork, and reached down to Specs. 'Easy does it,' he hummed. 'One hand at a time, alright? Once I've got a hold on, swing your leg up. Like I'm pulling you up onto me horse. Alright? We'll be down in the pub in no time.'

Specs stared, his blank eyes massive in fear. 'I can't. He won't let me.'

'Who, God? It don't matter about him. Gis your hand.'

Specs hesitated. He could see Wiggins meant to save him. The tension in his face dissipated. He relaxed his muscles, Wiggins readied himself.

But then the poor wretch, a spectacled man without his glasses, shook his head in a sad and tiny movement. He let go.

His arms stretched out, his body flattened, his eyes and face still up at Wiggins, his back hurtling to the surface. It took an instant. It took an age.

Thwamp! Wiggins heard the landing. He stared down, horrified. The spectacled man had landed on one of the steel rods that sprouted up from the sunken piles, like thin branchless trees. The rod had impaled him through the neck. His body hung limp as laundry.

Wiggins scrambled down the crane, slithering and swinging until he reached the platform. 'Man down, man down!' the cry went up. He slid down the ladder and raced to the fallen man.

A couple of the men had already pulled Specs from the steel stake that impaled his neck. They laid the body on the hard ground just as Wiggins reached them. A crowd began to gather, and Wiggins pushed through and knelt beside the body.

'He's dead,' the foreman said, joining the crush.

'Who is he?' someone else asked. 'I ain't seen him.'

'Must be a casual,' the foreman muttered. 'Come on then, aht the way. Ain't nothing to see here. Oi Wiggins,' he went on. 'I said he's dead. No need for no doctoring here.'

Wiggins shifted back from the body. He'd examined it as best he could in the time he had, pretending to act as a nurse of sorts but actually rifling the pockets. But now the foreman took an interest there wasn't much to be done. 'Tommy,' the foreman called out, 'get the cart over here, call a copper. Right, out of it. Day's over. I ain't paying for you dossers to work late, just to gawp. Got it? Got it!'

The crowd began to disperse, rightly realising that to be told to leave by the foreman was a rarity not to be missed.

'Get out of it, go on!' The foreman chivvied his charges away. It wasn't rare, for someone to die on the site, and the foreman was thankful that it was a casual who had fallen. No mates on the crew to cry 'poor conditions', no grieving widow after a payout and no facking union to cut his bollocks off. 'What you doing?' he barked at Wiggins.

Wiggins stepped back from the body. 'Checking he's dead, is all.'

'Checking he's dead! You fall on your head an' all?'

'Nah, it's just. You know when he signed on? I don't recognise him.'

'Neither do I,' the foreman said, forgetting himself for a moment. 'Anyway, it's none of your business. He would have come in with the casuals, wouldn't he? Why do you care?' He squinted suspicion at Wiggins, who shrugged.

He looked down at the fallen body once more. The neck a bloody mess, the head askew now, barely attached. His clothes didn't look like builder's clothes. If anything, he was dressed more like a cheap shop clerk, someone you might see at the labour exchange rather than on a site. Someone once with a half-decent job – the trousers weren't cheap, but had not been replaced for years. A half-decent job that he had no more. The glasses chimed with that, and his fingernails too. They were clean, unchipped. When Wiggins had felt his hands, they lacked the callouses and nicks usual for a manual worker.

Spectacles wasn't a casual, that was obvious. Wiggins had run his pockets and found nothing, other than a pawn ticket, which he swiped. That was telltale in itself. Who went to work with nothing? Not a bus ticket, not a latch-key, not even a tanner.

Wiggins nodded at the foreman absently, and slung his rope over his shoulder. He didn't want the foreman to see him hurrying, didn't want any more attention than necessary. But he knew the dead man had been there to see him, and he guessed why.

He also knew he had to get to Sherlock Holmes.

2

Men tumbled higgledy-piggledy from aeroplanes. Dogs yapped up at the great machines in the sky. A red-suited brass band bashed out a jolly tune. The ticket queue bulged. A Union Jack fluttered high and proud, as necks craned upwards. A nice day out. At least, that's what the poster promised.

Wiggins stared at the advertisement blankly. FLYING AT HENDON, it advised. A jokey, crazy picture that did not match his mood. All he could think of was the horrible death that awaited the jovial figures falling from the flying machines. He wasn't looking for a nice day out. He was looking for something that wasn't the end.

As soon as he'd given Specs the once over, as soon as it became clear that he wasn't a casual on the site, that he was there for a *reason*, Wiggins knew he had to warn Sherlock Holmes. Coincidences did happen. The world was crazy enough for that. But the man in the glasses was watching Wiggins, and had appeared the day after Kell visited the site and the afternoon following Holmes's visit. If Wiggins had been under surveillance from the morning, they would have seen Holmes. He was disguised, of course, but nevertheless. If Wiggins had been watching a target, and that target took fifteen minutes talking to a tramp, it would have rung alarm bells. The suspicion was enough to send Wiggins hurtling to the Hampstead

Railway station at Charing Cross. He now sat looking at the poster of the Hendon flying show as the train rattled and screeched northwards.

Wiggins got off the crowded train at Highgate station, which wasn't in Highgate at all but in Archway. He didn't look behind him. He'd scoped everyone on the train, out of habit, but he knew he wasn't being followed. The man who was meant to be following him had a broken neck, and was currently being carted off to the mortuary on Horseferry Road. Outside the station, he pushed through the commuters and hustled along Holloway Road towards the Mother Red Cap. He knew the pub slightly, as Holmes knew he would, because Wiggins knew most of the pubs in London – he hadn't been inside all of them, but he knew where they were. It was part of his mental map of the city, where others would demarcate areas by tram stops or underground stations or parks, he'd orientate himself by where he could get a drink.

The Mother Red Cap stood on a corner off the Holloway Road. Wiggins scanned the windows above – the small rectangular ones on the top floor. This is where Holmes would be renting a bed, under his cover name, and Wiggins looked for signs. It was like the old days, when the detective would use his violin to signal to the young Wiggins.

But there was no signal tonight – not even the all-clear. Wiggins didn't expect to see a violin – such an instrument would surely not fit into the cover Holmes was working under – but he would have stuffed a white handkerchief in one corner of the window if it was all clear. It was a signalling system between the two they'd developed years previously – when Wiggins was tailing one of the criminals Holmes set him on – and Wiggins knew Holmes would employ it now. He'd said as much. 'If you change your mind. The old protocols.' There was no signal now, no all-clear. He went into the pub.

He'd barely sat down before he felt the cold chill of those around him. This was a locals' pub. More than that, it was an Irish pub. He'd last been in Dublin two years earlier, but he hadn't forgotten that he'd left that city without his finger-nails. Ireland was no country for an Englishman just then, what with home rule coming and a big argument about that in the north. And the Mother Red Cap was a smoke-filled corner of Ireland for sure.

Wiggins positioned himself at the bar, his back to the room, and ordered a drink. As he waited, he scanned the customers behind him using the nicotine-stained mirror that ran along the wall.

'Do you know who she was, do you?' the barman barked at him suddenly.

Wiggins did not flinch. He eyed the angry man carefully as he took a gulp of the half and half. He savoured it, for the first drink of the day was always a holy moment.

The barman went on. 'Mother Red Cap was famous, so she was, for violently disposing of unwelcome guests.'

'Cheery,' Wiggins said at last.

'Just so you know, fella.'

Wiggins settled his eyes on the barman. He'd fixed in his head the layout of the pub behind him using the mirror; the two exits, the long vicious-looking club on the wall opposite, a tatty boxer's bill. Most of the customers appeared harmless inebriates, the kind of men who kept pubs in business countrywide. Most of them. 'I ain't looking for trouble,' Wiggins said to the barman, but loud enough for all to hear. 'I'm looking for money. I'm looking for a man named Altamont.'

'Don't know the man.' The barman glanced backwards. As he did so, Wiggins saw movement in the mirror. A young man with a bright green sailor's cap and dark stubble got up and slipped out of the door on the right.

'Sure you don't,' Wiggins said. 'And you don't know nothing about the money he owes me.'

'And there it is,' the barman sneered. 'We don't serve tick boys. Not if they're English too. Understand me? Finish your drink and be gone.'

But Wiggins was already on his way. He left the pub in time to follow the man in the sailor's cap. Wiggins caught sight of him hurrying up the hill away to the right. The bright cap caught in the glare of the electric lamps outside the large hospital on his left as he passed. Wiggins followed.

He'd been watching Sailor's Cap in the mirror of the bar, when he'd mentioned the name Altamont, and had seen the man's undoubted reaction. It was all the information Wiggins needed to follow him.

Sailor's Cap obviously suspected a tail. He glanced around often and hurried onwards, his hands driven deep into his pockets, his cap pulled low. Wiggins followed unseen. Always unseen. No one saw Wiggins when he ran a tail, a trick learned as a small boy at the foot of the master. Anticipation, knowing when your mark was going to turn around to look, knowing seconds before they knew themselves. Holmes taught him long ago and he'd honed it as he got older – if he couldn't do it, he wouldn't have got old at all.

Trees and bushes crowded in on the road. They bent and shook in the gathering wind. Rain began to fall. Sailor's

Cap pushed into the wind, faster, as the road tailed steeply to the right. Wiggins hurried on, a chill creeping down his neck, despite the heat. Up here, on the high bleak hill, it suddenly felt like he was in the deep countryside and not in London at all. He gripped the rope on his shoulder for reassurance and turned the corner.

The road ahead tapered onto a long, thin bridge, lit by old-fashioned gas lamps that flickered and fizzed in the rain-spattered night. Wiggins kept his eye on Sailor's Cap, who had stopped just short of the bridge. The man shouted out across the chasm. Then Wiggins saw them.

Two men, huddled together in conversation. They stood hunched by the parapet, in the downlight from a gas lamp. Wiggins recognised the first man instantly, even though he had his back to him. He'd know that tall, thin frame and angled head anywhere: Sherlock Holmes, albeit dressed in labourer's clothes. Next to him, a dark cloaked figure. His face was obscured by Holmes's body.

Sailor's Cap shouted again, and Holmes swivelled around instinctively. At that moment, the Cloaked Man stepped forward and plunged something into Holmes's side. Wiggins saw the flash of a blade. 'No!' he shouted.

Holmes slumped into the Cloaked Man's arms. Wiggins ran towards them. Sailor's Cap turned, surprised, and Wiggins drove a fist into his face but did not stop. Would not stop.

The Cloaked Man held Holmes across the midriff, almost comforting. He seemed not to hear, or heed, the onrushing Wiggins. Instead, like a friend, he held Holmes close – consoling, caring, nurturing.

And then in one swift movement the Cloaked Man pitched Sherlock Holmes over the parapet.

Wiggins roared. The Cloaked Man looked up. Without hesitating, he lifted his arm and—

Bang! Bang!

The bullets screamed past his ear. Wiggins slithered to a halt. He couldn't see the man's face clearly but he didn't need to. He had a gun. And Wiggins had nothing. He glanced behind, looking to escape. Sailor's Cap stood up, rubbing his chin. Behind him, the headlights of a motorcar came rattling towards them. A saviour.

A dark shape leaned out of the passenger side of the car. Flash, bang! Another gun, aimed at Wiggins. The car accelerated.

He ducked, and shrank into the parapet. The Cloaked Man raised his gun again and strode towards him. Trapped.

In an instant, Wiggins secured his rope on the railings and slung it over the side of the bridge.

'Hey, you!' a London voice shouted through the gun smoke and the rain. 'You're a dead man.'

Wiggins jumped off the bridge, clinging to the rope. As he did so, bullets chipped the paint on the handrail. He began shimmying down. Another burst of fire spurred him on.

As he swung down, he realised someone was working on the rope with a knife. But by now, shouts and cries came from the road below too – traffic had stopped. Wiggins slithered and swung. He looked up. His attackers – Sailor's Cap, the Cloaked Man and someone else, presumably the gunman from the car – suddenly stepped back from the edge into the darkness just as the rope gave way.

Wiggins fell the final ten feet to the road. He landed awkwardly. Up above, another barrage of shots rang out, extinguishing the lamps in a bright flair. The gunmen had shot out the gas and disappeared.

All was chaos. Two, three cars, a cart and a bus slewed to a halt. Men shouted. Lamps flickered in the sheeting rain. A bell began to ring. But Wiggins only had one thing on his mind, one horrible thing.

He pushed himself to his feet and waved aside the offers of help from the gathering passers-by. They could not help him now. Instead, he limped across the road to the body stretched out ten yards away. A small crowd ringed it, lit by the headlights of a stopped taxi cab. Rain lashed down now, pooling in the potholes. A woman started to scream. More motorcars stopped. Horns added to the bells. Someone ran past him. But all Wiggins could do was stare at the body.

Sherlock Holmes lay dying.

Blood oozed from his stomach wound, dark thick death. His body was crushed and crippled from the fall, a leg awkwardly folded under him. His eyes flickered in recognition as Wiggins knelt beside him. 'Schläge . . . schläge . . .' he muttered.

'I'm here,' Wiggins said.

'The doctor,' Holmes whispered. 'The doctor.'

'A doctor,' someone cried. 'A doctor.'

'Not that doctor,' Wiggins said softly and nodded.

Holmes's eyes caught once more, then relaxed. Wiggins could see the life ebbing out of him. His eyes cleared of focus, then closed, closed shut as the blood pumped out of his wound and pooled, pooled by his crumpled body. Wiggins held his hand.

He held his hand and wept.

3

'Shall we let the ladies go?'

'What's that?' Kell replied absently.

His secretary, Simpkins, stood at the door of Kell's office in Watergate House. He glanced up at the clock. 'Home?'

'What, yes, er. Of course,' Kell said, putting down the notes in his hand. It was almost eleven o'clock in the evening. As soon as he'd heard the news of Franz Ferdinand's assassination, he'd been asking people to work late, convinced that war was imminent. 'Wait! Yes, let me address them.'

He locked his office behind him. He always locked his office. Then he followed Simpkins down the stairs to the floor below and the Registry. Six women sat at desks, skyscrapers of notes in front of them, filing cabinets lining each wall, filled to bursting with Roneo cards. Kell wanted to say something profound, something stirring. But he always found it difficult talking to women in this way. If it were soldiers, or navy men, he would have found the speech, the oration. But women? Was it even proper to talk to them of war, of battle, of a literal fight to the death?

'Ladies,' he said at last. 'You may go home. I'm sorry to keep you so late. I would like to say,' he faltered. The women, who in his mind resembled the maiden aunts of his youth, were already gathering together their things, packing their handbags. He realised that these women were no older than him, not his aunts now, but he couldn't get that thought out of his mind – as if they were about to tell *him* off for an infraction, rather than be roused into great feats of chivalry and defiance. 'I would add,' he went on. 'Our work is very, very . . .' He paused again, distracted this time by the smell. Lavender? Rose water? A mixture of perfumes, so different from a room full of men. Pleasant and disorientating.

Constance had suggested he staff the registry operation with women, and by and large they seemed tremendously efficient – though he found it almost impossible to talk to them. For all that Kell lacked capable agents out in the field, the operation as a whole was spectacularly good at generating paper trails. It was as much an administration as it was a spy hunting service. There was an almost complete register of all male aliens over the age of eighteen in the entire country. He felt sure that no such complete record existed anywhere else in the world.

And then there were the reports. A few came from trusted agents in the field, but for the most part the system was stuffed to the gills with police reports. Each force in the country sent in information and details of suspected spies and enemy agents. Not only that, they forwarded any reports from *members of the public* about suspect activity. All these reports – the academic caught swearing in German, the water colourist accused of spying, pretty much every waiter in London – all this information ended up in the headquarters of the secret service home division, to be indexed, referenced, cross-referenced and filed by his platoon of severe, competent women.

One of them, a Mrs Jepson – he thought, though couldn't be sure – looked over her spectacles at him, her mouth set in a sharp jab of distaste, waiting for him to continue.

'Um, yes. Our work is very important,' Kell muttered finally. 'Well done. I will see you all tomorrow.' Kell often felt, when faced with these women, that they regularly read reports on *him*.

As he went back upstairs to his office, he reflected that although these women were marvels – and his indexing and cross-referencing system would surely be the envy of Whitehall (if any of them ever got to know about it) – this hive of efficiency and good administration was only as effective as the information fed into it. And that was his biggest problem. The service had one reliable source of information on German intelligence – the Pentonville Postman – and the rest was puff and blow-by. Scurrilous rumours mostly, racialists motivated by petty envy, spy fiction fanatics seeing shadows at every turn. They'd picked up a couple of agents over the last two years – Graves, Schultz – but they always felt like small fry. Even the enemy agents he suspected now could not be the full extent of a German network, he was sure.

Of all the people in the service's employ, only Sherlock Holmes was on the track of a big fish. Since Kell first set up the Bureau five years earlier, he and Wiggins had divined the machinations of an as yet unmet and unseen German spy they knew only as Von Bork. He'd been meddling in both British and Irish affairs since at least 1909 – infiltrating the arms factory at Woolwich, fermenting unrest in London, running an upmarket brothel in Belgravia that turned out to be an illicit information exchange – but neither Kell nor Wiggins had managed to lay a glove on the man himself. They'd scotched some of his plans, but the man himself escaped.

Kell suspected that Von Bork ran the German spy network in the UK – or at least, he probably ran the most influential and important arm of it. Kell had been happy to arrest piddling artists making sketches of the ships off Portsmouth and such, but what he really needed to discover now – on the brink of war, he was sure – were the names of the inside men and women spread across the country. People in positions of trust; harbour masters, civil servants, army officers even. He suspected everyone. And Von Bork held the keys to unlock that suspicion.

Sherlock Holmes had been on the tail of the man for the last two years. Holmes had travelled to Chicago to establish a long-range cover story. The detective called this story, a narrative about his past as an Irish-American and fervent nationalist, a 'legend'. It had taken him more than a year, since when he'd come back to Europe and began to trade false secrets with Germany. From their latest conversation, it seemed that Holmes was close to meeting Von Bork at last – he'd lured him in with the prize of the Royal Navy signals, or at least he was on the verge of doing so.

The problem with Holmes as an agent was his inability to report back, as well as his antipathy to taking orders. Kell found it difficult even to contact him, let alone control him. He'd finally managed to leave a message for him at that horrible pub on the Holloway Road, informing him of Wiggins's refusal to heed the call. He had no idea what Holmes (or 'Altamont') would do with the information, nor how close he actually was to Von Bork and the treasure trove of information he possessed. But apart from the name Altamont, and where he said he stayed, all he knew about Holmes's activities was his concentration on Von Bork, and the urgency of his chase.

With these thoughts jumbling through his mind, Kell unlocked his office door and stepped inside.

'Where are the files?'

'Hey!' Kell stepped back in astonishment. For Wiggins stood in front of him, dripping wet from the storm, dark stains down his front, more bedraggled than ever. 'How did you get in here? The watchmen . . . I mean.'

'He's dead.'

'Look at the state of you . . . is that blood?'

Wiggins stepped towards him, agitation written on his face. 'He is dead.'

'Who?'

'Mr Holmes.'

Kell sat down as Wiggins paced the office and told him what had just happened. The dark stains on his shirt front, the great detective's blood. 'I need his notes,' Wiggins said when he'd finished. 'I need to find who did this.'

'One moment,' Kell said, holding up his hand. 'There's brandy in the cabinet there, oh, I see you've already found it. On this one occasion, I think we both need a drink. Sit down, man, while I use the telephone.'

As Wiggins drank and glowered and shook, the shock seeping out of him, Kell established which police station was dealing with the matter on the ground. He fired off a number of instructions, sent his own personal police inspector out and then replaced the speaking horn.

'You must come back to us now, Wiggins,' he said, trying to keep his voice steady. He squared off the foolscap on his desk, and carefully chose one of his fountain pens. Then set it aside. 'This is espionage run red. This is war. We shall keep it out of the papers of course.'

'I want it public,' Wiggins growled, rising to his feet once more.

'Do you think making it public will help you get the kind of retribution you crave?' Kell asked. A silence fell between them, filled by this thought. For Kell knew Wiggins would not lead these murderers to the Old Bailey.

'It's Von Bork, ain't it?'

'Holmes was on his tail, yes. But isn't it a mistake to theorise without data?'

'It's a mistake to get yourself knifed in the guts an' all, but that happened too,' Wiggins snapped. 'Don't give me any of that shit.'

Kell blinked but said nothing for a moment.

Wiggins continued to pace. 'I need his notes,' he repeated. 'That's where the data is, Mr Holmes's notes.'

'You'll come back?' Kell repeated in turn, eyeing his man carefully.

Wiggins stopped pacing, but his eyes danced wild. He'd lost his hat, and his hair fell wet and askew. He searched the room for answers. Kell had never seen him so lost, so agitated.

Finally, Wiggins realised something important and came to a halt. 'The doctor,' he said.

Wiggins had to help him into a chair. He thought the doctor was going to die there and then in front of him. The bluff old fellow, thickset now with a grey moustache that glistened in the electric lights of his consulting room, went as white as his hair. It took a few moments before he gestured at a cupboard. Wiggins knew what he wanted. Brandy. They both drank deeply from two Derby cups that sat either side of the sink.

'You are sure?' Doctor Watson asked at last. 'Quite, quite sure?'

'He died in my arms, doctor,' Wiggins said, unembarrassed. Death collapsed social distance, it collapsed time. Wiggins described the detective's death for the second time that night. Still it didn't feel real; the shadow figures, the flashing blade, the great, great fall. And that titan of a man, crumpled and crushed in the middle of the road, like an unlucky fox.

Doctor Watson listened as if in a daze. When Wiggins had finished his account, he handed his empty brandy cup back to Wiggins and then set his chin in resolution. 'Who did this? Who were the men on the bridge?'

'I don't know,' Wiggins said. 'Not yet, not for sure.' He didn't want to tell the doctor about Von Bork just then, as he felt sure Holmes had not told him either. For all that Watson had been the detective's great chronicler, Wiggins knew he kept his cards close when he was on a job.

'I shall solve the case,' Watson said, in a sudden burst of energy. 'It must be one of his enemies!'

The old man thrust himself out of his chair, seized by inspiration. 'That's it. Moriarty!'

'He's dead,' Wiggins said again.

'What was that? You don't know him, Wiggins, he is the Napoleon of Crime. His tentacles spread wide, through time itself.'

Wiggins put his hand on the doctor's shoulder. 'Easy,' he mumbled.

The doctor twisted around. 'What of his other enemies? He is the most hated man in London's underworld. There must be hundreds of criminals intent on his destruction. I must get to my notes. The clues will be there,' he cried again.

Wiggins moved his other hand around, and held the doctor by both shoulders. 'He's gone, doc, he's gone. Now, get dressed and I'll take you to Barts. One last time, eh?'

Watson searched his face, his eyes lost, looking for something. Something that wasn't there. 'Yes, of course, good old Wiggins.' He fingered the collar of his dressing gown absently. 'I will dress as you say.' He shuffled to the door, paused and turned. 'But surely, my notes . . .?'

'You look at 'em, doctor, let me know if you find any clues.'

'I will, Wiggins, I will.' He hesitated, his eyes drifting. 'Barts, you say?'

'The mortuary,' Wiggins replied. It was only when they were in the cab, thirty minutes later, did he remember. Barts: the very same mortuary where Watson had first met the Great Detective, and where he'd first written about him too.

Tuesday 30 June 1914. Of particular concern in *The Times* was the looming threat of war, the 'supreme calamity of civil war' in fact in Ireland, where the protestant followers of Edward Carson in the north of the country had armed themselves with illegally smuggled Mauser rifles. This has led to much consternation among nationalists in the South, though *The Times* hopes the imminent Home Rule Bill would avert disaster and ensure peace. It ran a small piece about the upcoming funeral of Archduke Franz Ferdinand, the assassinated Austro-Hungarian Emperor's heir.

'Captain Kell! Captain Kell!' Mrs Jepson screamed down the stairwell.

'I'm coming,' Kell called back. He took the stairs two at a time, alarmed already. The soldier normally positioned at the front door of the building was missing that morning. He'd barely slept a wink last night at home, tossing and turning as Constance slumbered. The shock of Holmes's death had not diminished, and the sense of unease it engendered had only grown. For despite his smooth working registry, Kell had no idea what to do. And now, it seemed, his very HQ was under attack.

'There's a man here,' Mrs Jepson urged as Kell approached. 'He's already punched Corporal Maddox. He's rifling the Registry.'

Kell burst in to see Wiggins pulling open a filing cabinet drawer. Rifling the files indeed. The ladies stood looking on, unsure. Maddox lay on the floor, massaging his chin – scared to get up, no doubt.

Mrs Jepson went on. 'He just came in, sir. We called Corporal Maddox, of course, but well, as you see, he is rather a force of nature.'

'Agent W!' Kell cried sternly. 'Agent W. My office at once.'

Wiggins turned to him, nodded and strode to the door.

'Carry on, ladies, Mrs Jepson. If you could clean up here. Agent W is, er, one of our field agents. He acts with my authority.' Kell looked down at Maddox. 'Except when punching soldiers. Get back on post, Maddox, don't slouch.'

'Calm down, Wiggins,' Kell hissed. 'You're out of control.'

'Me?'

'Have you slept?'

Wiggins looked at him, eyes wild. 'I've just taken Doctor Watson back from the bloody morgue, course I ain't slept. You ever seen a man like that cry? A man like that.'

'Sit.' Kell pointed at the chair opposite his desk. He waited while Wiggins slumped into it, exhaustion suddenly overtaking the nerves. 'Now, am I to assume you've come back to the Bureau? You're taking the shilling. Is that what that display downstairs was all about?'

Wiggins shifted his head in reluctant acquiescence. 'It ain't about the money,' he said, almost to himself. Kell could see the struggle in the man, the clenched fist, the way he wouldn't meet his eye when he mentioned the shilling. It wasn't that Wiggins was proud – you only had to look at the way the man dressed to know that he wasn't proud. He'd changed his bloodstained clothes from the day before, thank god, but he still presented shambolically. His shirt flapped untucked, his grey builder's coat was frayed at the cuff, and his plentiful hair hung almost to his neck. It was not a look Kell appreciated (his wife once called Wiggins 'Byronic', though it wasn't a view he shared), especially in anyone who worked for him. The Bureau was born out of the Ministry of War, and he'd much rather employ men who bore themselves in a manner fitting to the army. He much preferred, in fact, men of an entirely different class than Wiggins. Except none of them were in his class as an agent.

'Better?' Kell asked.

'Never.'

'Calm then? Good, so – state the case, the problem. Like *he* would do.'

Wiggins straightened his back. 'First off, we have to be clear who did it – and then who's *responsible*, and then we have to find them.'

'We could leave it to the police – I have my best inspector on it.'

'You think that's what *he* would do?' Wiggins glared.

It was a fair point, Kell conceded. Holmes had very little faith in the official police, even now with all the scientific advances and the record keeping. 'And you're convinced the man who wielded the knife was Von Bork?' he asked.

'No,' Wiggins said flatly. 'Not the man with the knife. Could be. But Von Bork's definitely the man behind it.'

'Reasons?' Kell pushed, although he agreed.

Wiggins sighed. 'Mr Holmes . . .' He stumbled on the name for a moment, his attention drifting again. 'Holmes.' Wiggins said the word as if it meant something else, Kell realised, as if he were talking about the real thing, a home, and not a man, a dead man. Wiggins breathed deeply and went on. 'Holmes had lots of enemies, course, but he's always had them. And he hasn't made new ones in years. Anyone wanting to kill him could have taken him out in Sussex a long time since. Anyways from what he told me, from what you say, his only case was Von Bork. He was *only* looking for Von Bork.'

'That's true.'

'And it's only Von Bork who would need to kill him. We know Von Bork's smart, and he'd know the only way stop Mr Holmes would be to . . . end him.'

'Why now?'

'Cos he was rumbled. Discovered that this cover, Altamont, is someone else, and the only way to silence him would be to kill him. Von Bork's responsible, sure as. It can't be anyone else.'

'I agree,' Kell replied. 'But it doesn't mean that he did the deed himself. There were at least three men, you say?'

Wiggins nodded, and looked away in thought.

Kell pressed on. 'The police, at least, have a look out for the men you described.'

Wiggins waved away the mention of the police. 'Anything from the ports?' he asked. 'We can find the others, I reckon. It's Von Bork we need, and he'll be running now.'

'There's been nothing from Dover, Harwich – certainly no one unusual. But, you must admit, we don't have much to go on.'

'Mr Holmes mentioned a book.'

'Did he?'

'"A little black book", he called it. Von Bork's list of agents, here in Britain. He reckoned it had the lot of them in there. Was going to nab it off him.'

'That's your mission,' Kell exclaimed. 'Get me that book!'

'I know my mission,' Wiggins muttered darkly.

'Don't be blinded, man. Holmes's best revenge is to complete his work, to best the man who bested him. With that book in my possession, we could seal up the entire German intelligence operation in the whole country. We could close it down in days. It would be the service's great victory!'

Kell could not contain his excitement. To learn that there was a central list of agents in Von Bork's possession was to finally understand why Sherlock Holmes had poured himself so ceaselessly into his work with the service. Because it was surely German intelligence's biggest mistake, if such a list existed anywhere outside Berlin, that Von Bork had it written down and held it with him.

Peacetime intelligence work had been frowned upon when he started doing it a few years earlier, and still many in Whitehall disapproved. It was ungentlemanly, sneaky even, and not at all to be encouraged. The high-minded men in the Foreign Office and the Admiralty were content enough with military intelligence as pertaining to war – as had been carried out for centuries – but the idea of secret intelligence gathering in peacetime was an anathema to them. Only Winston Churchill, currently the First Lord of the Admiralty, of all the senior ministers was positively enthusiastic about intelligence gathering in civilian and peacetime life. (When he was Home Secretary, it was Churchill who'd allowed them to start opening people's private post on the grounds of national security, and it was Churchill who'd helped force through the Official Secrets Act.) The rest of the cabinet tended to refer to such work as *spying*, a word said in much the same way as they might say *slurry*.

If he could obtain this book, the one that Holmes had been pursuing, then it would both lay to rest any of these prejudices – it would finally prove the extent of German infiltration, of German spying in Britain – and simultaneously crush the effectiveness of the German operation just on the brink of certain war.

One look at Wiggins, though, was enough to convince him that the man didn't really care about the book at all. Kell changed tack. 'Listen, Wiggins. Think of it. If you find the book, you find the man – yes? Isn't that what you want?'

'I'll find him,' Wiggins said quietly. Kell didn't need to know what he'd do to Von Bork once he caught him – as long as he had the book, he didn't care. Wiggins pondered for a moment, and then pointed at Kell. 'Now, where's his notes?'

'Holmes's? All I have is his expenses.'

'What?'

'Apart from the fact that he was chasing Von Bork, he told me very little. Except where I could reach him.'

'And did you?' Wiggins leaned forward. 'Reach him?'

'The day before yesterday in fact. After you turned down my offer, I sent a message to him.'

Wiggins cursed. A murderous look crossed his face and, for a moment, Kell thought he might attack him there and then. But Wiggins shook his head, resigned. 'Get me them expenses anyway.'

'I'm *your* boss, remember.'

'And the Postman, we'll need to shake that tree. I'll need his papers.'

'That'll take time,' Kell said, irked. Wiggins hadn't been back in the service ten minutes, and he was already issuing orders like he was Wellington himself. Except he lacked the manners.

'I've got somewhere to be first. I'll be back.' Wiggins stood up and patted his pockets. 'Got any blunt?'

Kell sighed. He took a petty cash box from the drawer in his desk, and slowly pulled the key from his pocket. He drew this operation out as long as possible, glancing up at Wiggins every now and then. He wanted to make him wait. Finally he asked as he handed over the money, 'How do you get in and out by the way? And why don't you use the front door?'

'So I'm not followed,' he answered, matter of fact.

'And I am?' Kell said, surprised and alarmed.

'Course you are.'

4

'Ach now, isn't it the wee tick boy back for his shilling.' The barman of the Mother Red Cap let out a theatrical sigh. 'I told you, fella, you're barred.'

Wiggins strode up to him, ignoring the implied threat and the large young man who stood up at the far end of the bar – clearly in the pay of the pub. Instead he leaned over, grabbed the barman's hair and yanked his face into the teak bar top. The violence was so sudden, so shocking, that no one moved for a moment. A pint glass rolled onto the floor and shattered. The barman clutched his bleeding nose and gestured to the large young man.

Stung into action, he strode towards Wiggins, head down, fists up. Wiggins waited, ducked the first punch, then drove his heel into the inside of the man's knee. He crumpled onto the beer-wet floor, yowling in pain.

'The key,' Wiggins said to the barman. 'Altamont's room.'

'Ya bastard,' the barman mumbled. 'You broke my nose.'

Wiggins held his hand out. 'I ain't got all day.'

'I . . . I know people.'

Wiggins glanced down at the young man on the floor, who clutched his knee still. 'Like him? Well, I know people like the OC – know him? Patrick O'Connell. My old boss, but I'm sure he'd do me a favour, if I asked like.'

The barman's eyes widened at the mention of the OC. Wiggins had worked for him in Dublin two years earlier, that city's most fearsome crime lord. Although they'd parted on bad terms, the barman wasn't to know that. He fumbled nervously at the key hooks behind the bar.

'Or else,' Wiggins went on as the barman passed over a key, 'I could report you for unjust measures. That cup there's a nailed-on shave.'

'Top floor,' the barman gestured to the door behind the bar.

As Wiggins pushed through it, he heard the pub gradually come back to life and someone said, 'What's this now, about unjust measures?'

'Shut you, Maguire.'

Holmes would leave nothing in his room, Wiggins knew. No clues as to his real identity, nothing that could be used by an enemy, no notes. He held everything in that vast warehouse of his mind. Still, Wiggins went through the motions. There was a single cot against one wall. A small fireplace. A messy pile of clothes, some papers strewn here and there on the floor. A line of empty liquor bottles on the windowsill.

Wiggins turned over 'Altamont's' clothes – the set of tramp rags he saw him in at the building site, a battered straw hat, the pockets all empty. They smelled of cheap booze, and Wiggins guessed that's what Holmes did with the liquid from the empty bottles. He wouldn't have been drinking the stuff, but using it to keep in character – first, if anyone looked up at the window but second for the smell.

The papers on the floor were mostly Irish Republican newspapers, propaganda sheets and a boxing bill. Nothing out of character. Under the bed he found a Royal Navy Signals book, dated that week. This must have been the fake, the final bait for Von Bork. Wiggins put it in his inside pocket to take back to Kell, and cast around once more. On the mantelpiece, a long thin pipe – still in use judging by the loose shards of moist tobacco on the mantel, and the fresh stamps of ash that lined it. Never cared much for an ashtray, Mr Holmes. The one part of his old life he must have allowed himself in the legend, a smoker until the end. Although he had no Persian slipper here to keep it in, nor a coal scuttle for the cigars.

An image of Baker Street flashed into his mind. The old detective stood at the window, pointing his pipe at Watson, laughing, getting the Irregulars to line up, detailing his instructions in that clear, slightly high-pitched voice. The smell too, tobacco and newspapers and fire smoke (the chimney at 221b never worked properly but no one seemed to mind). 'Come on your own next time, Wiggins. We can't have them all in here. It will never do!'

He shook the memory away, and knelt down to look at the fire grate. Fresh ash, but no coal dust or detritus of wood, it being June. He fingered the fine ash in his hands, burnt paper.

'Is he gone?' the barman asked.

Wiggins stood up. The barman now occupied the doorway, an oversized ceremonial sword held up ready to strike. 'Did Altamont get post?'

'He owes me a shilling for the room. I'll be wanting that, if he's gone.' Wiggins stared levelly at the man until he faltered, and the sword shook slightly. 'No post. Wires.'

Wiggins nodded. 'There was a lad, last night, bright green cap.'

'Sure, I don't know.'

'Do we have to do this again?' Wiggins twisted his neck. The barman's sword twitched once more and he took a step back.

'He was the telegram boy. He delivered the wire, for Alta-mont, then stayed for a pint. Altamont left, and the boy stayed.'

'Seen him before, the despatch boy? He local?'

'I ain't never seen him once, not even on the street like.'

Wiggins believed him. That's how they would have done it. Delivered a fake telegram, so it couldn't be traced, then sent Holmes up the road. He put his hand up at the bar-man, carefully, gently. 'I'm going now, and I reckon neither of us want no trouble. Alright?'

He walked slowly past the barman, down the stairs and away out into Holloway Road. He hadn't expected to find anything of use in Altamont's room. What he found was his past.

The door of the shop stood ajar. They almost always did, half in invitation, half in repulsion. The half-and-half nature is the pawnbroker's whole world – one set of customers eager, on the lookout for a decent bargain, better than the bric-a-brac stall down Petticoat Lane, the other set could barely bring themselves over the threshold, paying money to *keep your own* stuff, just because you didn't have cash on the day. Most of the people Wiggins knew were in and out of 'uncle' half their lives, it was what you did if you had a smite more than nothing, and needed a penny to tide you over. Wiggins never had the stuff to pawn in the first place.

He faced up to Garratt's on the Old Kent Road, his next stop after the Mother Red Cap in Holloway. It looked like any number of London pawnshops, only larger than most. The three golden balls hung heavy in the sky from a signpost jutting out into the street. The word PAWN-BROKER, in flecked yellow paint above the door, the plate-glass windows glistening with jewellery and silver, and sad pieces of crockery, silent musical instruments, a solitary clock, woodworking tools, used but unused now, given up by a carpenter who now could no longer work; the signs everywhere, painted on the brickwork: 'Money advanced on plate, jewels, wearing apparel, and every description of property.'

Wiggins noticed the entrance around the side of the corner shop. Another sad sign of the typical pawnbrokers. This was where you went with your goods, or where you sent the children with the last of your linen – if anyone asks, you're taking it to aunty. No one wanted to go into that door, but they wanted to be *seen* going into that door even less. A pauper's door.

Wiggins looked down at the ticket in his hand. The pledge. Garratt & Co, 160-166 Old Kent Road, it had printed across the top. 1914. Across the bottom, in large black numbers 8142, and printed in small red letters beneath Est. 1823 Fireproof Room, Stamps Not Taken. Scrawled on the ticket in a hurried hand was the date, May, scratched next to the 1914, the simple words 'ring' and the price of redemption '1 pound'.

He had found the ticket – the pledge – in the pocket of the dead spectacled man at the building site. It was all the man had on him. Wiggins was sure that the spectacled man had been at the building site to watch him – and further, that the reason he was there at all was because someone had been watching *Kell* the day before. Someone had seen Kell talk to him, which had given him the tail. This web of surveillance must be at the heart of Holmes's downfall. If Kell had been watched, then they might have put a tail on Wiggins and thus must have seen Holmes at the site – or if not, they could have followed Kell when he visited Holmes two days earlier. Consequently, there was a slim chance the owner of the pawn ticket – the man who died falling from the crane – could lead him to Holmes's killer.

Wiggins looked about him one last time, spilt petrol and horse dung catching in his nose. The Old Kent Road was wide, straight and busy. A tall tram rattled past. Beyond it a painted model swan in the shape of an 's' beckoned to him – the Swan tavern, taking a delivery of huge bulging beer barrels. Reeking of hops. He licked his lips, gripped the ticket and pushed through the half-opened door of the pawnshop.

'Morning, sir,' a snooty clerk trilled. 'Please take a seat at the back there. You'll be called up to a booth directly.'

A counter stretched along half of the back wall, with three partitions. It was shaded there, with low bright lights on the counter but the bench beside it in shadow. Wiggins could also make out the side door, which opened right next to the counter. A man and a woman stood hunched over at one booth, while another tall, long-nosed clerk eyed something suspiciously.

'I ain't here for money,' Wiggins grunted at the older clerk. The man's hair was heavily oiled and whipped over from one ear to the other, atop a polished bald pate.

'A buyer?' The clerk smoothed down a flap of hair. 'Please, how can I help?'

Wiggins stepped to the buying counter. To his right, he saw a doorway open into the back, partially obscured by hanging beads. He could just make out the vast storeroom, stretching into the distance, with gear stuffed any old how on high shelves, each object numbered with a paper docket. The stock that was still pledged, not yet come up for sale, the customers out there, still hoping to find enough money to get it back. Wiggins held out the ticket. 'I need to talk to the boss fella, about this.'

'I really don't think – is that one of ours?'

At that moment, a tall fat man of middle age appeared through the doorway. His belly rattled the beads before his face came into view. He had small black eyes, currants in a bun, and a wave of tobacco smoke gusted with him. 'A nosy parker is it, Phelps?'

'Yes sir, Mr Garratt sir,' the clerk said, nodding his head.

'Leave him to me, Phelps,' Garratt said, peering in disgust at Wiggins. 'I do so like dealing with scruff.' The older man rubbed his pink sausage hands together. 'Tell Dogger to run around the front. He'll be needed to scrape this shit off the step.'

Wiggins waited for this display of boss-ship to be over. Always tiresome, never scary. 'This pledge,' Wiggins said, showing the ticket to Garratt. 'I need to know the address. Just flip the book there, and tell us. Save any bother.'

'Save any bother? You're choice you are,' Garratt said. 'I'll enjoy watching Dogger rip you a new arsehole, I really will.'

'No one needs to get hurt,' Wiggins said, pained. 'Just the address.'

Garratt wiped at his armpits absently. It was early, but the day was turning into a hot one. And Garratt would sweat in the arctic. 'My clientele trust me, they's do. Good old Garratt, they say, is the finest uncle south of the river. The finest north too, 'cept my clients don't much make it that far. Ha ha. No, no, Scruff, I would never divulge such personal information. My word is my bond, my reputation is my business.'

Wiggins sighed at such canard. He pulled a banknote from his pocket, the blunt Kell had advanced against expenses and pay.

'No no.' Garratt put his hands up in mock dismay. 'I will not accept money, I will not break my word.' He said this loud and clear but his eyes told a different story. They almost sweated to see such a note.

'I ain't paying for information,' Wiggins said. 'I wouldn't want to offend, like. No, what I really want is a service revolver. An old one'll do.'

'Is that a five or a ten?' Garratt tried to peer at the colour of Wiggins's money.

'It's a ten.'

'Then we can do business.'

'And sharing information, between businessmen, is a normal part of business, yes?'

'I think we speak the same language,' Garratt twinkled. He roared at one of the clerks, who scuttled off to fetch the gun and came back a moment later, holding the piece with reverence.

Wiggins checked the action on the revolver – a service gun, an officer's gun in fact, he'd seen many during the Boer War and on and off ever since. He looked down the barrel. 'The billy?' he said.

The clerk pushed a box of bullets across the counter. 'Hop it now,' Garratt said to his underling. He licked his lips. Ten pounds was a great score for such an old piece of junk. He laid his hand on the leather-bound ledger, and said, 'And now to business.'

Wiggins pulled out the ten-pound note and pushed it across the counter. Garratt spirited it away with the speed of a conjuror, while Wiggins fiddled once more with the firearm. Garratt swung open the huge ledger, muttering to himself. 'Ah 8142. Yes, here it is. Oh dear, yes indeed. A wedding ring, so sad. I was so pleased we could help. Mr Pilch, of 42a East Street. Not a salubrious area, I'm afraid. The Walworth Road end of the street, if you get my . . . eh?' Garratt gaped in astonishment.

For Wiggins pointed the now loaded pistol, so recently purchased, right at his chest. 'Ta for that. Now, give me the dosh back.' He gestured with his free hand at Garratt's pocket.

'But . . . but, this is infamy. It's robbery!' he cried.

'I just want me tenner.'

Garratt handed over the note, gibbering. 'Call the peelers, Dogger,' he shouted. 'Get down the station. Police! This is theft.'

Wiggins took his money back. 'No it ain't.' He proceeded to unload the gun, and put it back onto the counter. 'Ain't nothing missing. Ain't nothing stolen.' He pointed to the gun.

'But . . . but,' Garratt spluttered.

'All that's happened here is that you've given me some information of a private and personal nature that you really shouldn't have. You wouldn't want that getting around, would you? Not a man of your reputation.' Wiggins sauntered out of the door, tipping his cap to the bemused heavy Dogger as he did so.

Wiggins decided to walk. East Street wasn't far, up Walworth way, and he was enjoying the feel of the sun on his back, so much so that he didn't even detour to the Swan. He didn't hold out much hope for this particular lead. The spectacled man who fell to his death was almost certainly this Mr Pilch, and had almost certainly fallen on hard times. He hadn't been old enough to pawn a wedding ring out of bitterness. Wiggins recalled the man's suit. Well made, once, but fraying. Nevertheless, it had been darned and repaired with a degree of care – as had the rip in his shirt, recently re-stitched with attention and what looked like love. No, Mr Pilch had still been loved by Mrs Pilch. He had pawned his wedding ring out of necessity, not spite.

Pilch clearly wasn't a professional either. He'd panicked at the first sign of discovery. He may have been part of a surveillance network, but presumably he was at the very edge of any web. He'd hardly have any knowledge of the centre. Had he lived. But if Holmes had taught Wiggins anything, it was to follow every lead and to follow it while it was hot.

Wiggins knew the better lead was the Pentonville Postman. Kell would be back in the office, digging up everything they had on him. It was around the time of King Edward VII's funeral, back in '10. Europe's big nobs were all in London, and one of the German contingent had taken a trip to Islington. On the off chance Wiggins had tailed him, and it had led to a barber's shop on Caledonian Road. The idea that a German diplomatic official – a Count no less – needed a haircut was too fanciful even for Kell. It turned out that the German who ran the place – a Karl Gustav Ernst – was operating a clearing house for messages between some German agents and their spy service back home. His barber's salon was literally a post office. They called him the Pentonville Postman because Ernst was also a visiting barber at Pentonville prison around the corner. He'd be in and out of the prison at least once a week, cutting the hair of the warders mostly but also – so they discovered – occasionally the hair of privileged inmates.

Rather than busting it open there and then, Kell had decided to continuously monitor the posting station. He'd persuaded the then Home Secretary Winston Churchill to let the Bureau intercept and read all the post that went in and out of Ernst's shop. (Churchill had to push through a law to make this legal, but legal it now was.) This surveillance operation became the single biggest source of information for the secret service bureau's domestic branch. In many ways, it *was* the Bureau.

Wiggins didn't care about the Bureau, he didn't care about the secret service and he didn't even care too much about German spies running around London. He cared about who killed Sherlock Holmes, and everything else could go to hell.

The thought of his dead mentor rose up in him again as he walked down East Street towards Walworth Road. It was hot now, and the smell of poverty caught in his nose. There was a sweet spot of being poor, weather-wise. Warm enough that you could sleep in your clothes without dying, but cool enough to kill off the stench of blocked drains, rotting food and the full, fat flies that hived around the slums. Today was a hot one – you could see the flies already, massing round the small piles of rubbish dotting these unloved streets.

'Looking for Mr Pilch,' Wiggins said. He'd stopped outside number 42. An old woman sat in the doorway, on a stool, her head uncovered, her scalp showing through thinned-to-nothing grey hair. Beside her, a tiny child clad in a too-big, dirty white dress squinted up. '42a?' Wiggins said again.

'Fack off, tallyman,' the child barked, like a mechanical doll.

'I ain't tally,' Wiggins said. He'd collected debts once, the weekly tally and the larger debts that needed the heavy mob. The child had, quite reasonably, mistook him.

'Tally's here!' the child barked again, this time back into the darkness off the hallway behind her.

The old woman scratched her chin, looking up at Wiggins. Then she nudged the child with her elbow. The child jumped. 'Hop it, tally!' the child shouted at him again. 'I'll get me dad.' Then she disappeared inside the house at pace.

'Market. His missus. Selling hankies. They owe rent,' the old woman spat out the words seemingly without moving her mouth, which was dry and raw and rough. 'Now git, 'fore my son come down and whip you.'

'Whip me?'

'I don't want no trouble with the beak.'

Wiggins glanced up at the house. A two-floor double-fronted tenement that housed four families at least. 'Alright, mum,' he said and went on his way.

A sparse market straggled the street at the Walworth Road end of East Street. Wiggins picked his way through it. People were fanning themselves against the heat. He could smell the rotting fruit. Flies bunched around the butcher's stall, feeding. Rubbish burned in a small brazier, wafting smoke across the market, smudging the wilted greens and reds of the greengrocer stalls.

Wiggins saw her on the corner of Walworth Road, squeezed between the rattling trams and the final stall. She had a blanket on a tiny patch of pavement, displaying hand-stitched handkerchiefs and little else. She sat on her knees, head almost bowed like a beggar, deliberately avoiding any-one's eyes. As he approached, he saw the unmistakable swell of her belly too. A pregnant woman fallen on her uppers, with now a husband dead.

'Mrs Pilch?' he said quietly.

She looked up sharply. 'Yes?'

He hesitated, the supplication in her eyes almost unbearable. She saw it in his face. She saw the pity. 'Have you seen my Jack? Do you know him?'

Wiggins set himself. Noted the oft-mended tears in her dress, the worn-to-nothing elbows, the fingernails bitten to the quick. 'There was an accident, up on the County Hall site.'

'An accident? What sort of accident? Where's Jack?'

'Work there, did he?'

'Oh my god, oh my god.' She began collecting up her wares. 'I knew something was wrong. Where is he, mister? Tell me where he is. Is he alright?'

Wiggins crouched down and stilled her with a gentle hand. 'Here,' he said softly. 'Take ten bob for the lot.' He gave her a ten-shilling note, at least twice what the hankies were worth. 'And you look after 'em for me.'

'But, but . . .'

'Who was he working for?' Wiggins asked.

'But Jack, where's Jack? I don't understand. Who are you?'

'The TALLY!' a small voice shouted loud down the length of the market. Wiggins stood up and looked back the way he'd come. The girl from number 42 pointed, unmistakably, at him. Behind her, a huge man with a wooden club stomped after her. 'There, Dad!' she cried again. 'The facking tally.'

Wiggins sighed. He liked the girl, but didn't fancy her dad much. 'Try Horseferry Road mortuary,' he said to Mrs Pilch.

She stared at him uncomprehending, as if trying to place the unusual word 'mortuary'. And then she found it, and let out a wail so loud and sudden it startled passers-by. Everyone turned to them, and Wiggins felt a stab of guilt. It pained him, but what else could he do? He was sure she didn't know a stroke about what her husband had been up to. He was pretty sure her husband didn't know much either, other than who to follow and where to report to when his day was done.

It was the London way, the world's way – these great games between powerful Empires, with powerful men like Holmes and Kell and Von Bork playing them like cards at the casino – and it was paupers like wretched, pregnant Mrs Pilch left sobbing in the dirt who had to pay for the chips.

The little girl and her large dad neared. Wiggins stepped away from Mrs Pilch, then out into Walworth Road just as a tram rattled towards him. Part of him wanted to fight the man mountain who approached, and his club. It enraged him, this blameless woman sobbing into the dirt, alone, with ten bob and fuck all else. The heat flooded his face, his heart pumped and his muscles tensed.

'Come here, Tally,' the man cried, the club raised.

Then Wiggins stepped back, out into the main road, and took hold of the pole on the tram's boarding platform as it sped past. He hauled himself onto the tram in one sleek movement and turned away from the man, the club, and the pregnant woman sobbing in the gutter.

These people weren't his enemies. He needed to use his anger for the real fight to come.

5

Wednesday 1 July 1914. London sweltered. It was so hot, in fact, that the Fleet Street newspapers devoted many inches to the weather. In particular, the society pages screeched with scandalised delight at the 'scenes' at Henley Regatta, as harassed chefs threw meat overboard and served only 'salad'. The foreign press, read in London only by such concerned polyglots as Captain Vernon Kell, busied itself rather with the deepening crisis in the Balkans. The extent of the Serbian government's culpability for the assassination of the Archduke was the key issue, together with the Austro-Hungarian Emperor Franz Joseph's appetite and ability to do anything about it.

'Let's pull the Postman,' Wiggins said as soon as he got into Kell's office. 'He's bound to know where Von Bork is. Let's rip him apart.'

Meeting Mrs Pilch had upset Wiggins. To see a woman, a widow, in such distress had unsettled him. The child inside her, coming into such a world. It wasn't as if her husband had done that much wrong, either. They were always going after the henchmen, the people at the bottom of the deck. He was working for the head of the Bureau, high up in the government structure – and no doubt the people making the decisions, the Von Borks of this world, on the German side were the same. Yet when the battle started, when push came to shove, it was the little men who lost their lives – and the lives of their loved ones were destroyed.

He'd gone straight back to Watergate House, raging still. Not just at the injustice of the world, but – perversely – he'd been hit once more by the death of Holmes. Unusually, one of the boss class had lost their life, and Wiggins was determined that his equivalent had to suffer. He wanted Von Bork, he wanted the German 'Kell' dead, not just the men in his employ.

'No. We will leave Ernst alone,' Kell said calmly. 'We will do as we've always done. Analyse his post, check the traffic. That's where we'll find the answers.'

'Do you know where Von Bork is?'

Kell hesitated. 'Not yet.'

'Nothing from the rozzers?'

'Inspector Melville is, ah, well, they have some interesting leads . . .' Kell tailed off. Trying to convince Wiggins that the official police might be of some help was harder even than doing the same for Holmes. Both men would rely on the Metropolitan police for muscle and actual arrests, but neither would trust them to investigate the origin of a fart.

Wiggins shook his head. 'They've got nothing. So I'll go and ask Ernst. Beat it out of him, simple.'

'You will do no such thing!' Kell pushed his chair away. 'We can't let on that we know who Ernst is, who he works for, what that barber's shop actually is. Do you know how much intelligence we get from that post office?'

'Why would Von Bork's plans be in any of those letters?'

'You can't just barge in there – it would be, well, it would be the death of the Bureau.'

'I don't give a fuck about the Bureau,' Wiggins growled. 'I'm just after a murderer.'

* * *

Winston Churchill was not aging well. His sandy hair had thinned, the lines around his petulant mouth had sharpened and the deep ridges on his forehead looked like they belonged on the side of a boar's head at a banquet.

They were not at a banquet, however. Kell had been given an audience with the First Lord of the Admiralty after he'd just finished a sumptuous luncheon at his club. Kell had been trying to meet him ever since the assassination – he'd been trying to meet with all the important men in government – and finally Churchill had found the time for him.

'Germany is preparing for war,' Churchill rumbled. 'Her navy is massing, her army is growing, the war bells are ringing.'

Kell sighed. He'd made this point only moments before, while Churchill ostentatiously lit his cigar and seemed not to hear. He went on (he always did). 'We must gird our loins, Captain Kell, we must be alert, we must be vigilant . . .'

'Yes, sir,' Kell managed to interject, for Churchill had reached for his port and therefore could not physically speak while drinking. 'If we could get back to the issue of, er, funds?'

The financing of the secret service bureau had always been a thorny issue, with the budget shifting from one department to another, with pots of money here and there, but never a steady, demarcated stream. Kell knew he needed more resources, he assumed war was coming and he'd been scouring Whitehall to find a cabinet minister who agreed. He felt some relief that, at last, he'd found one, if only it hadn't been bloody Winston. It was always bloody Winston.

'Strike all the blows you can, Captain,' Churchill said, stabbing the cigar at him. 'As hard and as fast, as deep and as telling as you may. I will back you.'

(He wouldn't, Kell knew, unless it would benefit him.)

'I will back you to the hilt.' (As he plunges that blade into my back when it all goes wrong, Kell thought but did not say.)

Churchill swallowed the remains of his port and Kell took the opportunity to ask, 'A facility for this, er, support?'

'Do I look like a man used to dealing in details? Do I look like I know the insides of a ledger? Do I, Captain Kell?' Churchill pushed his chair back and rose. 'Speak to Martindale,' he muttered, then waited as one of the attendants rushed forward with his coat.

Kell resigned himself to another internal administrative battle with the Admiralty paymaster, but at least he had the verbal support of the First Lord. That was Winston all over – he'd support you with words, but those words would suddenly evaporate if the political weather changed.

'Ah, Kell.' Churchill turned to him as an afterthought. 'Is Agent W in the field?'

Kell hesitated in surprise. He'd forgotten that Churchill knew of Wiggins, indeed regarded him as his own private agent. A few years ago, when Churchill was Home Secretary, he'd tried to use Wiggins as an *agent provocateur* during the Welsh miners' strike at Tonypandy. He clearly loved the idea of having an unofficial agent, a working-class 'non-gentleman', ready to carry out his own personal commands in order to further the government's cause. Since he had moved to the Admiralty, Churchill and Kell's paths had rarely crossed, and Kell realised he hadn't even told him that Wiggins left the service.

'Yes, sir,' Kell replied. 'He is in the field.'

'Good show, good show,' Churchill muttered. 'He can be the wrecking ball.'

* * *

Wiggins started on his second pint. He stood outside the Prince Arthur on Caledonian Road Islington and inwardly fumed. Sweat prickled his back, and even the beer could not quell his mood. Across the road, about fifty yards away, Karl Gustav Ernst's barbershop stood in open reproach. Reproach to the idea that he should do nothing, while Von Bork swans his way around London whenever he may. Reproach for the ten bob he gave that poor pregnant woman rather than the ten pounds. Reproach that he stood there drinking beer, in the hot afternoon sun, while murder went unpunished.

Kell had flatly refused to let him interrogate Karl Ernst. They'd got quite heated and, in the end, Kell had threatened to have him arrested if he disobeyed. He'd told him to cool off in the pub, while he went to get some real help for the cause. It was rare for Kell to advise him to have a drink, and Wiggins knew he'd pushed it as far as it could go. He understood, for without that barbershop-cum-post office, the Bureau's single biggest source of intelligence would be destroyed forever. He'd promised not to move in on Ernst.

But that didn't mean he couldn't get a haircut, did it? He put the empty pint glass on the sill, and headed for a cut and shave.

'Good morning, sir, please, come.' The barber, Ernst, gestured to a free chair. A bald man in his sixties, with a comfortable belly, a thick neck, and a leather apron. Wiggins sat as Ernst carried on with the only other customer in the shop. Wiggins took in the place. Two swivel chairs, a large mirror facing each; a grid of shelves covered the whole wall, with a tub of hair pomade peeking out of each one. *Brilliantine.* The back of the shop was guarded by a small counter and a gleaming silver till. A few stray papers sat by the till, together with an impressively large receipt spike. A thin young man in a striped apron sat on a stool and stared listlessly at an unlit stove. He bent forward, all angles, like the rickety metal chimney that spidered up to the ceiling.

Ernst pattered away with his client. He slapped on pomade, obviously just about to finish. A lemony, liquorice scent filled the air. 'She'll like this, no?' Ernst said in a jolly tone. 'The Greeks say it is aphrodisiacal, ya.'

'They can say what they like, as long as I get some,' the surly customer muttered. 'That'll do, Fritz,' he said.

'Wonderful,' Ernst said. As he headed to the back of the shop he clicked his fingers at the boy and pointed to the floor. 'Billy.' The young man leaped up and began to sweep away the dark curls of hair.

The surly customer shuffled to the counter and muttered something under his breath. Wiggins caught the phrase, 'French Letter'. Ernst smiled slightly and dug beneath the till before placing a paper bag on the counter. The customer spirited it away in a second, and paid his bill. Ernst wrote out a double receipt, handed one to the customer and then impaled the other on the large pin by the till. The front door rattled and trilled as the customer left, and Wiggins saw in the mirror that Ernst let his smile slip for a moment. Then he turned his attention to Wiggins.

'What can I do for you, sir?' he asked. 'Cut, shave, would you like something for your hair?'

Wiggins examined him in the mirror for a second. Ernst was a man who smiled often. You could tell by the crow's feet at his eyes, the lines under his fat cheeks. Fine beads of sweat dotted his forehead, and he had no hair apart from an immaculate moustache. He did not look like a picture of the German master spy, the ones he'd read about in *The Invasion of 1910*, or the silly stories in the *Daily Mail*. He looked just like a German barber, and London had dozens.

'Cut, shave, ta,' Wiggins nodded.

Ernst billowed a sheet under his chin, then took hold of Wiggins's hair in proprietorial fashion. 'Hmm, it's good, ya. Thick. I have cut your hair before, I think? I never forget a head.'

'Nah,' Wiggins muttered.

Ernst bent down and spoke softly. 'Not while you were a guest of His Majesty?'

Wiggins glanced into the mirror and then away, embarrassed. Ernst chuckled to himself. 'Don't worry, I won't let the cat out of the sack,' he said softly. Wiggins relaxed his shoulders. Best let a man think he's discovered a small secret about you – he's more likely to miss the big one. It was the same with most lies: a person's more likely to swallow a big one if they've found a tiddler.

He signed to the boyo. 'Ere lad,' he said, holding out a coin. 'Get us some scran, will you?'

The boy looked at Ernst, who nodded. Wiggins handed him the coin and went on. 'Bread and cheese'll do – but not from the boozer. Go to the Eyetie place down the road.'

The tall thin boy undid his apron, took the coin and left. The door rattled and the bell trilled loud, leaving Wiggins alone with Ernst and a sudden, heavy silence.

'Shave first, ya.' Ernst already had a razor blade in his hand. He stepped slightly to the side and began sharpening it on a heavy strap that hung from his belt. Swish. Swish. Swish, the razor went. It caught the light on every down stroke, sparkling in the mirror. Wiggins waited.

'Oil or cream?' Ernst asked.

Wiggins had to remind himself that this jovial barber, Ernst, almost certainly worked for the man who had killed Sherlock Holmes. He watched him as he put the razor down on the sideboard and reached for a bottle of Trumper's Old Original hair oil.

At that moment Wiggins leaped out of the chair and, in one movement, grasped the back of Ernst's fat neck and smashed his face into the mirror. It cracked into a crazy star. Ernst groaned in pain. Wiggins wrenched him back into the chair.

'Vas, vas . . . my nose is broke,' Ernst muttered, holding his nose and whimpering.

Wiggins yanked the leather sharpener at Ernst's belt and bound his free hand to the chair with it. Ernst began to shout, and cry out for help. Wiggins slapped him across the face. 'I'm just here for the money,' he hissed. 'But I'll cut your tongue out if you make another sound.'

Ernst shrank back in alarm. Wiggins strode to the till.

'Take it,' Ernst whimpered. 'Take it.'

Wiggins acted the wild thug. He picked up the till and brought it down on the counter in a riot of bells and coins and twisting metal. The tray sprang out, splashing small coins onto the floor. Wiggins grabbed a handful of them, thrusting the money into his pockets. 'Where's the notes?' he roared.

'No notes, no notes, please,' Ernst cried. 'I'm barber, not banker. Take the change, please. Go.'

Wiggins ripped out the drawers and threw papers everywhere, acting the wild man still. He knew he only had a second, a thief wouldn't tarry long, and certainly wouldn't meticulously rifle the counter – not with the lad returning in minutes and the hue and cry all but guaranteed to start. His mind raced. Not for the first time, he tried to imitate his mentor – where would someone like Ernst hide secret information? What would Holmes do? What was the short story the doctor had showed him once, about hiding things? As he thought, he swept the contents of the shelves from beneath the counter, shouting wildly about banknotes as he did so.

'Arrg!' Ernst cried out. Wiggins looked up. The old man had freed himself and now brandished the razor. 'Get out!' Ernst cried.

Suddenly inspired, Wiggins grasped the receipt spike by the till and leaped towards Ernst like a fencer. 'Behave!' he growled.

Ernst quailed behind one of the chairs and moved out of his way. Wiggins walked slowly to the door, his eyes and the point of the foot-long spike pointing at Ernst as he did so. 'One move, and I'll have an eye.'

'The police will . . .'

'What? Take this point in the guts for a couple of quid?' Wiggins shook his head grimly and kicked the front door open. 'Best keep schtum, eh?' he said, and then went out into the street.

The young boy was running down the street towards him, with a sandwich packet in his hand. The sight of Wiggins with the weapon brought him up short. Wiggins walked briskly towards him, gently took the package from his hand, and said, 'Keep the change.'

'Brussels!' Kell leaped up in excitement. 'You're sure?'

Wiggins plunged the upended receipt spike into the desk. 'I'm sure.'

'Mrs Jepson, Mrs Jepson.' Kell strode to his office door and called out down the stairwell. 'Please come up here at once.' He turned back to Wiggins. 'How do you know?'

Wiggins pointed to the spike. On it, like the ridges of a decaying bottle brush, the many white and yellowed receipts of weeks and months of haircuts. Wiggins held one of these receipts in his hand. It was like all the rest, a small white oblong with a printed header and a few scribbled numbers or words.

Kell took it from him and examined it. It had the word 'Brux' scribbled on it, with a PR next to it. Beneath it, the numbers 14 07 04. 'What's this?' he asked. 'Where did you get this?'

'Ernst.'

'I told you not to go!' Kell cried in frustration. 'You've played our one trump card, for nothing.' He wiped his face with his hands and took a breath. 'This is a disaster, Wiggins, you absolute fool. I expressively forbade it. This is the greatest catastrophe that we've faced since Agadir, it's, it's . . .'

Mrs Jepson poked her head around the door to interrupt this flow. 'You . . . summoned me, sir,' she said.

Kell looked up at her, sensing an air of insubordination but unable to substantiate such a charge with evidence. 'Mrs Jepson ah, yes could you . . .' He glanced back at Wiggins. 'You are sure it is Brussels?' Wiggins nodded. 'Could you check with the passport people at Dover, Folkestone, Tilbury? Get a list of German-named passengers going out to the continent, as soon as possible.'

'Shouldn't I check at Charing Cross and Victoria first, sir?' Mrs Jepson asked, brow furrowed. 'I presume the boat train would be the quickest way for anyone to escape

London. If I got a list of those who boarded on the, er, night that you're investigating then maybe . . .'

'Maybe?'

'Well, sir, it might be worth noting the names of those who bought a ticket on the night itself. Rather than booking beforehand. Perhaps the journey was improvised?'

Kell sighed. Did no one look to him for expertise these days? Wiggins's influence already exerted on the staff. 'Yes, yes,' he said vaguely and waved her away. 'But check the port logs too.'

He tried to regain his composure. This was turning into the worst week of his professional career. He fixed his eyes on Wiggins. 'I cannot believe you blew Ernst. That post box was everything. It was . . .' Kell struggled to convey the calamity of the situation. He might even lose his job. '. . . all I had.'

'I didn't blow nothing,' Wiggins said. 'First off, he thinks he's been robbed of a couple of quid, not rumbled. Second, he thinks I'm an old Pentonville lag not some bloody spy. I mean, look at me.' Wiggins gestured to his torn trousers and dirty shirt. 'Do I really look like I work for the British government? Do I look like I work for anyone?'

Kell shifted his head in acknowledgment. He then listened as Wiggins told him what had happened at the barbershop.

'You're not going to get arrested again, are you?' he asked when Wiggins had finished. 'I don't think I could face having to extract you from a police cell again.'

'Nah, I'm clear. I doubt old Karl Gustav will kick up much of a fuss neither.'

Kell sighed. He'd always hoped that his secret service would be a smooth-running, invisible machine, the

workings of which would never be known to the general
public or, indeed, most other authorities. Wiggins operated
on the edge, though, and he was neither controllable nor
contained. He reminded Kell of his wife. It was infuriating.

'What makes you think Von Bork has gone to Brussels?'
He held up the receipt. 'This? Come on.'

'Look at it,' Wiggins pressed. 'It's new. See how white it
is, ain't curled up at the edges, nothing. Now see here, on
the spike. I took it from near the bottom.'

'Yes . . . and?'

'They're yellowing, brown, curled up. They've been
there weeks, months even. You can tell by the date on some
of them an' all. But not this one. This one's new.' Wiggins
looked at the note again.

It had come to him, the old story, when he was rifling
that till in Ernst's shop. The best place to hide something
is in plain sight. Doctor Watson had even shown him some
Frenchie detective story about it. He'd been at Baker Street
once and heard the doctor and Mr Holmes arguing about
the story. 'Dupin is an inferior fellow,' Holmes was saying.
'The mind reading is but a cheap trick.'

'But Holmes,' Watson replied. 'Surely there's some truth
in this, about hiding the letter?'

'Perhaps,' Holmes muttered.

Wiggins had remembered. The villain in the story had
hidden a stolen letter on his desk, out in the open, amongst
all the other papers – in other words, hidden in plain sight,
hidden by virtue of not being hidden at all. And so it was
with Ernst's fake receipt.

'I'm telling you,' Wiggins went on to Kell. 'Ernst took the
top ones off, placed that on the spike, and put the old ones
back on.'

'But what does it even mean? I can see the Brux, I suppose, but the numbers mean nothing and what are we to
make of PR?'

Wiggins exhaled theatrically. 'You're the one that speaks
German.'

'And French, Russian, Mandarin actually, Italian too, of
course.'

'It's a postal address, ain't it? Brussels, poste restantay'

'Restante,' Kell corrected the pronunciation in reflex.
'And the numbers?'

'A date, ain't it? 14 07 04. Don't the Germans write it
that way round?'

'My god, you're right!' Kell cried. 'July 4th. But how did
you know that?'

'Noticed when we was in Germany back in '10, cleaning
the arse of Mr Cumming and his pair of jokers.'

He notices everything, Kell thought. Damn the man.
'But what does it mean?'

'It means I'm going to Brussels.'

6

The red, blue and white tricolour fluttered in
the light of a burning, open torch. First one
torch, then a second, then a third. And more flags,
held up above a swelling crowd. The tricolour was
smudged with a coat of arms, a double-headed
eagle off-centre, the national flag of Serbia. At
the heart of the central blue band, a dark circle
appeared, then grew red and hot until the flag
was in flames; and the second, then the third.
Across the heaving Viennese crowd, Serbian flags
burned like beacons. Tossed and cursed with anger
and intent, as those in the crowd chanted for
action while the aging Emperor dithered. The
crowd would riot, for they believed as one that
the Serbian government was behind the assassination of Franz Ferdinand, that Princip and his
conspirators acted upon express Serbian orders.
The newspapers across continental Europe led
with stories such as this. In the British press on
Thursday 2 July 1914, however, much is made of a
campaign to make more women OBEs, and the great
explorer Shackleton is back on the front pages.

Wiggins looked out of the window as the train rolled slowly
into the station in Brussels. Great bundles of imported
English newspapers lay ready to be despatched across the
city. He'd read most of them already, from yesterday, on

his way over from London. The train came to a halt, and he waited for it to clear. Better to come out with the last of the passengers, rather than show your face in the hustle and bustle at the front.

'You English, ya?' The man opposite finally spoke. He'd been reading his own newspaper for hours, and tossed it on the empty seat beside him. He too was waiting for the crowds to depart before getting off.

'London,' Wiggins said. 'Not the same.'

'Ha. I see you looking at the newspapers,' he went on. 'I love England. I wait the tables at the Macclesfield, in Soho, ya. You know it?'

Wiggins always got this when he left London. People assumed that he knew all the people there, and all the pubs too. Didn't they know it was a city of four million? 'Oyster bar,' he said in reply. 'Posh.'

'Ya ya, that's it!' the Belgian said. 'Papa De Hem will be so happy you said "posh". His dreaming coming true, ha. From sea captain to high society, for sure.'

Wiggins smiled sadly. The last time he'd been in the oyster bar was fifteen years earlier, when it was a plain old pub. He'd tailed a bent stockbroker in there, at the behest of Sherlock Holmes. He wondered if such echoes would ever stop.

The carriage and corridor had now cleared enough for them to get up and leave. Wiggins reached up and took his luggage down from the rack. He slung the knapsack over his shoulder, and then held up a large bicycle wheel, wrapped in brown paper.

'Are you a cyclist, ya? Do you like the Tour de France?' the Belgian asked.

'You what?'

'The cycling race? Thys will win. He's Belgian.'

Wiggins nodded slightly. 'It's for a friend,' he said, and gestured for the Belgian waiter to go first out of the door. As he did so, he noticed the discarded newspaper – a Belgian one he guessed, VOORUIT. 'What does it mean?' he asked.

'Vooruit? Forward.'

'Nah.' Wiggins shook his head. 'I mean the headline there, Rake Kogels?'

The waiter hesitated for a moment, finding the right word in English, and then said, 'Good Bullets.'

Wiggins had worked hard to be on that train, to get to Brussels at all. He was convinced that the fake receipt at Ernst's barbershop meant something, and the link to Von Bork made the most sense. It was the best lead he had on Holmes's killer, though, and it was the kind of lead that needed to be followed hot. Von Bork would not have stayed in London after such a deed. And as for the accomplices, they could wait. He had plans for them. As it was, he'd lose two or three days at most if the trip to Belgium came to nothing. But he didn't think it would come to nothing. If he were Von Bork, or whoever else it was for that matter, and he'd killed Sherlock Holmes, he'd be out of the country like a shot.

Convincing Kell hadn't proved so straightforward. They'd argued about it back at the office, when Wiggins had first produced the note.

'I can't send you off across the channel on such flimsy evidence,' Kell said. 'It's a wild goose chase.'

'What's the point of me being here,' Wiggins simmered, 'if I can't hunt?'

'The expense,' Kell said. 'An overseas trip? Besides, I have absolutely no authority to act – or to commission action – outside of the United Kingdom.'

Mrs Jepson interrupted at that moment. Wiggins noticed her properly for the first time. He'd been through the office a couple of times and he approved of the number of women Kell now had on the staff. In his experience, women were smarter than men – or at least, better suited to analytical and intelligence work. They didn't have cocks to lead the way for them, didn't constantly need to show you how clever they were. And they'd been taught to notice everything since they were children, notice and keep schtum.

Mrs Jepson was the smartest one of them, Wiggins realised. She was younger than the rest too, not much older than him, though her clothes aged her. She wore a heavy dress, despite the heat, with dark green fringing. Spectacles hung from a thin cord around her neck, and she frowned constantly, a facial expression extenuated by the severe bunning of her hair. Deliberate subterfuge. And Wiggins guessed there was no Mr Jepson, lest you count her father. Underneath the frowning and the dowdy clothes, she looked too happy to be married, too confident and content to be worrying about some wastrel drinking her pay packet away at home. The disguise was just a feint to put off men. He didn't blame her – being a looker as a woman was a curse. He'd been beautiful once, as a young boy in the workhouse, and he wouldn't wish that on anyone. Women had that shit their whole lives, or at least until they got old and grey and invisible.

'Captain Kell,' Mrs Jepson said again, as Kell appeared not to hear her. She stood at the doorway, and almost tapped her foot in frustration.

'What's that?' he said airily, without meeting her eye.

'You asked for the passport lists at the ports, and . . .'

'Ah yes, thank you, Mrs, erm, um yes just put them on the desk.'

She glared at Kell but he did not notice. Wiggins stepped forward. 'And what else?' he asked.

'I asked for the last-minute passengers, as I suggested. The ones going on the boat train, all the way through to the continent.'

'And?' Kell drawled, finally taking notice of the woman.

'Three men turned up, on the lists. One man came with his wife, the other two were alone. Booked all the way through.'

'This is all useless, without the names,' Kell waved his hand at her.

'I have the names, sir, of course.'

'Give 'em here,' Wiggins urged. He smiled at her, a conspiracy of competence.

'Aren't they confidential? I know we can get the passport lists, but this? How on earth did you get them to tell you?' Kell wondered aloud.

Mrs Jepson just looked at him. Like any woman who looked at a man who didn't understand how women got things out of men. Wiggins cackled. 'Diamond,' he said. 'You're pure carat. What you reckon?' Wiggins said this to Mrs Jepson, not Kell.

'A Mister Athelney Smith, a Monsieur Maxim DuPont and a couple, Mr and Mrs Herman Wolff.'

'No Von Bork?' Kell asked. He got a contemptuous look from both Wiggins and Mrs Jepson for his pains.

'Well, no sir,' she said. 'But he'd hardly be . . .'

'Yes, yes,' Kell interrupted, impatient. 'Check the names against the registry, will you?'

Mrs Jepson sighed almost imperceptibly. 'I've already done that, sir. Smith is a commercial traveller, for Pears Soap. He's in our list because he travels to Germany among other places. He was debriefed two years ago, and there is nothing irregular about him. The others don't show at all.'

'Anything interesting from the passport lists?' Wiggins asked.

'Not as suspicious as these names. I mean, I don't think I would buy a continental train ticket at the last minute, would you? Unless it was very urgent. And why would it be urgent?'

'What's your instinct?' Wiggins asked. 'With these names?'

She paused, and the lines of her forehead wrinkled. 'I prefer to base any, er, insight I might have on evidence rather than instinct. I do not believe in relying on intuition.'

Wiggins nodded. He'd heard that before, from Mr Holmes, although Holmes would hardly have credited a woman with such a thought. That was Holmes's fault of course, one of his blind spots. Wiggins had no such prejudice. Although he was more inclined to follow his gut. He tapped the desk as he turned to Kell. 'I've got to rule out these two. DuPont and Wolff. And his wife,' he added, with a nod to Mrs Jepson. 'Brussels it is.'

Kell stared at Wiggins evenly. Then he dismissed Mrs Jepson with another wave of his soft hands. He waited for her to leave, then turned back to Wiggins. 'I can't pay for it, man, you know that.'

'Then we'd better go and see *him*,' Wiggins said.

Mansfield Cumming stared at his desk. He moved a piece of paper from one side to the other and looked again. Then he lifted up the blotting pad and readjusted its position. His eyes strayed to the drinks cabinet. His clerk, Michaels, would be going home soon, and he wondered if he could have a whiskey now. It was one of the drawbacks of living and working in the same set of apartments. You couldn't have a peg at a perfectively reasonable hour without someone thinking you were some kind of soak. Irksome.

He turned his liquid eyes to the telephone. Best not have a drink, not yet. That blasted man Kell had just rung, and insisted on coming round in person. As pushy as ever, he always wanted something. And yet he was the one with the staff. Why should it always fall to Cumming, the head of the foreign secret service, to do Kell's bidding? Surely his was the senior service, for all it must remain secret. Damned impertinence. His eyes shifted once more to the decanter of scotch on the side. Perhaps a quick snifter.

'I wouldn't if I was you.'

Cumming gasped in surprise and swivelled in his chair. 'Who the devil are you?' he cried, and then called out to the door. 'Michaels, Michaels. It's an, an . . . intruder!' He got up with surprising speed and reached for the umbrella stand.

'Steady on,' Wiggins said. He thought the old man might do himself an injury.

Cumming whipped a walking stick from the stand, and began struggling with it in panic. Wiggins stood by the open window from whence he'd entered, and waited. Part of him wanted to introduce himself properly, to put the old man's mind at rest. Another part of him was having too much fun.

'Ah, at last,' Cumming cried. He'd finally freed the sword from his swordstick and brandished it at Wiggins. 'En garde.'

'Easy, sir. We have met. Down the boozer on Victoria Street, and again, in Borkum. Yous call me Agent W, or double O, something like that. I'm with Captain Kell.'

'Michaels,' Cumming shouted again over his shoulder at the door. 'INTRUDER.'

The door finally opened to end this stand-off. 'You called, sir. Can I help?' Michaels asked.

'Are you deaf, man? We've an intruder! Look, there.'

Michaels, a blinking, fat-lipped man, glanced at Wiggins without curiosity. 'Yes, sir. Agent OO if you remember, sir. Captain Kell is on his way up. He said you were expecting him.'

Cumming peered at Wiggins over his sword point. 'You! Double O!'

'Careful with that,' Wiggins replied.

The truth slowly began to dawn. Cumming peered some more at Wiggins. The two had met, more than once, including a rather embarrassing episode in Germany that Cumming had rather expelled from his memory. It didn't do to owe the lower classes. 'How did you get in here?' he rasped. 'Through the window? Why?'

Despite his tone, Wiggins could tell the old man was intrigued. He held the sword by his side and walked over to the window, looking out and down at the small parapet that ran along the windows of all the top-floor flats. Cumming glanced upwards. 'From the roof?' he asked, marvelling now, his anger quite subsided.

'Captain Kell, sir,' Michaels announced.

Kell came in, noticed Wiggins there before him. Again, blast the man. It was as if he clambered from roof to roof to get about the place. It was most disconcerting. 'Cumming,' he said. 'Good evening.'

Cumming didn't notice. He was too busy looking out at Wiggins's means of entrance. 'Remarkable,' he said again. 'Secret of course. Very good. Evading any sort of surveillance.' He was excited now.

'Cumming,' Kell said again.

The old man gestured out of the window and spoke to Wiggins. 'Do you always come and go like this?'

'Only when the gaff's like as not watched.'

'Yes, no one saw you come in, very good,' Cumming said in excitement. 'Michaels! Can we arrange something similar for me?' he said, looking from his secretary to the open sixth-floor window.

'Your wooden leg, sir. Might be a problem.'

'Hmmm. Ah Kell, there you are. Late as usual. What do you want?'

The conversation didn't go well at first. Wiggins could see the two men detested each other, and detested the 'office' of each other as well. To Cumming, Kell was a sneak, a man prepared to spy on his own people, the worse kind of dishonour. The fact that Kell (and his underling Wiggins) had saved him didn't help. For it was Wiggins and Kell who extracted Cumming from a disastrous expedition to Germany four years earlier. Cumming's two agents were arrested in ignominious circumstances, and imprisoned. Wiggins, Kell and Constance had managed to smuggle Cumming out of the country by the skin of their teeth.

Wiggins could feel the weight of that expedition now, could almost see the sag in Cumming's shoulders, though it was never mentioned. It would never be mentioned, but everyone in the room knew what happened, knew the debt Cumming owed, and knew the depth of incompetence the whole escapade revealed. Nevertheless, Kell launched into an explanation of why they were there, and what they wanted from him.

'No, no, Captain Kell.' (Cumming always liked to use his rank, given that he himself was a Commander.) 'The service simply cannot afford this kind of expenditure. To send a man to the continent in such a way? We are stretched tight. Besides, it seems to me this pursuit of a "little black book" is very much a domestic affair. Not part of the foreign service's competencies at all.'

'At least we can agree on something,' Kell said. Wiggins glared at him, so he went on. 'But this is a matter of national security, Cumming.'

The old man scowled. 'It's a wild goose chase.'

'It ain't no chase,' Wiggins said finally. 'It's a hunt.' He'd let the two toffs argue it out long enough. He'd seen the twinkle in Cumming's eye when he'd stepped through the window. 'Captain Kell here is a bit squeamish, like, a bit careful. He likes to step gently round the dirt in the road, likes to keep his kid gloves spotless. So he don't tell you the truth of this mission.'

Cumming glanced across at Kell, then back to Wiggins. He nodded. 'Go on then, if you must.'

'You and me, we's men of action, men of war. We know that this world, this whole spy malarkey, ain't about faint-hearts and Queensberry Rules. The Captain here has to follow those rules, he's the home service, he can't break the British law. But you, you're a man apart.' Wiggins could literally see his chest swell. 'Soon as I cross that channel, I'm *your* man, and I can do *anything*.'

'Anything?' Cumming asked. His eyes danced.

'All I ask is the chance to . . . get that book the Captain wants.'

'And . . .'

Wiggins glanced between Kell and Cumming. Kell knew what he was going to do, and obviously didn't approve – he was a straight die in that respect. Any hint of illegal violence and he'd blanch, though probably as much at the illegality as the violence. Wiggins judged that Kell was ultimately happy enough for Wiggins to do most things, as long as the more distasteful elements of any extreme action weren't discussed. It was the *discussing* it that was the thing that lacked taste, the making explicit of what should be implicit, making the covert overt.

He couldn't say that then, though, he could not verbalise what he wanted to do. But he needed Cumming to agree to fund him on the hunt, and anything that made Kell look weak was good with him. 'You can see it, guv, you've got the vision. Picture it, a freelance agent working for the Crown but not of the Crown – totally deniable, a Whitechapel scruff, an oik – able to go, on your orders, anywhere in Europe. In the world, even.'

'Yes, yes,' Cumming nodded excitedly. 'You might need special equipment,' he went on, eyeing his discarded sword-stick.

'Course. And in the execution of such missions – as this one here proposed – an agent (an unofficial agent mark) might have to, well, act on the edge, or even outside the law.'

'You must, yes.'

'Even if those actions are of the extreme nature.'

Cumming frowned for a moment. 'I don't follow . . .'

Wiggins flicked his eyes at Kell, who stared back levelly as if to say *you've dug this hole, I can't help you*. 'You know, the kind of thing that might happen . . . in a war?'

'Ohh!'Cumming finally got the point. His eyes widened. He clutched his chest. 'You want me to give you permission, even licence to . . . kill?'

And so it was, the following day, that Wiggins found himself getting off the Brussels train. As soon as Cumming had understood that he was doing something unprecedented, the height of espionage sophistication, something that only he, Commander Cumming, could agree to – given the nature of his bureau and his brief – he couldn't give Wiggins enough money, together with a stream of fairly minor instructions. He loved it, the old fool. Wiggins had finally left Cumming's office with the old man muttering to his secretary about rigging a rope ladder so he could also enter and exit by the window.

While Kell and the admirable Mrs Jepson spent the rest of the night and the next day arranging his tickets, identification and information, Wiggins put in place the London part of his plan. He would leave nothing to the police unless he had to, and he had no faith that they'd run to ground any of Von Bork's conspirators. The money Cumming had advanced him was significant, and he put it to good use. Cumming, like Kell, seemed to have no real conception of the cost of anything and assumed that Wiggins would run on a similar budget to them. This gave him the slack he needed.

Once his papers were in order and his pocketbook full, Kell had seen him off at Victoria and now – having left the friendly Belgian waiter on the platform – Wiggins traversed the concourse at the grand Gare du Nord, Brux.

He headed straight for the postal counter, where he posted the bicycle wheel and managed to ascertain how long it would take to be delivered. Then he went to the telephone counter. Inside the booth, concealed by frosted glass, he sat down for a moment. He did not take the horn. Instead, he flicked through the various directories. He selected one, then ripped out all the pages in three great tears. He placed the papers in his knapsack, put back the emptied almanac, then picked up the horn.

'*Le numéro, s'il vous plaît*,' a French voice came on the line.

'What!' Wiggins shouted. 'English! Understand English?'

'*Numéro, s'il vous plaît*,' the irritated voice repeated in French, and then in a German-sounding language.

'Ah, sod it,' Wiggins cried. He strode out of the booth, looking at the telephone clerk in angry exasperation. 'No one speak English?' he said, without expecting an answer, and walked on. It wasn't hard to play the Englishman abroad.

As he continued to the front entrance, he glanced up at the huge clock that hung above him. Seven at night. The note from Ernst's shop said 4 July, which was the following day. He reckoned he had until then to be sure of finding whoever left that note. He was shocked when Kell told him that he didn't have a telephone directory for Brussels, or any of the major European cities. But no matter, at least he now had money sewn into his trouser band, a directory in his bag and the names to follow up from Mrs Jepson and her sharp-as-needles brain. He wondered for an idle moment about the non-existent Mr Jepson, and what manner of being stood in for him.

The station opened out onto a large and busy square, with traffic whizzing around it. Trams, cars, vans, horse-drawn carts still, a troop of cavalry, delivery vehicles. Large

news-stands bookended the station entrance, and he could
see the bundle of international newspapers already being
opened. The air crackled with energy, the cafes across the
way hummed and the light from the dying sun cast a golden
glow, smudged and dancing in the traffic dust. A line of
taxis waited, but he did not take one.

Instead, he rushed to get on a stationary tram that was
about to depart. Wiggins got on at the back door and handed
a coin to the conductor just as it jolted forward. He carried
on down the busy tram, pushing past the throng, towards the
doors at the front. As the tram jumped forward and braked
into the natural corner of the square, Wiggins skipped out of
the front door (on the other side of the tram), took two steps
and smoothly leaped onto the back step of the tram going in
the other direction. He tipped his cap at the bemused conductor and proffered his fare.

He was certain he wasn't followed, and he wanted to
make sure it stayed that way.

Bordellos radiated vice. You could walk past a nondescript,
otherwise anonymous building, but if it was a knocking shop
you could almost feel the throb of sex as you went past – certainly, if you had your wits about you. And Wiggins almost
always had his wits about him.

He knew the building he was looking for instantly. He
could feel it from the end of the street even, that special
hormonal thrum. This particular whorehouse was unusual, though, for it stood out as a building in and of itself.
Fully electrified light fizzed out into the street. A big round
window stood in for the first floor, casting blue-green
light through its coloured panes. The large terraced house
was magnificent, with long, bending lines up to the roof,

asymmetrical angles and twisted, decorative metal work. It made Wiggins think of melted candle wax, allowed to seep away untended to dry in strange elongated forms. The building was a work of art.

He had rounded the block twice already, waiting for the long lowering of the sun as it finally gave way to the electric streetlamps. In was an area of the city that was well kept, wealthy without being top rank, but certainly not the kind of neighbourhood where you'd find scruff. The buildings gave off an air of money and secrecy, as if the people in them wanted you to know they were rich but didn't want to give away much else. Like the city itself.

He entered the street for a third time, eyes on the bordello. This time, a large brown motorcar with a cream hood stopped outside the building. In a blink of an eye, the occupant of the car flitted into the front door, and the car purred away. Wiggins caught sight of the hallway and shared a look with a muscly doorman. It was not a friendly look. It was also a look of recognition. The doorman had spotted him.

Wiggins kept his step even, turned the corner again, but this time he darted into an unlit alleyway that ran behind the terraced row of buildings. It ran left then a sharp right, with high fences either side, and very little room. Two broad-shouldered men couldn't pass without shifting, and Wiggins had a feeling that one particularly broad man was on his tail. Only the lights from the backs of the buildings on either side illuminated the alleyway, but Wiggins could tell where he was going. The whorehouse was obvious to anyone who knew, for the music if nothing else.

When he reached the wrought-iron gate behind the bordello, he didn't break stride but stepped up onto the gate's handle and hauled himself over with little effort. Rigging and maintaining the cranes kept him as fit as he'd ever been, barely a scrap on him other than muscle. An eight-foot gate was nothing, even on the two large glasses of excellent beer he'd had on the way there. (He'd stopped to eat, but couldn't resist the great flagons of beer that came with the delicious meat paste the cafe had served him. The beer was a miracle, and he'd ordered another. Rude to the gods not to.) He swung into the long, thin, paved courtyard that opened up to the house.

The back entrance looked closed, and the basement window dark. Above that, though, light spilled from the magnificent building. Party noises drifted down – a roaring gentleman, tinkles of women's laughter, a sudden thrum of guitar, and someone starting softly on the piano. Wiggins hesitated. He could either break through the back door, or climb to one of the dark windows at the very top of the house, the servants' quarters. As he eyed up a potential route, a stench of strong tobacco caught in his nose. Not the smoke, but the deep reek of the heavy rolling kind; then he heard the soft shuffle of feet behind him. He stepped aside just in time.

'*Merde!*' the doorman cried, as Wiggins avoided the cosh swipe.

The huge man stumbled forward, cosh clattered to the cobbles. He wheeled around and this time swung a hammer fist at Wiggins's head.

Wiggins shifted his chin back and caught the fist in his hand. In an instant, he reached his other hand on the doorman's elbow, straightened the arm, then twisted.

'Arrgh!' The doorman cried out, bent to the ground in agony. Wiggins didn't let go. He kept twisting, pinning the titan in pain.

'Get the chief,' he said.

'Eh? Ah . . .' The doorman gasped, his eyes wide. 'No no . . . *Français*?'

'The Captain. The boss? Le big chef!'

'Monsieur Carriere?'

'No.' Wiggins found the right word at last. 'Get me le Madame?'

'Qui, qui . . . ah, s'il vous plaît, s'il vous plaît.'

Wiggins released his grip. The doorman gasped and fell back in relief. Even in the darkness, Wiggins could feel resentment ooze off him like cheap cologne. The doorman massaged his enormous, wounded shoulder for a moment and then retreated through the back door.

He waited, unconcerned. The doorman was big, and had that nasty look about him that all door staff needed to deter time wasters. But he didn't have the devil in him. His mama must have loved him, once. Instead, Wiggins thought of Vernon Kell and envied him his education, his six or so languages. It would be useful to speak the lingo, all the lingos. He suspected he had more in common with that doorman than he did Kell, but they'd never get to find out.

'Fack sake,' Wiggins said in disappointment. 'Ain't no need for that kind of nonsense.'

'*Allez, allez!*' The doorman had returned. He carried in front of him a pistol, pointed at Wiggins. He flicked the gun at the back gate and shouted again.

Wiggins tutted in resignation and disappointment. He stepped towards the doorman confidently. 'Nah mate, nah. It's alright.' As he walked he put his hands up, unthreatening but advancing still.

'*Allez!*' the doorman shouted. He brought the gun up higher.

Wiggins carried on advancing and in one swift movement reached up and disarmed the man. The doorman's shoulders slumped. A look of shock and humiliation flashed across his face. 'Don't worry,' Wiggins said gently as he emptied the barrel into his hand. 'But never point a gun unless you're prepared to use it. Now, where's le Madame?'

He put his arm around the doorman now, not aggressively but to comfort him, for all the big man's bounce had gone. He stood shrunken like a burst balloon. 'Come on, lad,' Wiggins urged. 'Le Madame?'

A voice cut through the night from the dark doorway behind him. 'Is it you?'

Wiggins swivelled and peered through the open back door.

A woman's voice spoke again. 'Is it you?'

7

Friday 3 July. A bombshell hits the British press,
the death of elder statesman Joseph Chamberlain. He
was a great man, a politician of such stature that
he managed to split not one but both major political parties. A rarity too, in that he was a self-made
businessman, a titan of the Midlands with sons set
to make a mark in government too. Whitehall mourns.
Fleet Street mourns delightedly, for the gentlemen
of the press like nothing better than death. The
news reaches the Continental papers, which report
it soberly enough while ignoring those other, more
sensational, morally panicked pieces about mili-
tant suffragettes defacing great art. The Belgian
journals are dominated by the fallout of Archduke
Franz Ferdinand's assassination and what it might
mean for the precarious balance of power in Europe.

'Off!'

Wiggins opened his eyes. Martha stood before him at the
open door.

'That is my chaise,' she went on. 'So hop it.'

Wiggins scrambled off the velvet chaise longue and into
a swivel leather chair. Martha lay down and closed her eyes.
He looked over her as she lay before him, like a posed paint-
ing. An electric bulb fizzed and cracked. He hadn't seen her
for four years, and she wore the time well. He couldn't help

but look at her body, stretched out in front of him, in a dark green tight dress, low cut.

She was the Madame now, having been funded to set up this particular knocking shop by Mansfield Cumming and the British secret service. It was modelled on the very same brothel that Martha was working in when Wiggins first met her, called the Embassy, back in London. An intelligence gathering operation, ultimately run by Von Bork, Wiggins and Kell had managed to shut it down without getting their hands on Von Bork himself. But, as Wiggins noted bitterly once again, looking down at Martha at 5 a.m. on that crisp Brussels morning, Cumming had liked the idea of prostitution as a means of accruing gossip.

'This is my own private room, you know,' Martha said at last, opening her eyes. 'The punters do not ever see this room. They like the big bed, they like the thought of sex. They like to think of me on my back, on my knees.'

Wiggins looked away, heat rising in his face.

'I forgot,' Martha said more softly. 'You don't like that kind of talk. This place, it makes you . . .' She whirled a tired finger around. 'The only man who's allowed in here is the chief of police.'

Wiggins raised his eyebrow.

Martha smiled a half-smile, weary, knowing. 'Not like that, I don't have to do *that* any more. In any case Monsieur P is not the kind of man who likes to touch anything, least of all women.'

'How does it work, here?' Wiggins asked, gesturing around him at the room, for it was very oddly appointed. It had a fine desk, with locked drawers, the leather chair he sat in and the beautiful chaise, all very normal, very working woman's office-cum-boudoir. But it was the walls that made the place stand out. On two sides there were a number of square holes in the wooden panels, together with what looked like unconnected telephones – a bit like the servants' hall but in reverse, for this small room was nestled at the top of the house.

'Don't you know already?' Martha asked. 'Ah, but you'll like me to tell you. That's your thing, isn't it, I remember now. You like to treat me like a person. How is Bela?'

Wiggins blinked, surprised by the sudden mention of Bela, and the sudden surge of emotion it brought in him – years later. He'd forgotten he even told Martha about her, and mixed in with this shock was the thought that she, Martha, had remembered the name. A name no one else knew. He shook his head shortly, tightly. 'She died,' he said. 'Factory fire,' he added, despite himself. He didn't like to give out information about himself. But he couldn't deny her. 'Few years back in New York. I never saw her again.'

Martha took this in for a moment. She didn't condole. He didn't want her to – what would be the point? Instead, she sat in silence for a little longer, looking at him with her dark, wide eyes, weighing up something. Then she came to a decision and stood up. 'Let me show you how it works, even if I'm sure you already know.'

She stepped over to one of the square holes in the wall and pulled open a small shutter. 'These are the sight lines. Here, look – if you haven't already. We built in small mirrors and it's properly lit. I can see into every one of the rooms in this place without leaving my very own, private office.'

Wiggins put his eye to one of the holes. 'Not that one,' Martha said. 'The light's off. Here, look at this. A Monsieur Raymonde, should be getting his dress in order right now.' Wiggins peered through the hole. Sure enough, the peephole operated like a reverse periscope, a small tunnel of dim light with a view of the room at the end. He couldn't even tell which floor the scope led to, only that he could see a small depiction of what was going on inside. A portly man stood in the middle of the floor tucking in his shirt tails, while behind him a woman lounged on the bed. The picture was very small, and lacked detail, but nevertheless any observer could see what was going on in a general sense. Wiggins wondered about photographs.

'Here,' Martha said at his ear. She held out one of the strange horns hanging from the wall. He put it to his ear.

The man, Raymonde, was talking in French but Wiggins smiled at Martha. He could hear it alright. She replaced the horn and propped herself on the desk, while Wiggins sat back down in the chair and looked up at her.

'The girls know I'm up here, they know I could be watching at any time, and listening in. They wouldn't want to work anywhere else in Brussels, this is the . . .' She paused. 'Crème de la crème of whorehouses in the city. We only have the best clientele.' She searched Wiggins's face for a moment, for approval or something else, maybe even for a complaint. 'I treat them well, the girls I mean. Better than anyone ever treated me, anyway. Apart from you.'

'And this is all financed by the Bureau – they's pay for it all?'

'This is the hottest information exchange in Europe. I have royals in here, ministers, generals. And not just Belgians. This is a knocking shop très diplomatique. We have the French, the Dutch, the Germans, not to mention Austrians, Russians and even Italians. We cater for all religions, all races, all ages of man. And in and out of those revolving doors come half the secrets of Europe, military, political. Sexual, obviously. Don't blush.' Martha laughed softly. She told him not to, but he knew she liked it when his face reddened. 'Brussels is the spy capital of Europe, and this is the city's information exchange. Of course, the punters don't think they're sharing information; they think they're making the girls hot for them. It's pitiful really.' Martha reached down onto the desk and found a cigarette. She lit it, and then exhaled a lazy stream of smoke towards the ceiling, showing him her neck. 'But to answer your question, the Bureau paid to set it up but it pays for itself now. And some.'

'And you report to C?'

'What does that stand for by the way?'

'A few words come to mind,' Wiggins said.

She laughed. 'I've only met him twice. Once in London and once when he came out here to check up on the building. He wore a ridiculous false beard, and refused to refer to me by name. He barely talked to me at all, in fact. I think he was a bit embarrassed, as he had to pose as a customer to come in.'

'He wouldn't know what to do with you.'

'I don't know. His swordstick was quite impressive.'

At that moment the door opened, startling Wiggins. It was a lad, fourteen or so. He in turn was surprised to see Wiggins. The boy drew his hand up, and anger flashed across his face. Wiggins felt it was jealousy, or similar, for all the boy was barely into teenage years. 'Madame,' he said, ducking his head slightly.

'*Le lanterne rouge est fini?*' she asked.

'*Oui.*'

'*Dites à Paul de se verrouiller. Obtiens un petit-déjeuner. Et vas au lit.*'

'*Oui, madame,*' the boy said. He gave Wiggins another glance of suspicion and disdain, then left.

'That boy,' Wiggins said.

'Someone had to look after him,' Martha said casually. 'Don't worry, he's discreet. This business is built on discretion.'

'What, spying?'

'No, survival.' She slipped off the desk and pulled what looked like a large hearing horn out from underneath. Then she screwed the short end of the horn into a small hole in the wall next to the desk. Immediately a soft buzzing sound of conversation filtered into the room. Three or four people spoke, in French, and he could hear the click and clank of plates and people speaking over each other. Martha swayed past him back to the chaise, and nodded over her shoulder at the horn. 'Just the girls, having breakfast before bed. I like to look after them.'

'Yeah, I can see.'

'As I say, the business of survival is hard. And it's going to get a whole lot harder.'

'War?'

'C, London, whoever, they ignore every message I send.'

'How do you send messages to him?'

She waved away the question and went on. 'Even before that kid in Sarajevo set off his gun, there was going to be some kind of war. Now it's certain.'

'Do you have anything solid?' Ever since they'd started talking, Wiggins had tried to get an anchor on the conversation. And Martha gave the impression of honesty and openness. Mansfield Cumming had told him to make contact with her, debrief if necessary and pass on anything he thought she wasn't telling him.

And she wasn't telling him something. She was so good at it, as all great deceivers are, because she told him so much. There she lay, stretched out before him once more, continuing her situation report on Western Europe. He grinned, despite himself, as she went on. 'Ain't nothing solid here, handsome, this is the demi-monde. But I will tell you this. No one's mobilised yet. All the soldiers that come in here, mind, talk of nothing else. And the soldiers we get in here aren't real soldiers, they aren't the fighters.'

They shared a look of recognition. They'd both been pawns in other men's games, they still were, the people who actually did the dirty work for those that only talked about it. 'But they will mobilise. God knows who first, but they will. And once they do, the wheel will keep turning and no one can stop it. I've seen it a hundred times, once a man has a hard-on, you better be sure he keeps it in his trousers. If he takes off those trousers, then that's it, it's all over.'

Wiggins raised his eyebrows, but she went on regardless.

'Well, Germany, Russia, Austria, Serbia – they'll all be harder than a bishop on Easter Sunday. Soon as one army mobilises, that's the trousers coming off – they all will and it's goodbye Christmas.'

She rubbed her brow wearily. It was more lined than he remembered, and he suddenly saw the flecks of grey at her temple. The morning light had now completely taken over from the electric, and he even heard the birds sing over the faint chatter of the women through the horn. 'Is that why you're here? Does someone in London finally believe me?'

'They'll never believe you,' Wiggins said flatly.

'And yet here you are – taking the shilling.' She lit another cigarette and eyed him through the smoke. 'I thought you quit,' she said at last, smiling at him as he coughed. It was a smile he could not read.

Wiggins felt stung again, on the wrong foot once more. When they'd last seen each other, years earlier, he'd urged her not to work for the Bureau, to get out of the whoring business and to leave spying alone. She'd argued, quite correctly, that she had to eat. And as for him, for all his high words and principles, he too had gone back into the service, had taken the King's shilling again to dissemble, to fool, to double-cross, all in the supposed name of the Empire. That was back in '12, although he left again soon afterwards, but Martha was right – he'd turned up at her door once again in the pay of a government he supposedly mistrusted. Working for an organisation he warned her against.

'I'm not . . . well, it's personal.' She raised an elegant eyebrow as he stumbled on, wilting. 'I'm looking for someone. He's got something we need. Nah, that ain't right. I'm looking for *him*.'

'Does this man have a name?'

'Von Bork.'

She shook her head slightly. 'I don't know that name.'

'Yeah you do,' Wiggins snapped. 'He was the money behind the Embassy. German fella, at least so we's think.'

'I told you before,' Martha said carefully, 'I never met him. How do you know he's in Brussels?'

Wiggins worked at his knuckles slightly, a bad habit that only surfaced when he didn't know the answers. 'I don't, I just feel it, you know?'

'That's a bit of a new development for you, isn't it? Feeling not thinking.'

'How about Maxim DuPont or Herman Wolff – know either of them? Scratch that last one, he's a banker. I staked him out earlier. But what about DuPont?' Wiggins stressed the final t.

'DuPont? Yes, I know someone of that name. Only a little. He comes here, sometimes, with one of the old buffers from the French embassy. He's not official, some sort of aristocrat or other. Has money. He hasn't been here for ages, though. Are you sure he's in town?'

'I ain't sure of nothing.' He let that sink in for a moment. The straightforwardness of Martha's questioning wasn't as easy to evade as Kell's, or Cumming's. He had so little to go on, so little data. He could picture the great old detective shaking his head at him: 'Data, Wiggins, data.' But the old man was dead, and he didn't have time. Besides, although he lacked data, he didn't need to convince a court of law to exact the kind of justice he intended. And he was sure of his reasoning. Whoever killed Holmes – surely Von Bork or one of his agents – would have made the journey to the continent as soon as possible after the murder. And Mrs Jepson's manifest was the best lead as to what name that killer may have travelled under.

He was on the verge of telling Martha about the Poste Restante lead, where in fact he was going to head that day, to find out whether Maxim DuPont or Von Bork or whatever name he went by might pick up their post. She broke in on his thoughts.

'Why is this personal?'

'Huh?'

'You said, earlier, that this was personal. I can believe that. I mean, look at you . . . you look, I don't know, angry?'

'I am.'

'No, that's not you. It's the others, those . . .'

At that moment, a loud buzzer went off on the desk. Martha shot up to the door and flung it open. A louder bell rang repeatedly from some floors below. 'Not again,' she cried, and dashed to the staircase.

> *3 July 1914*
> *Dear Wiggins*
> *Forgive me for writing, against your express wishes. Putting pen to paper is a habit of a lifetime, and one I cannot shake. Besides, I simply cannot believe that Captain Kell would open a letter addressed to you. The man is a gentleman, a servant of the crown, and a staff officer – such duplicity is unthinkable.*
>
> *Please contact me at your earliest convenience. Various names have already come up in our investigations. The remnants of the Bishopsgate Jewel Gang is a possible line of enquiry. Adams from the Manor House Case. Wilson the notorious Canary-Trainer is now out of prison. And, of course, Jonathan Clay's accomplice, in the case of the Red Headed League. He was sentenced to 20 years back in the '80s, and I remember still the look of hatred on his face when he was found guilty in court. Holmes and I attended. He vowed to bring down the very devil onto our heads.*
>
> *We shall keep searching for clues. Please see me when you can. The game is – very reluctantly – afoot.*
>
> *Yours in expectation and sorrow*
> *Dr John H. Watson*

Kell put down the letter on his bedside table. Blast that man Wiggins. Even from abroad, with the distance of days, he'd predicted his actions and even – the impertinence! – informed Doctor Watson that he was a sneak. Worst of all, of course, was that Wiggins was right.

He'd read it many times since it arrived at the office the evening before and now, as he lay in bed reading by the dawn light that crinkled through the curtains, he thought again of Wiggins. Probably sleeping off a binge of Belgian beer in some flophouse in Brussels. Doctor Watson's letter had unsettled Kell, for it reminded him that Wiggins's mission was a deeply personal one, that his agent would be driven by his heart – a wild, raging heart – and not by the reason and rationality that normally characterised his actions. He was hot-headed of course, he had no schooling, no class, no breeding, but he had a mind to match the dons. He had been sure-footed in his previous missions. But this mission was different, and Kell suspected that even if Wiggins were to track down Von Bork, he would far rather follow that man into hell than save the Empire, stop the war or even save himself.

In fact, Kell was convinced of it when he framed it in those terms. Wiggins would choose his own destruction, if it meant guaranteeing the destruction of Von Bork. Any intelligence – the list of agents in that little black book – that could aid Britain's cause would be a mere irrelevance. He sighed. Beside him, Constance snored gently, her jaw turned away from him, her long neck exposed. At least she was still beside him, although Kell wasn't sure how long that state of affairs would last. They'd argued the night before.

'Calm down, Vernon,' she'd said when he came back late into their bedroom and started fiddling with his personal items on the chest of drawers. 'You're all nerves.' She sat propped up in the bed with a pamphlet.

'And why do you think that is, eh?'

'Is that a specific comment, pointed at me? Or is it a more generalised lament, you know the kind, whereby women shouldn't be allowed to comment, shouldn't be allowed to vote but should somehow, as if by unthinking magic, be able to read the minds of the men around them?'

'I didn't mean . . .'

'Because I'm quite prepared to try my hand at mind-reading, I'll muck in like a good girl, but I do so need a guiding hand. Some training, by a man of course, to set me straight, to show me how it's done. So, can you work out what *I'm* thinking?'

'I've been struggling to do that for years.'

'I am sorry, to present such an enigma, it must be *so* trying. Perhaps if you asked me occasionally what I thought, that might help?'

'Would it?'

'You know, I'm not so sure it would.' She turned off her bedside light then and drove her head into the pillow. She killed the light rather than carry on the conversation, for sooner or later she'd have to admit why her mood was so off. She'd spent the day at Bow Street Magistrates, in the public gallery, desperately supporting her fellow campaigners. Women of all ages, thrust into Holloway prison, hunger striking, forcibly fed, with rough rubber tubes jammed down their throats. Women like Mary Richardson, who she had known since 1910, and Sybil Thwaites, who she'd marched with many times. Their bodies emaciated, their throats shredded, their minds surely damaged by the horror of it all. She'd shouted at the judge, she'd cheered when Richardson had declaimed the justice of their cause, of votes for women, shouted and cheered uselessly as those heroes were led away once more.

It was this, as much as anything Kell had said or done, that made her snap and – with a tiny stab of remorse – she offered one final word that night. 'I am going to Wimbledon tomorrow, so I may be back late.'

'Wimbledon?' Kell groaned, remembering the admiration Constance had expressed for Emily Davison – the mad woman who killed herself in front of the King's horse at the Derby – and various other high-profile suffragette protests. 'Oh Heaven, please no. Sport and politics absolutely do not mix.'

'I beg your pardon?'

'I simply cannot have you disrupt the tennis – it will cause me immense embarrassment, you'll probably be arrested and . . . and . . . it's just the absolute limit. Think of those poor men competing, think of all the hours of work they've put into their games.'

A deep, dark silence descended after this outburst. Constance stared out of the side of the bed, away from him. She finally spoke, without looking at him. 'I intend to watch it, Vernon, not ruin it.'

They spoke no more that night. Kell squeezed his nose between finger and thumb in embarrassment at the memory. He folded away Watson's letter and glanced once more at his sleeping wife, at that long neck with a twinge of guilt. He knew of the force-feeding in Holloway – how women, women like Constance (!) were being brutalised by the doctors there, all in the name of democracy. No wonder she was angry with him. He decided to get up without waking her. He would leave his wife to enjoy the tennis, and get straight back to the office. Although, with Wiggins gone and the rest of Whitehall intent on a long and indolent summer – or else a trifling little civil war brewing in Ireland – he didn't really have the tools to fight the real fight, to ready the country for war in Europe.

War with Germany, a war that Britain might not win. Yet again, he found himself betting on Wiggins, because Wiggins was his only horse in the race.

Wiggins was not slumbering hungover in a Belgian flophouse, as Kell supposed. He was rushing after Martha as she sped down the twirling staircase of the Brussels bordello. He'd noticed the beauty of the house the night before, lit by fans of electricity, but now, as sunlight filtered into its hallways and landings, Wiggins saw once more the elegance of the construction – as if it had been drawn with one unbroken, bending line, non-stop, poured almost by liquid brick and iron.

'Paul, Paul,' Martha shouted as she leaped the last few steps and dashed to a heavy, locked door.

Paul – the doorman who'd tried so unsuccessfully to eject Wiggins the night before – appeared from below stairs, rattling a bunch of keys. '*Il l'a verrouillé, madame.*' They could all hear the screaming now, a woman's, coming from behind the locked door.

'*Qui est-ce?*'

'Block.'

A couple of the girls came up after Paul, and Boy too. The girls ran to the door and began to beat on it. Martha scowled at Boy and barked at him in French.

He shrugged and muttered something back.

Wiggins did not understand the words, but knew the gist – and he knew enough to ignore it. Instead, he pushed past the fumbling Paul and delivered the heel of his boot with thunderous force against the lock – once, twice and CRACK, the door split open. He barrelled in.

A girl, on her knees at the end of the bed, her back arched, screamed. Behind her, a tall man in shirt sleeves and underwear had hold of her hair in one hand. In the other, he held a riding crop. Blood streaked the girl's back.

As Wiggins came charging in, the tall man – Block – looked up, surprised. 'Hey,' he shouted, but he was unafraid.

Wiggins drove his fist into Block's neck. Block flew backwards, letting go of the girl as she screamed again. He crashed to the floor, crying out. Wiggins kicked him in the head, once, twice, until he stopped crying out and cowered silently.

'You're alright, love.' He turned to the girl and handed her a sheet. She quivered. 'You did good, to ring the bell. He can't hurt you now. You did good. Bon,' he said again. He ushered her towards her waiting friends at the door.

Martha stood just inside the room staring at him, aghast. Wiggins shot her a black look, then turned back to Block. 'Get out of it,' he shouted. He reached down for Block's hat and trousers.

'His coat,' Martha said weakly.

'Fuck him.' Wiggins pulled up Block by the scruff of his shirt and frogmarched him towards the door.

'*Non, non,*' Block muttered and tried to scramble free. Wiggins punched him brutally in the ribs with his free hand. 'Next one's your nose,' he said.

He forced his way through the fluttering girls, Boy and the ineffectual Paul, and violently bundled Block into the street. 'Fack off – get it? Sling your hook, connard!' he shouted, and threw Block's trousers and hat at him.

Block got up. Blood streamed from his nose and he held his hat to stem the tide. For a moment, he turned to face up to Wiggins – a pathetic figure, in his underwear, scowling – but he stepped half forward, as if in challenge. Wiggins made to step forward again, like a boxer about to deliver the killer blow, and Block scuttled clear, casting hateful glances behind him as he disappeared around the corner.

Wiggins slammed the door shut and walked back to the room. The hallways were full of young women now, and Boy and Paul watched on as Wiggins went back to Martha. They looked at Wiggins in awed silence, the sudden burst of total violence shocking still.

Martha waited for him, furious. She strode past him and cried out something to the onlookers in the hallway. '*Allez, Allez. Lit* . . .' Then she carefully closed the busted door as best she could, turned back to Wiggins and hissed. 'Do you know who that was?'

'A nasty fucking nonce who hurts women. Is she alright?'

'That's Herman Block. He's one of the most powerful criminals in Brussels.'

Wiggins wiped his hands on a towel. The adrenaline was subsiding but the anger had not. It always got to him, men and the women they hit. 'I said, is she alright?'

'She's new, she didn't know what he wanted, what to expect.'

'He's done that before?'

'This is *my* business. Do not barge in here and wreck my business.'

Wiggins took a step towards her and almost whispered. 'Your business is carried out at His Majesty's pleasure. And His Majesty can take it away, like that!' He snapped his fingers, the implication clear. 'So let's stop fucking around, eh? You gonna tell me how to find this DuPont bloke or what?'

8

'She ain't got no clothes on, hardly,' Wiggins whispered.

'Why do you think they're all here?' Martha replied. 'It's not for the choreography.'

He stood at the crack of the open door, and watched the performance. A woman danced. She was clad in a long transparent skirt, a turquoise headdress and two tiny, tinselled discs covered her breasts. A pianist and a couple of other musicians played the music, something German-sounding Wiggins thought. The dancer, though, looked anything but – she swayed and dipped; slow slow, quick quick slow, she threw veils in the air, she suggested, she turned away, and sashayed forward. The male-only audience – six or seven sitting, and a few hangers-on at the back of the room, were all paying rapt attention. Wiggins let his gaze shift from the magnetic dance to these men, mostly older than the dancer (who looked in her thirties), and almost all in uniform, and all with their hats clamped into their laps. A still old man in the front row, with a large red and grey moustache and small quivering spectacles, even had the markings of a general – of the Belgian army by the look of it. Dirty fuckers.

'Put your tongue away, before someone cuts it off,' Martha said.

Wiggins stepped back, embarrassed. He sat down on a stool opposite Martha in the improvised dressing room set up for the dancer. The room was a side chamber off the grand salon where she danced, and Martha and Wiggins had reached it through a back staircase that led up from the servants' entrance at the side of the house. 'I said you could talk to Margaretha, not eat her.'

He tried to smile at that. He regretted pulling rank on Martha that morning, threatening her with the power of the secret service. But his blood had been up, and he was running out of time. If Kell was right, and Martha for that matter, then a European war would be upon them any minute and trying to find Von Bork in the midst of such a thing would be impossible. But Martha was an ally, in some sense at least, and he didn't want her to think ill of him.

'I don't know what you're smiling about,' she said. 'I had to spend most of the day prostrating myself in front of Block, who is not a pleasant man. All because you wanted to swing your big dick around.'

'Why don't you just tell him to fack off?'

She exhaled, more in exasperation than anger. 'He's one of the most powerful men in this city. When it comes to *my* city, anyway. It was all I could do to stop him torching the place.'

'What did you tell him?'

'That you were a jealous former lover. That you tracked me down. That you've left town. And that he has my permission to kill you if you should ever meet.' She looked at him steadily for a moment. 'He will do that, too.'

Wiggins shrugged.

'Why *haven't* you left town?'

'I told you. I'm looking for somebody.'

He would have said more, and used Von Bork's name again, but a maid came in at that moment. Martha nodded at her. 'Claudette,' she said.

Claudette gave a cursory nod of her head and began fussing among the wardrobe rails and trunks. Wiggins took her in for a moment, the slight hunch of the servant, the worn threads of her long dress, the premature aging, the grey eyes that would sparkle once the boss was out of the way. She couldn't be more than twenty-five, but she had a world-weary air about her and the plainness of her clothes was a stark contrast to the feathers, jewels and gaudiness of the wardrobe among which she worked. Only the faint dusting of powder on her cheeks marked her out as a maid of someone unusual. Although he suspected the powder was doing quite a different job on Claudette than it was on the dancer in the room next door.

The music quickened up, big rising notes heralding a crescendo. Martha glanced towards the sounds, and then back at him. 'Boy turn up anything?'

Wiggins shook his head. After the fight with Block, and after he'd threatened Martha with the British secret service, she'd actively agreed to help him find Maxim DuPont, the man who took the boat train on the night of Holmes's death. The man Wiggins assumed was Von Bork. She'd also offered him Boy's help, in particular, with staking out the Brussels central post office and the Poste Restante. Wiggins had taken Boy there on a tram, reasoning that – much like in London – a child is much less conspicuous than a foreigner, certainly when hanging around in public. Sherlock Holmes must have had the same thought about him, all those years ago.

The surveillance job was simple enough. Wait and watch, watch and follow. As long as one had eyes on the Poste Restante desk of the post office, anyone who left that desk carrying the bicycle wheel wrapped in brown paper would be the one to follow. It was the parcel he posted yesterday at the station, expressively for that reason.

Boy sat quietly with him on the tram to the post office first thing that morning. Wiggins still felt hot from his exchange with Block, from the way he spoke to Martha. For the last few days, Wiggins had felt his emotions running hot and cold, his mood up and down. He hadn't yet made the connection in his own mind, did not fully realise that these mood swings were probably grief. After all, he'd been dealing with death his whole life. Holmes was just another on a long list. And yet, he did not feel quite in control of his feelings.

Wiggins felt confidence in the boy, though. It was the way he listened to the instructions quietly, intense, picking up every nuance. Wiggins made him repeat everything, twice. When they'd done, the boy waited a moment and then looked up at him directly. 'What have you got on my mother?'

'Martha? What you mean?'

'Why is she helping you?' Boy asked. Wiggins noted the frown pinch in his forehead, the clear steady eyes, a lad beyond his years. Wiggins knew the feeling. When he and Sal started the Irregulars, they were only seven. Holmes had given them the idea, had staked them cash, but it was the two of them who put the gang together. By the time they reached double figures, they knew London better than any cabby, had seen more human frailty than the hack lawyers down the Bailey, and had an intimate acquaintance with death, disease and casual violence. Where Wiggins came from, all the kids were wise beyond their years, and none of them had fathers neither. At least, not ones they knew.

'Don't you remember me?' he asked.

'I remember,' Boy said. 'At Delphy's with my first mother in London. You came and it all ended.'

Wiggins opened his mouth to reply, to argue that, no, in fact he did not 'end' that particular whoring operation, but that people had died, it was a spying hub and that he'd in fact saved the lives of at least two people – including Martha – by intervening in the hellish and twisted mess. Of course the little boy, Boy, knew none of that. He only knew that Wiggins had steamed in there and brought the whole thing crashing down. Martha had taken him with her when she went to Brussels.

He was going to tell the small boy all this, as the busy commuter tram rattled into a square, and the sunbeams caught and sprang off the glass shopfronts, when the words 'my first mother' stuck in his mind. For Martha wasn't Boy's mother, he knew, and neither was Delphy – the Madame of the London joint – but Boy now spoke of her as such. It gnawed at him, this 'first', as if mother or father were mere roles to be taken by whoever was nearest at the time. He couldn't forget his own mother, died when he was seven, from her own hand; troubled, unable to look after herself let alone him, but definitely his mother, even if she did top herself. He could still picture her, the death tableau, but the other times too: dragging along the street from a copper, holding her cup out for a gasp of gin, it rattling, rattling, rattling as she shook. He had a mother alright, only the one.

Boy didn't have neither, other than Martha, he realised, who only took him on a couple of years earlier. 'I ain't got nothing on her,' Wiggins said. 'We were friends once, and I'm in a bad spot, so she's giving me a helping hand because, well, she's a good 'un. Is this here?' He pointed to the large building which had the look of a central post office.

The boy glanced out of the window, then back at him. Finally, he nodded sharply and they got off at the tram stop. Wiggins explained the plan once more in an undertone as they walked together – though not together. The square hummed with early-morning commuters, people rushing to and fro, and Boy looked like any other young kid on the streets of a major European city. A possible pickpocket, a bored kid playing hooky, or on an errand, barely seen by those looking straight at him and invisible to everyone else. 'Look out for the bicycle wheel, right. It's large, in brown paper. Whoever picks that up at the counter, follow 'em. You can do it sly, I know you can. I see you, round Martha's. You're a natural. Follow whoever picks it up. Wherever they go, the next address, follow 'em there.'

'What about the fares?'

Wiggins grinned, and palmed the boy a couple of coins as they turned into the post office. 'Soon as it's dropped off, back to Martha's with the address. Tell me or her. On you go.'

Boy disappeared into the crowd, as Wiggins knew he would. A childhood living in a brothel had equipped him with all the skills necessary for observation without detection. Wiggins himself went to the Poste Restante counter and collected the letter he'd sent himself yesterday, a pretext to allow him to check out the place without suspicion. He then left Boy to it.

'Boy saw no one,' Wiggins said to Martha across the dancer's dressing room. 'At least, that's as he told me.'

'I don't know how you expected him to spot the right person anyway, that post office is busier than Piccadilly.'

'Easy,' Wiggins said. 'Plant something distinctive in the PR, can't miss the fella who picks it up. But no one did.' He glanced again at the maid, Claudette. She was fussing with the contents of a huge trunk, and seemed totally oblivious to the conversation.

'No English,' Martha mouthed at him as she shook her head. The music from the other room suddenly finished and gave way to a burst of applause, shouting and cheers. Martha gestured at him. 'Stand up, by the back door there. Like my butler,' she added.

As he did so, the door to the salon flew open and the dancer came in, pursued by the clapping of her admirers. She closed it behind her in a great flourish and Wiggins saw her close-up for the first time. She still had the head-dress on, with dark hair pinned back behind it, but with longer tresses around her bare shoulders. She had very little on her top half, other than the bronze discs covering her nipples. Her long skirt shimmered, transparent. Wiggins couldn't help but look, couldn't help but look away. And then she smiled, and all the distractions of her body melted away. She beamed at him, this strange man in her dressing room, and then fell upon her friend. 'Martha,' she cried, and offered a stream of effusive greetings.

'Margaretha,' Martha said, in English. 'You danced divinely, you lit up the salon. No, you lit up the world. As ever.'

'*Qui est le beau?*' Margaretha turned to Wiggins. She smiled at him again, like the full beam of the sun, dazzling, dangerous, impossible to look away. Wiggins felt the heat in his face once more. She barely had any clothes on, but he was the one feeling embarrassed.

'An Englishman,' Martha said in English. 'With little French. We call him Wiggins.'

'Wiggins, *enchantée*. I am Mrs Margaretha MacLeod,' she said in good English. She offered her hand, which he took, as a child might. Then she turned back to Martha and, without warning, took off her skirt and handed it to Claudette. Wiggins gulped, and glanced at Martha in dismay.

She smirked slightly, as Margaretha muttered to Claudette and began rifling through a wardrobe rail. She gave out a couple of commands to her maid, and they discussed various clothing options, Wiggins assumed. All the while Margaretha stood there almost entirely naked, as if he – a man – wasn't there at all.

'Martha, I have no time,' she said once she'd decided on the clothes. 'The Little General is waiting. He says he must take me for supper.'

'Is that what they're calling it now?'

Margaretha laughed. 'Don't worry, I will make him pay, for sure. What do you think?' She turned suddenly to Wiggins and held a shimmering turquoise dress across her otherwise near-naked body.

'Er . . .' Wiggins, forced to look at her, could only shake his head slightly.

'He doesn't talk much, does he?' she said, jolly and sly. 'He doesn't need to, of course, ya, Martha.' She said something else in French, and the two women laughed again, revelling in his discomfort.

'Margaretha,' Martha said, glancing at Wiggins and then at Claudette. 'May I ask for your help? I think you must know everyone in Europe.'

'Of course, darling, for sure. But why are you boasting for me? I don't know everybody in Europe. I only know everybody who is anybody, ya,' she said with a tinkling chuckle.

'Do you know Maxim DuPont?'

'French? Soldier, no?'

'*Bien sûr.* He's come in before, with a French delegation I think.' Martha passed a hairbrush. 'He didn't avail himself of the facilities, though, if I remember. He was a sort of hanger-on.'

'A spare prick,' Margaretha said. 'Is that the phrase, no?' She looked at Wiggins when she said this, and he could only nod. 'I am not sure. I think, maybe. Not French, Austrian maybe or something like that. And maybe not a soldier, for sure. A tall man, yes? Handsome – not as handsome as you, of course.' Wiggins averted his eyes again, feeling the heat in his face once more. Not only did Margaretha's constantly amused eyes unsettle him, she was getting dressed quite unashamedly, clearly enjoying his discomfort.

With a cough, Wiggins willed himself to speak. 'Is he in Brussels?' he managed. 'This French, Austrian, whoever he is. This DuPont.'

'No, for sure no. I doubt it. He will be going to Paris. We all will be,' she said, wrapping feathers around her neck. 'I take the train tomorrow.'

'Why?'

'Bastille Day of course. The celebrations. Everyone will be there.' Now fully clothed – or what passed as fully clothed in this kind of place – she turned to Martha, thrust out her hip and said, 'And now, I must go. The Little General demands it.'

'On your own . . . with . . .' Wiggins gestured to the door.

'Of course. I am, how you say, a grown-up.'

Martha, who'd stood up to embrace Margaretha in farewell, suddenly caught the thrust of Wiggins's point, and certainly the urgency of his tone. She held Margaretha by the shoulders. 'He's right, darling. You need someone to look after you.'

'Martha, a very powerful man looks after me. He just happens to be a different man every night.'

'Be serious. Last time you were in Brussels, you moaned to me every day about the trouble you had travelling, about the need for a man of some description. A bodyguard, say.'

'Bodyguard pshaw!' Margaretha scoffed. 'But someone yes, to carry bags, to look out for my things, to keep an eye. For sure, yes, but you know it is not easy to find this kind of man if you are the kind of woman I am.'

Martha stepped back and motioned at Wiggins. 'Here is a man, Margaretha. He will be able to look after you better than any rich or powerful man could.'

Margaretha turned her dancing eyes back at Wiggins. 'I am not sure I could afford him. Not such a fine, how you say, specimen as this.'

Wiggins found his tongue, at last. 'You don't have to pay me,' he blurted out. Her eyebrows arched in scepticism at that, but he went on. 'I mean, I'll help you to Paris. When we get there, you show me where to find this DuPont geezer, and we're even.'

'Geezer?'

'This bloke, Maxim DuPont. I find him, I owe you.'

Margaretha smiled quizzically then looked at Martha, who nodded encouragement. 'Do you wear a uniform?' Margaretha said to him.

'No.'

'Could you?'

A pause, then Martha and Margaretha burst out laughing at Wiggins's confusion. Margaretha smiled again and put a hand, an electric hand, on his shoulder. 'Be at Gare

du Midi at nine tomorrow morning. I am hoping to catch
the connecting train for Paris, for sure. Look out for Claudette at the station, you can help her with my luggage – and
at Quévy, it is always such a bother at Quévy – and you
can chaperone me to Paris – a bodyguard, no? – is that the
word? Good, ya,' she turned to Martha and hugged her.
'Now, the Little General,' she said. 'Goodbye, my lovely.
And you,' she pointed at Wiggins as she reached for the
door with her other hand. 'Don't forget a uniform.'

With that she was gone, through the door and back out
into the salon in a great whoosh of patchouli and rich eastern spice that made up her perfume. The air hung heavy
with the scent, cloves and something muskier, for Margaretha sweated in her dance routine and Wiggins fancied he
could smell this mixture of perspiration and perfume. But
the energy swept out of the room after her, like the cold
dark night after a day of hot sunshine. She left you waiting
for the sun to rise again.

Wiggins and Martha looked at each other, both suddenly
empty and bereft. 'Why are you helping me?' he asked,
suddenly.

'I want you out of town. You're bad for business.'

'Sorry,' he said.

'Sorry about beating up one of my most influential
patrons? I should think so too.'

'Nah, he deserved it,' Wiggins replied. 'I'd do that again.
No, I'm sorry about the way I spoke to you. Threatened
the business with, you know, London and that. I'm all up
and down.' He fell silent. Claudette clattered and shuffled
behind them, busying herself with the monumental task of
packing up Margaretha's wardrobe. Finally, she grabbed a
carpet bag and scuttled away through the side door.

Martha readied herself to leave, though she kept a close eye on Wiggins. He could tell she was trying to get a read on him, and his mood. 'What do you make of your new boss?' she asked, once Claudette had gone.

'Dancer, obviously. She's spent time in the tropics, that's for sure – I reckon the East Indies, at least part of the time. Had the rough end of the stick – been beaten, I mean, probably by her old man. She's had kids an' all, though she don't really care for them now – if they're alive.' He shrugged. 'I reckon she was brought up proper like, Christian, schooling all that, but she's had to fight since. Fight 'em off, an' all,' he added, almost as an afterthought.

Martha nodded. 'I didn't know half of that,' she said. 'And though she doesn't live with Louise, she does pay her way.'

'Louise the daughter?'

Martha nodded.

'I'll also say that she don't look like no MacLeod I've ever met.'

'True enough, but that was her married name.'

'Was?'

'Don't you know?' Martha raised an eyebrow. 'The name she goes by now? She's famous throughout the dance halls and salons of Europe. I think I've even heard her say it herself, she's the Belle of the Belle Époque!'

Wiggins shook his head. 'No clue.'

'My friend Margaretha,' Martha said with a flourish, 'is Mata Hari.'

9

He wasn't there to catch a train, that was for sure. The man, with a light blue jacket and no luggage, had walked up and down the concourse at the Gare du Midi three times. He had exited out of the east door, and come back in through the main entrance. He had stopped at the postal counter, but deposited or picked up nothing. He had taken a telephone booth but made no call. Now he sat, sipping a coffee at a cafe table on the concourse, scanning the three main entrances to the station.

Wiggins knew all this because he himself had turned up at the station two hours before he was due to see Margaretha (he couldn't think of her as Mata Hari – what would he call her? Mrs Hari? Mata?) It was a point of protocol to turn up to any meeting early, but his two days in Brussels had put him on high alert. Margaretha, his new boss, may have seemed carefree enough when they met the night before but the speed with which she identified Maxim DuPont, her easy knowledge of his movements, and the way she then waltzed off to a rendezvous with one of the Belgian high command told their own story. She was a woman who moved in powerful circles. And power meant danger.

As soon as he'd arrived at the station, he reconnoitred the entrances, checked the platform where the Quévy train was due to depart. He had a Bradshaw in his pocket and knew they would have to change on the French border, to connect with the service to Paris. Once he'd found every exit and entrance, every nook and cranny of the station, he melted into the growing crowds, waited and watched. Which was why he knew the Man in the Blue Jacket was waiting for someone and, like him, watching.

He wasn't the only suspicious-looking person there that morning. Wiggins, who had London and Londoners so ingrained in his very soul that he could tell who they were, where they were going and where they came from at a glance, had to adjust to the new environment. The Belgians obviously had a similar class system to the British. The posh folk, with eyes only for other posh folk, glided through the station oblivious. The haughty middle classes, so anxious to let everyone know they were not working class, that they could not walk anywhere oblivious – shown by the choice of carriage, the class of travel, the way they spoke to the porters. Then, spread throughout the station, were the people who did the work: porters, waiters, clerks, railwaymen in soot-stained overalls with blackened faces, a works crew heading to the tracks, the servants, tending their owners like an owner might in turn tend to a pet. And finally the most visible to Wiggins, the most invisible to everyone else, were those beneath the class of worker: the beggars, flitting in and out of sight of policemen; the children, pretending to run errands but looking for scraps, change, anything; the flower-sellers, a paltry offering that was as good as begging; the short lines of men outside each entrance, showing the hunched submission of an unemployed man desperate for work. Wiggins recognised this desperation, the men in those lines, just as he recognised the invisible children.

For all this, though, Wiggins couldn't be sure of everyone in that station. He knew the blue-jacketed man was definitely there on the lookout for something, but in his bones he felt another presence – perhaps one more skilled in the art of watching than this man, perhaps someone as skilled as him. Even the film posters stripped across the advertising bollards outside the station unsettled him. *CHARLIE CHAPLIN GARÇON DE CAFÉ*, a moustached Chaplin looked out of the poster with an unusual malevolence, dressed as a waiter with a teetering bottle on a tray. Wiggins remembered his brush with the star on a music hall stage four years earlier, before Chaplin had made it to the moving pictures; a London urchin like himself, now made it to the top of the world.

A large motorcar pulled up at the station and Claudette got out. She began remonstrating with the driver about the luggage. Two huge trunks jutted out of the back of the car, with another strapped on top. Inside, he could make out more carpet bags and a holdall, rammed in any which way on the passenger seats. The driver, though, had no interest in helping Claudette and simply shrugged in the face of her entreaty. She looked around, shouting for the porter. Wiggins sidled up from the road side of the car and began to take the trunks off the back. Claudette saw him and puffed out her cheeks, but let him do it as she hailed a porter with a cart.

Wiggins let the porter take over and melted back into the crowds while Claudette went with the porter across the concourse and onto the platform. He didn't want the Man in the Blue Jacket, or anyone else for that matter, to think that he was with Claudette and thus Mata Hari. It wasn't a connection he wanted to advertise, given the swirl that surely existed around her.

He wasn't particularly confident about Cumming's system of information either. When he was briefed in London, the old buffer had seemed much more concerned with the conduct of secret service work rather than the content. It took Wiggins over half an hour to talk him out of accompanying him, then a further twenty minutes convincing him that no, he did not need a swordstick, nor did he really want to go with another code name. Cumming had become struck with the idea that Wiggins's code name – originally marked as Agent OO – should be something more fitting. He preferred 'Ruffian'. This idea so seized Cumming that he even began to refer to Wiggins as such until his secretary finally chimed in with the information that, in fact, one of their other agents was called Ruffian and so, abashed, Cumming dropped the idea.

Instead, the head of the secret service's foreign bureau tasked Wiggins – Agent OO – with two liaisons in Brussels. While Boy staked out the post office the day before, Wiggins met with these other agents. He was not impressed. In fact, the only thing that had impressed Wiggins about these meetings was the quality of the beer served by the cafe. Drinking beer in Belgium was on a different plane of quality, transcendent, as his old pal Symes at the British Library might say.

What was very much on the same plane as mundane earth, however, were the two no-marks Cumming had sent him to debrief. The first one, a sweaty, black-haired man with sallow cheeks and pungent body odour, went by the codename of Rasher. According to Cumming's briefing, Rasher was a travelling salesman of Danish descent with an intimate knowledge of German heavy industry and a devotion to the British Empire. According to Wiggins, he was a drunk on the make.

Rasher (so named, Wiggins correctly guessed, because Cumming must have associated Denmark with bacon, hence Rasher the Dane) spoke good English, but that was the only thing about him that Wiggins trusted. He had no information about a German advance – 'they are plotting, I am sure of this fact, but plotting what?' – he had no information on potential agents – 'why, what is wrong with me? You think you need more agents, this disappoints me' – and he had nothing else to say other than an extended plea for more money.

'I ain't got no money,' Wiggins told him sourly. 'And if I did, I wouldn't give it to you.'

After this, Wiggins moved cafes and took another excellent beer, which proved more interesting than Agent Pikestaff. A thin wreath of a man with wire spectacles and an undersized bowler hat, Wiggins spotted him as soon as he entered the smoke-filled Café Le Cirio. He took a moment to admire the flowing lines of the mirrors about the tables, the long curled bar and the intricately tiled floor – a site more beautiful than the piss, phlegm and stale beer of the Kings Arms. Unlike Rasher, Pikestaff had lots of exciting intelligence. He talked of a cell of Indian nationalists plotting in Berlin; he talked of French duplicity in Alsace; he talked of a plan to assassinate the King of England. What he did not talk of, though, was evidence.

Cumming thought him a telegraph operator for the Belgian army, but Wiggins knew this to be false as soon as he saw him. He had none of the telltale indentations in his fingers, so pronounced in those of that profession, he did not hold himself like anyone with military training, and he refused to give any concrete information other than vague mutterings of 'interceptions'. He, too, was most exercised about the matter of money and whether Wiggins could supply him with more. Their interview ended soon after, but it left Wiggins with a very low view of Cumming's organisation in Europe.

As Wiggins made his way back to the platform, through the crowds, he tried to put the memory of these two 'agents' out of his mind. Cumming's network was almost certainly going to be little help in his search, his hunt. The fact that the name Maxim DuPont had rung bells with both Martha and Margaretha gave him hope, though. That these two women knew of him, that he moved in the circles of the rich and powerful (and immoral), made him a chief suspect in the search for Von Bork. He clearly had contact with the French military, and possibly Austrian too. Why would such a man leave London in such a hurry, barely hours after Holmes's death? He may not be Von Bork, but Wiggins had to eliminate him as a suspect – or a killer – one way or the other.

He wasn't overly concerned that both Martha and Margaretha seemed to think he might be French. Von Bork, almost certainly an upper-class German, would be well able to pose as an upper-class member of any number of European countries, including England. Like Kell, half of them spoke at least three languages perfectly, and they had more in common with each other than they did with the likes of him.

DuPont was the best lead, alright. He was worth chasing. And Margaretha was the person to lead him there. If she ever showed up. He glanced back down the platform and saw Claudette getting into a first-class carriage and busily ordering the porter about, but still no sign of the mistress.

As the porter left, Wiggins finally ghosted next to Claudette. 'Where is she?' he hissed.

She turned to him sharply, but did not answer. Instead, she glared at a Gladstone bag on the floor of the compartment, and indicated for him to put it up on the luggage rack. Wiggins stepped in, and hoisted it aloft. As he did so, the whistle of the engine pierced the air in a great shriek. He turned to the maid again and pointed to the platform clock. 'It is time,' he said.

She shrugged. '*C'est Mata Hari.*'

Wiggins stepped back onto the platform. He saw a station master type striding down the platform, waving his arms at the guard, who held a flag aloft but did not drop it. The two men engaged in a heated conversation, gesticulating at the clock. The driver, a short man with a long drooping moustache, stepped down and slowly walked towards them. Wiggins took the moment to reconnoitre the rest of the train. As he did so, passengers disembarked from the other platform in a riot of rushing steps and luggage carts.

He went up to the engine. It was a magnificent machine, a powerhouse that could march across a continent in hours, glistening, all brass and iron with an ugly square funnel at the front. It idled, ready to go. The fireman gave him an odd look and he moved on. The engine made him think of René Lequin, the French spy he and Kell had run to ground in West London and literally chased to his death under the wheels of an underground train. But that was a small engine – this one here was huge and glowering, like the artillery guns Wiggins had manned in South Africa but much bigger. It looked like an instrument of death.

As he glided back down the platform, checking the carriages as surreptitiously as possible – for the blue-jacketed man, for anything out of the ordinary and, of course, for entry and exit points – he finally heard Margaretha arrive at the far end. He could feel the wave of charisma as a knot of people surrounded her. Laughter cascaded down towards him. Clearly, she had the station manager, the ticket clerk, even the driver, eager and happy to please. He got on the train and walked the connecting corridor to her compartment.

Claudette sat waiting for her mistress and barely acknowledged his entrance. He went to the door and watched Mata Hari (for in public, it was obviously Mata Hari now and not Margaretha) at work. Wiggins saw it at once, the change in demeanour, the way the light simply oozed out of her, how she shone like a jewel in sunbeams. The station staff couldn't do enough for her, clearing the way, calling for a cart, until finally, she stepped upon a luggage trolley and they wheeled her to the carriage.

She reached the compartment door and turned in thanks to the bowing station master. The driver scuttled off to the engine. The whistles screeched. Mata Hari, dressed in an outrageous tight ball gown with a wide brimmed hat and voluminous pink feather boa, stood at the carriage door and waved. 'Adieu,' she cried. 'Dag, Salut, Auf Wiedersehen, Arrivederci, Goodbye!' Then she pulled the door shut just as the great train shuddered forward.

Margaretha slumped onto the seat, gestured for Claudette to close the blinds and exhaled. '*Ah mon dieu, la BELGIQUE!*' Then she caught sight of Wiggins, who hovered by the compartment door, unsure again in her presence: 'Ah, Martha's Englishman. Here, sit.'

'No ta,' he said. 'It ain't proper.'

'Ha,' she replied. 'I do not care for proper. Sit. Come now, am I not your employer?'

The great train had begun to sway and clank as it picked up speed, and Wiggins realised he had no choice but to do as she said. Part of him enjoyed the attention, for she had the knack of turning her gaze upon you in such a way to make you feel like the most important thing in her world. He knew it was a trick, this charm, but he was not immune. He sat down and watched idly as Claudette fussed with the luggage. She and Margaretha exchanged a few words in French and then she hauled open the sliding door into the corridor and left, studiously ignoring Wiggins as she did so.

'She is French,' Margaretha said by way of explanation.

'And what are you?'

She smiled, and bent her head. 'I? I am the jewel of the East. Trained from a child in the Hindu temples of India, expert in the art of ancient and exotic dancing. I am a pearl, I am a feeling, I am the mystery of the Orient. I am Mata Hari!' She struck a pose with her arms and grinned.

Wiggins grinned back. 'Out there you're her, I can see that. But what about in here, what about in your head?'

'You do not believe me, Mr Wiggins?'

He didn't. For one thing, she'd got the wrong continent – it was Batavia, Sumatra, somewhere on the archipelago, not India, that her styling came from. Her perfume too. He knew that from the odd shift down the docks after he left the army – when the spice ships came in from the East, smelling like heaven and looking like hell. Martha had told him her real name, and her accent was Dutch, just like the captains of those spice ships. She was also clearly a purveyor of dreams, illusions, like a fairground act – it wouldn't be wise to believe anything she said about anything, certainly not about herself. Instead, he just smiled again – he couldn't help smiling that morning – and said, 'Does it matter?'

H.B. Lyle

'That you believe me? Of course. Now, tell me something else, Mr Wiggins. Why does our beautiful friend Martha push you upon me?'

'I can go if . . .'

'Do not be so English,' she interrupted. 'I do not want you to go anywhere. You are too nice to look at. I want to know why you are here, and why Martha insisted? Does she want you to be her lover? Does she owe you money? Or are you a spy?'

Wiggins arranged his face into a surprised expression. He was ready for the question, had been ready ever since he started working for Kell, you always had to be ready. Only once before had he actually been asked this question so directly – are you a spy – and his failure to answer convincingly had cost him a fingernail. But Margaretha wasn't the type to torture you, at least not like that. 'Do me a favour,' he laughed. 'Do I look like a spy?'

She shrugged. 'What is this like anyway?'

'Martha's worried about you is all. She sent me along as a bit of muscle, you know.'

'Muscle is always a help, for sure.' She let a half-smile play across her lips as she looked at him. Wiggins didn't think she was truly attracted to him, but it was a habit, a reflex almost, the way she let her eyes dance and linger over him. And it worked. 'You will be my knight in shining armour, no? If I am in danger.'

'Are you in danger?'

The carriage door clunked open. Claudette returned and sat down, heavy and discontent. Again she did not look at Wiggins. Margaretha asked her something and she responded sullenly. 'You see,' Margaretha turned back to Wiggins. 'Claudette has walked the train. There is no danger. There are no monsters to be feared, for sure.'

'And no one's after you?' Wiggins knew his mission lay with finding Von Bork, tracking down this Maxim DuPont in the first instance, but he couldn't help thinking about the Man in the Blue Jacket, the sense of threat in the station, that group of men who'd been watching her dance the night before, including the Little General, while she took off her clothes. He couldn't help thinking this woman needed protection. 'No one wants you for anything?'

'Ha! Men want me all the time. It's my job to make them feel that way.'

Throughout this conversation, she'd been idly plucking at the feathers of her boa – absently but continually working her fingers. And though she'd laughed at his suggestion about her being followed, Wiggins could see that she was not relaxed. Her eyes flitted to the corridor every now and then, and up at her luggage. She asked a question of Claudette in French, and they burst into a discussion. Wiggins sensed the tension between the two women, and that what made them tense was not what they were discussing. Perhaps it was his presence, he thought, but then his mind wandered to Mrs Jepson back in Kell's office, and Constance Kell herself – he could imagine their responses: isn't it just like a man to think two women are talking about him.

'Mr Wiggins,' Margaretha said suddenly. 'We have two hours before we reach Quévy at the border. You will help Claudette with the luggage as we must change onto a French train for Paris. Oh so tedious. Will they ever invent a machine that will transport you, like that!' She clicked her fingers.

'I've seen the aeroplanes,' Wiggins said. 'Up at Hendon. They goes at a fair nip.'

'You like them, these flying machines?'

'I like the idea of them. It must be peaceful up there, quiet, just you and the sky.'

'But are they not dangerous?'

'Everything's dangerous. Unless you stays home and drinks tea.'

'There's other things you can do at home.'

Wiggins grinned. He couldn't help it.

'But please, Mr Wiggins,' Margaretha went on.

'Just Wiggins.'

She nodded. 'Wiggins,' she said the word with a hint of a v at the start. 'Tell me why you are here . . . no, no not about why Martha wants you here. Why are *you* here?'

'Actually, I should take a look-see, on the train – see that all's safe.'

'No. You will stay here with me. Claudette. She will go, we will have *caffè* yes?' She spoke to Claudette, and gestured at the door. Once the maid left, Margaretha turned back to him. 'Now, why are you really here?'

'I'm here to find Maxim DuPont,' Wiggins said, reflexively as if it was obvious to him. Otherwise known as Von Bork, he thought. And once I've found him I'll kill him, he did not add. But Margaretha's gaze settled on him. She did not accept this answer, and made him search for a deeper truth. 'I'm here,' he said at last, 'to right the worst wrong of my life.'

Wiggins had no choice but to help with Margaretha's luggage at Quévy, the stop beyond Mons. He didn't mind, except it was now clear to anyone watching that he was travelling with her. They all had to get off the train, go through customs, and board a new train to Paris. And Mata Hari – this is how Wiggins now thought of her when she was in public – travelled with more luggage than the rest of the passengers put together.

He and Claudette did their best to haul the trunks onto trolleys at the station while Mata sashayed to the customs house. It was while Wiggins pushed the luggage through the wide doors that he saw what he did not want to see – the Man in the Blue Jacket from the Gare du Midi. This may have been a coincidence, the Quévy train and the Paris connection was one of the biggest departures that morning and quite a few people were clearly travelling on. Wiggins had noted a number of other passengers from Brussels who were filing through the customs shed ahead of them, or rather around them, as Mata and her luggage dominated the whole show.

The trouble was, the Man in the Blue Jacket was no longer wearing the blue jacket.

He'd changed his hat as well, and now wore a farm worker's short coat and a flat cap, rather than the more rakish boater he'd worn in Brussels. But Wiggins recognised him all the same. Blue Jacket now hovered by a post as the rest of the passengers went into the customs clearing house. That was the move of a professional – to change jackets, change hats, mime a limp, whatever it took to change your appearance. Wiggins had done it many times himself. He doubled back, hiding behind a beer cart as he did so, and came around behind Blue Jacket. Blue Jacket threw a cigarette to the ground and shuffled into the customs house himself. Wiggins followed. The man walked slowly, and glanced much too long at Mata Hari and Claudette as he passed them. Clearly, he was following Mata.

As he rejoined Claudette and Margaretha, Wiggins reasoned that now at *least* one person was following her. They waited for the customs officers to clear Mata's luggage – a short while, as Mata laughed and joked with the men, to their obvious delight – Wiggins once again felt that feeling on the back of his neck, the hairs rising, the hunted animal. Eyes on. It was the same feeling he had at the station earlier, and now that he was sure one man followed, it made sense that someone else was looking out too. If you are a professional enough outfit to have a spare coat and hat ready for a tail, then you're probably organised enough to have at least two men on the job – especially for a train job.

He gently touched Mata's arm. She didn't turn, hardly acknowledged him at all but as Wiggins stepped back he could tell she was winding things up with the customs men. Blue Jacket wasn't the only pro in Quévy that day.

It was gone midday now, and the heat pressed down on his head, flat and constant. Flies buzzed here and there around the windless dusty tracks, and the walk across to the French train – to France itself – was an empty, desolate experience. The other passengers, with presumably Blue Jacket too, had already boarded the train by the time Wiggins and Claudette pushed the trolley to the luggage van and began to unload. A railwayman helped Wiggins lift the great trunks, grumbling and moaning in a low, rough dialect that Wiggins wouldn't have understood even if he did speak French.

Despite Wiggins's nerves, and his warnings, Mata Hari made no attempt to keep a low profile. She sashayed along the platform, towards the front of the train, like a cat asking for more cream. She made her body purr, and heads popped out of the line of windows as she passed.

She didn't turn her head once, but Wiggins could tell she knew every head on that train was arching after her – drinking in the great Mata Hari.

'You do know you're being followed,' Wiggins said as soon as he was back in the compartment.

'Of course I am being followed,' she said airily. 'I am Mata Hari.'

'Nah, nah,' Wiggins replied. 'Not like that.' He took a breath. It troubled him that this woman was in danger and seemed so blithe to it. Having at least one man wait for you at a railway station, then follow you into another country, was not the act of a dancing enthusiast, or even a jilted lover – not to do it on the sly, anyway.

'You're in danger,' he said.

'It's part of my appeal.'

He sighed and turned to Claudette, as if to enlist her support. But she simply stared out of the window at the light green and yellow fields whipping by as the train picked up speed. Wiggins tried again with Margaretha. 'Do you have any enemies?'

'You mean, apart from the many men who I do not wish to spend the night with?'

Wiggins hoped he would not blush. 'I see, the other night. Thems is powerful people. Is that your sort, is it?'

'I rather think *I* am their sort, wouldn't you say?' She seemed greatly amused by the conversation, and Wiggins's interest in her. He, on the other hand, couldn't get a read on her motivation. 'Look,' he went on. 'I don't think it's safe.'

'You have a remarkably, how you say, detailed, opinion of what is or is not safe for me. We have only met, for sure, less than one day. And you . . . you are a humble, handsome porter, no?'

'Bodyguard, Martha said. And I take it seriously.'

It was her turn to sigh. 'All anyone wants from me is, well, what you see.' She gestured at her body. 'And what I can do with it. I am not so young as you think. I have had men wanting this from me my whole life. I know what to do.'

He glanced out of the window again. The patchwork fields had given way to forest, deep dark forest. The kind where they buried bodies. It still didn't sit right. 'Do not worry so much,' she said. 'Let us enjoy the journey – we will be in the city of light by the evening, and I will show you how to meet your friend Monsieur DuPont.'

'Not friend.'

'So gloomy, is this the word? *Betrokken*. Ha! Now, I am hungry. Claudette, *mange*, no?'

'I'll go,' Wiggins said quickly and got up. He was eager to see who might be on the train, and he certainly didn't have Mata's blasé attitude to the threat.

'As you wish.' She waved her hand absently, and looked out into the brooding forest speeding by.

Margaretha travelled in first class, at the Paris end of the train. Which meant she was up by the engine. Wiggins buttoned his coat and slung his knapsack over his shoulder. The train rattled and screeched along at a fair clip and he bumped his shoulders on the thin corridor as he went towards the restaurant car.

The train picked up pace. Click clack, the windows rattled. They were going downhill. He pushed through one car, then the next into an open carriage. It was hot, despite the speed of the train and the breeze that whistled through the windows. Too hot for anyone in first class to spare him much of a look.

Click clack, the carriage jerked and swung as he stepped through the connecting doors into the restaurant car.

'*Non . . . monsieur. Non!*' A waiter, sweating in a heavy dinner jacket and tie, held up his hand to stop Wiggins.

'It's alright, lad,' Wiggins said without breaking his stride. The waiter watched on powerless as Wiggins kept an even pace. He kept walking. The glasses rattled in the bar, plates skittered together. A great blast of steam gushed from the galley kitchen as he passed. He looked in, saw the guard stuffing some kind of pastry into his face. Click clack, the train sped on.

His shoulders bumped against the sides of another tight, tilting corridor and then he opened the door into a busy third-class carriage. Wooden seats, all sorts of people. A man on the left-hand side flinched at the sight of him, and pretended to be asleep. Wiggins didn't break his stride but he knew people did not move like that in their sleep. He wore an open shirt, unshaven, a mass of blond hair with big bucket hands and shoulders fit for punching. Wiggins pushed on, through the heat hum of conversation, the squawking of chickens. An older woman held a cockerel to her breast and hummed a tune. Tobacco smoke swirled in the breeze of the open windows as the train sped on. Wiggins's mind snagged on the man with the blond hair. He hadn't seen him before, but the glare of his eyes, the sudden slump of sleep, suggested he knew who Wiggins was.

The next carriage had even more people in it, locals mostly he guessed, crammed onto the benches with bundles and crates, and two or three men standing. As he entered, a man got up and turned towards him, only to turn away on sight. It was the Man in the Blue Jacket, wearing the short coat he'd had on at Quévy. The man pretended to change his mind and turned to walk the other way, away from Wiggins towards the end of the train. Wiggins followed.

They lurched around a bend as the train sped on, click clack.

He pushed through the final carriage and still the man didn't turn, but went straight through the doors into what Wiggins knew was the luggage car. Wiggins kicked open the door.

CRASH! Blue Jacket swung for him with a cosh, but Wiggins expected that, twisted his shoulder and sent Blue Jacket into a pile of luggage.

'I don't wan—' Wiggins began, but the man leaped at him again. Wiggins sidestepped him and drove a right fist into the side of the man's head, sending him flying once more. 'Listen, mate,' Wiggins tried again.

The man scrabbled to his feet, crouched in the confined space and charged again. He let out a great cry as he came forward. Wiggins feinted, then lifted his shoulder into the man's belly and threw him against the carriage wall.

'Enough,' Wiggins said as he pinned him to the floor with his knees. 'Just tell me who you are, who you work for, and I'll let you go.'

The man struggled and writhed. Wiggins adjusted his knees on his chest. 'Tell me!'

BANG! BANG!

A sharp pain stung the tip of his shoulder. Wood splintered at his ear. Wiggins sprang back from the man on the floor, and tumbled away into the back of the luggage. The bullet had only grazed him, thank Christ. Blondie stood at the entrance, a revolver in his bucket hand. He squeezed off another shot at Wiggins, who dived behind Margaretha's huge pile of trunks.

The train lurched over the points, and he heard Blondie grunt at the man on the floor. Another lurch, and a stumble, and Wiggins leaped for the back door of the carriage. He scrabbled the latch open, as the train dipped into a corner.

He swung out of the door, just as another bullet clipped the frame. Wind rushed in his ears. The distance posts whipped past, the forest a green blur. Wiggins clung onto the small ladder at the back of the carriage and began to climb. The train was going too fast to jump, and Blondie meant business.

Fft! Another bullet flew up into the sky as he hauled himself onto the roof of the carriage. He heard the man shout out, the words fading in the roar.

He looked along the length of the train ahead. There was nothing for it but to run. Blondie would be able to climb up that ladder, lean over the top of the carriage and take a clear shot. If he was clinging to the roof and crawling, the man would shoot his bollocks into his belly. If he ran, he'd have a chance.

Sure enough, Blondie grunted into position behind him. He caught site of the shock of blond hair before the pistol came into view. Wiggins rose to his feet, angled his body severely into the onrushing wind, and ran.

He had a sudden surge of familiarity – running the cranes in high wind felt like this – and his feet stayed true. He loped, low, fast, then glanced back. The shock of blond hair had gone, presumably running back through the train. He had to get back to Margaretha, to warn her, to defend her if necessary.

He loped into the wind and then leaped across to the next carriage. As he did so a hand, a bucket hand, caught his ankle and yanked him back in between the carriages.

The gun exploded, BANG in his ear, muzzle flash blinded him, smoke in his nose. He smashed the gun away with his free foot. Blondie cursed. He swung a fist, a glancing blow. Wiggins grabbed the blond hair and smashed his head against the carriage. Blondie let go, loose enough for Wiggins to pull himself back on top of the carriage. He began to crawl.

Blondie came after him. Wiggins lay out on his front, tried to turn but the huge man was crawling on top of him now, bearing down with his massive weight, clawing at him with those bucket hands.

'If only, if only . . .' Wiggins thought as he tried to twist once more. And then, the cord was on him.

Blondie had a garotte around his neck. Wiggins squeezed his thumb underneath it just in time, but he knew he only had moments before the pressure became too much. Blondie throttled the life out of him, pulling, pulling. His eyes watered. His neck rang out in pain. The wind rushed in his ears. His head was about to explode, blood seeping into his eyeballs. His thumb bled. He had seconds.

Through a misted gaze, eyeballs huge, barely seeing a thing, Wiggins suddenly realised what he must do, an end-of-life clarity that had reached him once before and now, now, he needed that clarity . . . he released his thumb, let the cord bite and relaxed.

Blondie cried out in triumph and pulled harder still, as Wiggins went limp. Blondie rose up almost to his feet, heaving at the cord around Wiggins's neck, unheeding of the engine's whistle as

THWUMP!

The train careered into a low brick tunnel, and Blondie's body was no more, destroyed on impact and splattered onto the tracks below as the express rushed on.

Wiggins clung on. Breathing hard, heart thumping. His arms stretched wide, his cheek to the metal of the carriage roof. The tunnel barely inches above his head, the air was mostly steam and soot and smoke from the engine, billowing along the tunnel, washing over him like a high-speed sauna. But it tasted sweeter than the air on Salisbury Plain, fresher than an Atlantic breeze, for that soot-filled smoke tasted of life itself.

Whoosh – the train burst out of the tunnel, the smoke streamed upwards and away from him and Wiggins breathed easily. He lay there for a few moments, not scared of the movement, the rocking and rolling of the express, so much as resting, reacquainting himself with being alive once more. Then he remembered Margaretha and the Man in the Blue Jacket, and began to crawl to the end of the carriage roof.

Wiggins swung down to the door at the next carriage and rushed back through the train, hoping he wasn't too late. Blue Jacket was nowhere to be seen. No one seemed to miss Blondie. He either acted alone or in concert with Blue Jacket, but he could not see a third accomplice.

As he barrelled down the connecting corridor to Margaretha's compartment, he saw her door hanging open. He rushed in there to find her stretched out on the seats, unconscious. He knelt down to her, calling out her name. A searing pain exploded on the back of his head, and everything went black.

IO

Sunday 5 July: the leader of the Labour Party, Keir Hardie, argues in Manchester that it is time for women to have the vote. He goes further and states that all adults – working men, women, and not only property owners – should now have their say in democracy. It is not a message that the Fleet Street press is keen to carry. As self-appointed bastions of democracy and the British way of life, they see no reason to let the workers speak.

Wiggins woke up. Or rather, he opened his eyes briefly. He lay on something soft, comfortable. A faint outline of light framed the window in front of him. Above, a plain white ceiling with ornate cornicing, just visible in the gloom. He closed his eyes again. His head pounded. His mind fogged.

A door creaked. Footsteps and shuffling, and then that unmistakable smell of spice, jasmine and musk, the smell of her. He barely had the will or energy to open his eyes, until she placed a cold flannel on his forehead. 'Where am I?' he asked, tilting his head to the side.

'You are at the Élysée Palace,' Margaretha whispered, almost proudly.

He tried to focus, but his eyes closed again. 'What happened? I . . . I . . .'

'Shush. My Claudette she is, how you say, handy with a clothes iron. But rest now, yes?'

Wiggins tried to raise his head off the pillow but the effort made him slump down once more. At the Palace, in Paris? He tried to remember the last moments on the train, rushing back to the compartment. 'There was a man,' he gasped. 'He had a blue jacket. But no, wait, he took it off, he . . .'

'Shush, Wiggins, I am here, I am safe. Sleep now, I think you have a fever, for sure.' Her voice was soft and susurrous, as warm and enticing as her movements, and Wiggins drifted out of consciousness again.

She started to sing. She did not start to sing. He did not know, but he heard a song all the same, a lullaby, but not in Dutch or French now, in English, in London, a younger voice, cradling his head, the voice? Cradling, no a young woman, but he is younger, a child, his mother. Like a child too. A small hand holding his, an even smaller one disappearing, dragging, dragging along the street, through the horseshit and the mud and then she's screaming. What do you mean? One shift is all I asked for. I can't have my girls drinking. Fack off, fack off. Is that my father? 'Im? Cackling, cackling, don't think much of me, do you, scruff? Away, away. Ere mister, tanner for the boy, tanner for his poor head. Boots, punches, running again, running.

It was night when he woke again. The sounds of an argument merging with his dreams. The window opposite still emitted light, but the fizzing, yellow kind of electric street lamps. The argument grew more heated, in French he guessed, between a man and Margaretha coming from the other room. He pushed himself off the cot where he'd lain, and crabbed weakly to the door. He knew enough about Margaretha's life not to interrupt her, and besides, while the man in the argument sounded annoyed – angry almost – she still had a lightness to her voice, a half-amused tone, that made him think she wasn't in immediate danger.

He could not understand what they were talking about, though it seemed as if the man was demanding something of her, and she was lightly refusing or downplaying the significance of whatever it was he asked. At one point she laughed, which made the man shout in annoyance. Wiggins squeezed his eyes shut and tried to shake the visions of his mother from his head, the fever dream he'd been in. He tried to pick out familiar words, straining to hear what the man said. He could only really make out one, oft-repeated phrase. *Tu travailles pour moi.*

'Ladoux, Ladoux, Ladoux,' Marguretha said, and then something else he couldn't get the gist of at all.

He put his eye to the gap in the door frame. All he could see was a mirror, at the far side of the room, with no furniture in between. It was lit by electric lights, and the wallpaper was white and pink florals, expensive. The gilt-edged mirror contained nothing in it other than a white panelled door, the door behind which he stood. And then Margaretha flitted past, perhaps walking to the window.

'Mademoiselle Hari,' the man said, and then stepped into view himself, striding after Margaretha, and barked something else. He stopped, long enough for Wiggins to get a good look at him. He was a big man, barrel-chested, military for sure, an officer judging by the cut of his coat and the entitlement with which he spoke. He had a square face, and a small black moustache like a printed stamp on a piece of paper. When he finished speaking, he turned and looked directly at the door behind which Wiggins stood. He stared for a moment longer, hat in his hand, mind whirring, until Margaretha said, 'Ladoux, Georges.' And something soft and conciliatory.

Wiggins cursed again his lack of French. The man, Ladoux, continued to stare at the door behind which Wiggins stood, as if he knew he was being watched. But Margaretha's words finally got through to him, and when she swept back into vision, the two of them moved off, obviously to the door. He heard them complete a muttered goodbye, and so hurried back into the bed and closed his eyes.

Immediately after Ladoux left, Wiggins heard Margaretha at the door. She pushed it open gently and peered at him in the bed. He could see through slitted eyes her dark shape, partly silhouetted by the light filtering in past the window's blinds. She pattered slowly towards him, her spiced scent drifting over the bed. He relaxed and closed his eyes, made his breathing a shade heavier. He did not want her to know the extent of his knowledge, for all he liked her. He felt her hand on his brow. A second later, she placed a cold flannel onto his forehead. The shock almost made him twitch. He realised he was sweating, and the cloth felt like a band of ice. A fever still.

She muttered something in Dutch, and then he heard her soft steps withdraw. She closed first the connecting door and, a few moments later, his ears still twitching, he heard the other door open and close. After a moment, he went directly to the window and poked behind the blind.

The sky was dark, but the street blazed with yellow light. And this wasn't just any street. It was at least double or triple width – at least twice as wide as Piccadilly even. It was so wide that in places it had two lines of trees, on each side of the road. Dead straight, the trees like a line of soldiers on parade, arranged for show rather than for fighting. The window from which he looked out was on the third or fourth floor, Wiggins guessed, and as he craned his neck he could see down the long wide boulevard, lit as it was by a succession of crackling electric lamp posts. The street was busy with traffic, mostly motorcars, and the pavement below flitted and buzzed with people. It was dark, but it couldn't be that late for so many people to be out and about. Across the street, the buildings were as grand and large as the one he found himself in, though any fevered thought that it was the Élysée Palace was surely just that. Perhaps Margaretha had been playing with him.

On the pavement directly below, an awning jutted out from his building onto the street. He waited for a few moments, until what he hoped for transpired. Margaretha, wearing a cream dress, came out from underneath the awning. He recognised her easily at this distance given the way she moved and swayed, with so much more confidence and front than most women. She also wore a hat adorned with a number of peacock feathers, and a wide brim. She consulted briefly with a footman of some sort, then sauntered across the wide pavement out under one of the trees to the traffic. There, he could just make out a car pull away and drive off down the street.

His head pounded. He stepped back from the window and held onto the sill for a moment, dizzy with the effort of standing for so long. He clearly hadn't recovered from whatever had happened to him on the train, and he shuffled back to the cot and sat down. He didn't have the strength to get back up and turn on the light, but he could see from the outside light that he was in a small anteroom, a dressing room of sorts but without the clothes. By the cot, he found a jug of water and a thin, round baton of bread. He drank deeply from the water, scoffed a hunk of the bread, and then searched under the bed for the pan.

Before he relieved himself, he took the empty porcelain bowl up to the window and managed to read the lettering etched around the side. *Élysée Palace Hotel.*

As he slumped back into the bed, exhausted by the effort, he smiled to himself. Margaretha hadn't lied. She'd just given the impression of a little bit more glamour than was real – they were in the Élysée Palace after all. All she'd done was leave off that one word, hotel. It was with this thought, and the smile on his face, breathing in those oriental spices, that he went to sleep once more, wondering vaguely about the French army officer who'd bullied her.

'Where is Wiggins?'

'Eh?' Kell looked up at his wife, surprised.

Constance sat at the other end of the breakfast table, reading *The Suffragette.* 'It's just here, look, Keir Hardie the leader of . . .'

'Hardie's an insurgent.'

'The leader of the Labour Party, here – he supports us, of course – but he's saying *everyone* should get a vote! And, well, I thought of Wiggins.'

'Why?'

She snorted. 'Can you think of a man better able to choose a member of parliament than him?'

'It's not as simple . . .' Kell trailed off. She was right of course. Wiggins was an exceptional judge of character. But then, if they gave the likes of him the vote, he wondered how the Conservatives would ever get in again.

'I marched the other day with the ELFS,' Constance went on.

'Don't tell me about your political activities! I may have to arrest you,' he said. 'It's best that you don't tell me what you get up to. Politically, I mean. I must be able to play the ignorant fool.'

'A stretch, I know,' she said, raising a slither of toast.

'Elfs?' he said after a moment, unable to contain his curiosity.

'Keep up, Vernon. The world is turning outside White-hall. The East London Federation of Suffragettes. A fantastic young organisation. *They* are agitating for universal suffrage *and* poor relief.'

'The government's already given the rest of us income tax, what more relief do they want?'

'Relief from being poor, of course. Which I can quite understand.'

'Yes dear, you were exposed to the elements for hours at that Wimbledon final. Mrs Pears told Soapy that she even got sunburned.'

'Silly woman refused my parasol,' Constance replied, deliberately ignoring Kell's jibe. 'I thought she'd faint. But I suppose you're right.'

'I am?'

'I shouldn't want to embarrass you with the chaps. You can tell them quite truthfully that you have no knowledge of my participating in suffragette activity. No knowledge at all.'

Kell thought of his wife's words later that morning when he left the Foreign Office. It was actually the chaps in

Whitehall who were embarrassing themselves, so blind were they to the coming storm. He had nothing to fear about Constance's political activities. They'd all be put to shade by what was to come, if only the others in government would believe him.

He'd finally got a meeting with an old acquaintance, a bumptious self-regarding fool named Carruthers. Kell would come across him every now and then at the club, and the man would always bore on about his yachting prowess, or else shooting in Bumthorp-by-Blazers or wherever it was; and he constantly complained about the poor servants at his chambers; all the while, Kell noted with dismay, Carruthers rose in the ranks of that most arrogant and self-important of government departments: the Foreign Office.

The reason why Kell wanted to meet Carruthers was quite simple. Ever since he'd first known the man, bragging on as he did over cigars and extra brandies, Carruthers would tell 'his story'. He'd always preface it by saying, 'This is highly confidential, old boy, don't you know.' Kell had heard the account at least three times – Carruthers did not seem to remember having told it before, or if he did then he did not care – and each time Carruthers would swear him to secrecy as if he, Kell, alone was fortunate enough to have this confidence shared. The truth was, half the club had been regaled with this story at one time or another, but that never deterred Carruthers.

When he was a younger man ('Much better shot then, of course. More time for sport. Affairs of state weigh heavy, all that.'), his story would start, as he stared into the middle distance, he chanced to take up an offer to go yachting in the North Sea at the end of one summer. 'Had to work in

August, of course, one must when I had such a position of importance.' The details of this story would vary, but the essentials remained the same – that Carruthers was invited on a yachting holiday with a friend 'more of an acquaintance, can't tell you his name of course, national security et cetera, et cetera' (he really spoke like that), but that he ended up doing most of the yachting. 'X was a terrible duffer with the boat, of course.' Carruthers goes on to say that, during their sojourn off the coasts of Germany, Holland and Belgium, he began to suspect the German navy was planning an invasion of Great Britain. 'I was right, by god!' And he would go on to relate how he had thwarted the initial plans and reported back to London. Subsequently, the Admiralty had strengthened its defences and embarked on a radical, upscaled shipbuilding programme. Carruthers, so he said, had saved the Empire. 'That's how I got on in the F.O.,' he'd say, completing the story with a sideswipe at colleagues who owed their position to previous connections. He didn't mention his family homes in Yorkshire and Aix-en-Provence.

The story was preposterous, but Kell knew there was a grain of truth in it from other contacts in government. Carruthers had indeed stumbled across German naval manoeuvres that suggested a greater build-up of naval strength than had hitherto been imagined, and he did indeed owe an early promotion to this intelligence. Consequently, Kell supposed that if anyone in the Foreign Office was likely to take his warnings of war seriously – in particular his fear that Germany would end up at war with the British – it might well be Carruthers. Lord Grey, the Foreign Secretary, was no fool, but in order to gain an audience with him he needed to persuade Carruthers. And

Carruthers was undoubtedly predisposed to think much of German military ambition.

'No chance, old boy,' is what he actually said. 'It's a little local difficulty in the Balkans. Blow over in a couple of weeks. That's what we've been advising Grey, sure he thinks the same.'

'But, can't you see,' Kell replied, exasperated by this buffoon, by his office laced with gilt picture frames, fabulous Persian carpets, and lavish knick-knacks from around the globe. 'Austria has to declare against Serbia. Russia has to defend Serbia. Germany has to defend Austria. And voilà, grand European war.'

Carruthers leaned back in his seat and smiled. 'Look old man, I know – better than anyone, but that's another story that I'm not at liberty to share – that the Germans are hell-bent on military expansion. But not over this trifle. Cigarette?'

'If I could just talk to Lord Grey, I think he'd under—'

'No, no, no.' Carruthers wafted smoke in his face as he interrupted. 'Listen, I'm not arrogant enough to suppose that the Kaiser does not have advisers just as clever as us. They'll be telling him the same as I'm telling Grey. Germany will never support an Austrian war against Serbia, it makes no sense. No sense at all.'

The day before this meeting, while Kell tried in vain to press the case for greater urgency in the United Kingdom's response to the growing European crises, while Carruthers and his colleagues blithely dismissed all threat of major war, Kaiser Wilhelm explicitly offered Austria his unwavering support in whatever route it chose, a blank cheque for any military action whatsoever. The clubbable

gentlemen of Whitehall might think such a move irra-
tional, but the Kaiser has heard the nickname his
troops have for him after the last such crisis –
Wilhelm the Timid – and he will be timid no more. He
has let the Austrian government know that he will
back it in the dispute with Serbia come what may.
He signs this devastating blank cheque, and then
departs for a well-earned yachting holiday.

The fever broke. With a great burst of light, Claudette
furled the blind. Wiggins cried out in surprise. She cried
out in equal surprise. '*Mon dieu*,' she said, twisting around
and holding a hand to her chest. She said something in
French.

'I near shat m'self an' all,' he said.

She turned away, suddenly embarrassed. He realised it
was because he was in bed, in just his underwear. She must
have seen him earlier, must have helped Margaretha put
him into the bed and had probably nursed him too. She
would have seen him dishevelled. But that was when he was
ill. He'd woken up now obviously in a much better state, his
illness had broken and the embarrassment had returned.

'Speaking of which . . .?' he said, with a question in his
voice. 'Where's the lav? Er, toilet?' He continued to gesture
awkwardly but she got the point. Claudette pointed him up
through the door and into a door on the other side of the
hotel room. Wiggins sped across the wide and lush room,
which had a large double bed, a sofa and a writing desk all
just so. This was a hotel with swank, and Margaretha had a
suite. Thick floral wallpaper, gold-flecked paint on the picture rail, and hot and cold running water in the bathroom.

Hearing Claudette clatter around in the room, he locked
the door and turned on the shower – a marvel in itself.

He'd had them before in public baths, and once or twice in the army, but he'd never seen a private shower before. He stank, and such a smell seemed all out of place in a hotel like the Élysée Palace. The bathroom gleamed with hot and cold taps, a large brass showerhead and was tiled to shoulder height all around. It also smelled divine, clean, fresh and still with that hint of eastern spice, that scent of Margaretha.

Not only that, someone had also laid out a suit of clothes for him. Not too showy, not too cheap, cotton trousers, shirt and a dark green canvas jacket. Margaretha (or Claudette) had guessed his size perfectly. He carefully transferred his cash into the waistband of the trousers and got dressed.

When he came back out into the room, he saw Claudette carrying gowns into the anteroom. She was clearly re-commandeering the space as a dressing room, and from the way she cast disapproving glances at him, Wiggins was in no doubt that she expected him to sleep there no more.

'You hit me, didn't you?' he said. 'Where'd you learn to do that?'

'*Ne parlez pas Anglais. Pas Anglais! Français.*'

'Nah, don't speak French.'

She sighed. '*C'est Paris,*' she said in annoyance, and began folding a pile of underclothes together, ready to take them next door.

Wiggins watched her carefully for a moment. She finished folding, then put her hands flat on the top item and looked at him questioningly. 'What's that on your thumb?' he asked suddenly.

Her thumb twitched, she looked down, then up at him aghast. It was an old trick told him by an officer in army intelligence, back in the Boer War. A sure-fire way to find out if someone can speak a language – surprise them and it's almost impossible for them not to twitch.

'Don't worry,' Wiggins said, hands up. 'I knows you speak English. I ain't gonna hurt you.'

'But . . .' She presented a picture of dismay. Her eyes were downcast, like a child caught out in an innocent deception.

'Why don't you let on?'

'I can't . . . the Madame. It's . . .' She looked lost for a moment longer, then lifted her chin up steady, as if she'd come to a decision, a commitment to a course of action. 'I kept it secret once from the Madame, the first time. And then, I don't know, what do you do? A maid should be invisible, no?'

Wiggins nodded, grinned slightly. 'You hit me something rotten with that iron.'

'I thought you had attacked the Madame,' she said. 'She was lain out, you stood over her, so tall so . . . I am sorry, to hit you so hard.'

They both stood, looking at the floor between them for a moment, thinking about the blow that felled him or perhaps thinking about other blows they both had taken before and that may be yet to come.

She coughed, breaking the moment. 'But please, monsieur,' Claudette went on. 'Do not tell the Madame about, that I speak English. I think she would not like it, she would not trust me again, I think.'

Wiggins nodded slowly, and opened his mouth to say something when the door to the hotel room swung open.

'*Bonjour.*' Margaretha breezed in. 'Ah, Mister Wiggins. You look clean, for sure. And much better. But do not blame Claudette, ya? She is my bodyguard, ha. She thought you were attacking me, ya.'

'I . . . I thought as much,' Wiggins said, glancing at Claudette, by way of keeping her secret between them.

Margaretha waved Claudette into the dressing room and sat down on the purple sofa, so elegantly, like a happy cat, that Wiggins could almost forget the full, electric-blue dress she had on. She'd already windmilled her straw hat onto the bed (Claudette will put it away later of course), and she shook out her hair.

She eyed Wiggins for a moment, as he stood in front of her like a school child, unmanned somehow by her gaze. When he looked at people, like his mentor Sherlock Holmes, he observed intently every twitch and tell, checked their kneecaps, their cuffs, fingernails – all the details that lead to reliable deductions. Margaretha gazed at him with a similar amount of attention, but somehow didn't seem concerned with the details of his appearance; she seemed to gaze into his very soul, and weigh it up for value, there and then.

'Well,' Wiggins said at last, desperate to break the silence.

She blessed him with a puzzled smile. 'And? Well, and something, no? You say this in English?'

'Where are we?'

'The Élysée Palace Hotel, of course. I told you, for sure. Paris, *mon cher*, the centre of the world. To Parisians,' she added. 'You like it?'

'Course I like it,' he said as he looked back at her, sitting on that sofa just so. 'I meant what should we do now?'

'Oh, Monsieur Wiggins, what would you like to do?'

Wiggins took a pastis at a cafe on the corner of Rue du Faubourg Saint-Honoré. The drink itself was disgusting, a herby piss water, but he wanted to make himself as inconspicuous as possible, and this was one of the most fashionable areas in Paris as far as he could tell. He couldn't make head nor tail of the wine list the waiter waved in his direction, so pointed to a neighbour's glass and nodded. He sat with a long view of the street in either direction, and took in the height of Parisian chic; the women wore long, light dresses that swayed and drifted as they walked; colours more varied, brighter than the London set, but more precise too, and well-fitting; and they were prepared to show their upper chests. The women, in short, looked a million pounds; the men, meanwhile, looked at you like you were dirt. If they looked at you at all. Wiggins had quickly realised that sitting at a cafe table was the Parisian cloak of invisibility that he needed. On the street, or in the parks he imagined – that was to be out in public; to sit down at a cafe table was to sit down in your own house. Like the pub, only outside.

It didn't take him long before he settled his eyes on number 39. A magnificent pale stone building blackened by soot, the British Embassy fitted in perfectly on the grand boulevard. It stood a short distance from his cafe table, but Wiggins had a clear view. If he were the type to be proud of Britain's acquisitions and attainments, he would have been proud just then. Instead, he kept his eyes not on the imposing double-height doors in the middle, but on the smaller staff entrance to the left. He ordered another pastis and waited.

As midday approached, a young Englishman came out of the side door and crossed the road north. Wiggins threw down a couple of francs for the drinks (ruinous Mayfair prices, though the money wasn't his), and set off after him. The Englishman was as easy to follow as a snail with gout, for his Englishness, above everything else, shone out of him. He wore a light linen suit, a boater, and the bright red face of a pale man burnt. Whenever he turned to cross the road, or glance back (as he did every now and then), Wiggins could see this flash of red, a man unused to foreign sun. He looked little older than a student, and had that air of wonder and entitlement. As if *he* were discovering the world for the first time ever, as a pioneer of humanity.

They continued north, away from the wide, airy boulevards and into a warren of streets behind the Gare Saint-Lazare. The Young Englishman walked on with purpose, through ornate intricately tiled arcades and across a small square dotted with trees. They finally arrived in a district far less salubrious, and one Wiggins recognised from his own upbringing. Just as the whorehouses of Soho and Covent Garden were only a short walk from St James's in London, so this area they'd come to wasn't far from the British Embassy and the streets of Parisian high society. Like their counterparts in London, the French upper crust kept their vices close.

The tight streets here were stuffed with hotels, at every second door were bars and mysterious shops with blacked-out windows. The Young Englishman, whose gait had become more furtive and jumpier, took a seat at a pavement cafe and fumbled his order. Wiggins sat behind and managed to order something better than the aniseed nightmare of pastis. He'd found the word for beer. He was enjoying this particular tail, not least because he'd found an area of Paris that felt like home.

Almost instantly, a middle-aged woman crossed the road and made a beeline for Wiggins. But before she reached him, he made full, stern eye contact with her and shook his head slightly – not in disgust or disapproval, but in a world-weary way that Wiggins did not need to fake. The woman veered off course and approached the Young Englishman instead.

First, to Wiggins's total astonishment, the woman asked the Young Englishman if he was interested in sleeping with her. He jilted his head back sharply, but quickly recovered his manners and offered the woman a drink. She sat down, accepted a cigarette and waited for her glass of wine. The whole exchange had taken place in English; the woman's heavily accented, halting. The Young Englishman spoke haltingly too, though for different reasons. Wiggins's astonishment did not arise from the fact the woman was a prostitute, for this was obvious, but in the way she announced herself so openly and straightforwardly.

It was clear that the approach was not unwelcome by the Young Englishman, although his attempts at further conversation were painfully naïve. After a while, a younger woman came into view. The older woman stood up and kissed her (as Wiggins noted the French did, on two cheeks – something he'd rarely see back home). Wiggins heard the word 'sister' mentioned, then the younger woman sat down and another drink was ordered, and another cigarette smoked. Presently, the older woman stood up and gestured for the other two to follow – first calling the waiter over and getting the Young Englishman to pay. The three of them trooped off. Wiggins followed them at a discreet distance. After a couple of minutes, all three entered an open doorway of a hotel, with the words Hôtel L'Alsace painted across the top.

Wiggins had to smile. Though he was surprised by quite how forward the women were, he knew the old trick they were about to play on the unsuspecting, lustful mark. He needed the Young Englishman to learn his lesson, so he took a turn up and back down the street. He stopped at a row of posters lining the wall at one end. Wondrous colour and light, and paintwork. They looked like something you'd find in a gallery, Wiggins mused to himself, just slapped up on the wall like an advert for Bovril. But these posters said things like RICARD, LA MARQUISETTE and MOULIN ROUGE: CONCERT BAL. This last had a picture of a woman with long, frilly knickers, on one leg as the other kicked out karate style.

He walked back to the hotel, and then stormed up the stairs in the manner of an outraged cuckold or similar (he guessed the hotel was used to such interruptions) and tried each door on the way up. The first, second and third were all locked but on the second floor, the door opened and in he went.

The older prostitute, totally naked, looked up at the door, startled. She had a roll of notes and a wallet in her hand, as she bent over the Young Englishman's suit, which hung over the end of a chair. The Young Englishman was too distracted to notice Wiggins's entrance, for he lay atop the 'sister', going at it like billy-o. His pale, freckled arse rose and fell, rose and fell, like the pistons of the great steam train which had carried Wiggins to Paris. All he could see of the 'sister' were her knees and thin white shins, splayed either side of the ginger express.

'I'll have that back, ta.' Wiggins pointed at the money and stepped towards the older woman.

The Young Englishman leaped backwards and up on to his feet. 'What! Who?'

Wiggins, with the money in one hand, slung the trousers at him with the other. 'Put 'em on, we're off.' The sister, lying back in the bed, looked supremely unconcerned. She pulled the sheet up to cover her lower half, and said something flatly to the older woman. The older woman, for her part, had given up the money to Wiggins without complaint. She too seemed unconcerned by this turn of events, and shuffled into her dress without embarrassment.

'What was the price?' Wiggins barked at the Young Englishman.

'Er . . . it wasn't,' he spluttered, hopping into a trouser leg. 'I got the wrong end of the stick, I thought, language lessons . . . you see? Colloquialisms, that sort of thing, it all rather got out of hand . . .'

'The price?' Wiggins said again.

'Ten francs,' the man replied, quietly.

Wiggins whistled. 'They saw you coming.' He peeled off a ten-franc note from the retrieved bundle and gave it to the older woman. Then he looked at the Young Englishman, and gave her two more francs. 'Let's go,' he said, and handed him back his wallet.

The older woman took the money without complaint. You win some, you lose some. The sister in the bed said something in French.

'*Douze*,' the older woman replied, and they both shrugged.

By this time the Young Englishman was fully dressed. He turned to both the women, and said in loud English, 'I do beg your pardon, madame et mademoiselle, for the misunderstanding. My French is not what it should be.' He bowed and walked past Wiggins to the stairwell.

Once they were out on the street, walking side by side back south towards the British Embassy, the Young Englishman turned to Wiggins. 'Who are you?'

'I'm a friend to Britain. And in this case, I'm a friend to you an' all. That old bird was about to clean you blind.'

'Er, yes, I can see that now. But it was true, what I said back there, I only wanted language lessons . . .'

'Save it for Bertie,' Wiggins muttered.

'You won't tell His Excellency, will you?' the Young Englishman gasped. 'If the ambassador were to hear of this, I should be sent home, in disgrace.'

'Which is why you're going to do exactly as I tell you,' Wiggins said.

Forty minutes later, an angry middle-aged official marched out of the British Embassy. The sun was high in the sky by this time, and heat bounced on the pavement. Despite this, he wore a full frock coat and a felt hat, beneath which his impressive side whiskers bristled like a pair of squirrels. He muttered to himself as he walked, as if being dragged down the road by an invisible hand.

On the platform, he looked about him often, still muttering, frowning, a picture of discontent. If it weren't for his bearing, and the undoubted quality of his clothes, the rich fabric, the glistening gold watch chain, it would be easy to mistake him for an itinerant. The train rattled into the station and, again reluctantly, the official got on and sat down on a set of four seats, facing towards the engine.

'That was quick,' Wiggins whispered into his ear from the seat behind.

'What the?' The man gasped in surprise, and rounded angrily. 'Who the hell are you?'

'You're Augustus Millfield Browne, chargé d'affaires,' Wiggins replied. 'Mind if I call you Gus?'

'Yes I do mind,' Browne snapped back. 'Netherfield sent me out here with some cock-and-bull story about the Empire in grave danger, and all the time it was to come and talk to god knows who.'

'I think you know who I am,' Wiggins said. And it was true enough, for Browne's face had relaxed somewhat and he hadn't got up from his seat as they pulled into the next station. They both watched an old man creep off the train in silence.

'Captain Kell did mention that I might be approached in an . . .' He looked at Wiggins as he paused. 'Unusual way. But where are your bona fides?'

Wiggins shifted his head to one side and raised a shoulder as if to say, 'Come on.' Browne nodded. Clearly Wiggins fitted Kell's description to a tee. 'Well, why all this cloak-and-dagger stuff, Agent W? Am I followed?'

'No, not today. But you've got to get used to it. You're the head of intelligence, there'll be someone on you soon enough.'

'Poppycock! This is France, we're allies and we are at peace.'

'Paris ain't just full of French, and we won't be at peace for long.'

'I really think I know more about affairs of state and European diplomacy than . . . than . . .' Browne looked again at Wiggins, struggling to find the words to describe him.

Wiggins put his hand up to stop him. 'I ain't here to argue. And I ain't here to find out what you know about European diplomacy neither; I just want you to tell me what you know about Maxim DuPont.'

'Who?'

'DuPont. Hanger-on with the French military, so I'm told. Ducker and diver in toff circles like. Big bloke, might speak with a German accent. Kind of bloke who kills people he don't like.'

'Never heard of him,' Browne said, aggrieved. He obviously didn't like to be asked questions he didn't know the answers to. He didn't like being asked much.

Wiggins thought to press him further for a moment, but then let it pass. He'd met men like Browne in the army, the officer aristocrat class, who instinctively tried to make a virtue of their own ignorance. Wedded to arrogance, it made such men powerful and deeply useless; unable to advance anything except, possibly, their own careers. For by and large, their superiors were of the same stamp. That such men existed and thrived in the machinery of the greatest Empire on earth was a constant mystery to Wiggins.

As he was about to terminate the interview, Wiggins had a sudden thought. 'Do you know anything about Mata Hari?'

'The dancer?' Browne asked in surprise. Then his eyes began to shine beneath his bushy brows. 'Exotic. Beautiful. Very beautiful.'

Wiggins sighed. 'Is she a player? A spy?'

'She knows *everybody* and she goes everywhere. I've not tried to recruit her myself, never got close. Totally unreliable of course – I mean, most women are, but Hari in particular I should imagine. Absolute fantasist, so I'm told. Will say anything to make herself more, you know . . .' Browne waved his hands around suggestively. 'I suspect Ladoux has tried.'

'Ladoux?'

'Head of French intelligence. Their Kell, sort of.'

'Square face, postmark moustache, military?'

'That's the chap. Has an eye for the ladies, most French-men do.'

Wiggins got up as the train rattled into the next station. 'What are you doing?' Browne asked.

'This is my stop.'

'But . . . but, what should I tell Kell? Is there a stratagem?' He dropped his voice. 'A ruse? What are your plans?'

'Oh yeah, here's my bona fides,' Wiggins said. 'He'll know it's me. Tell him I'm planning to get blind drunk.'

11

Up went the legs, down went the legs. Across went the legs. And back off the dance floor went the legs. The crowd cheered, the waiters whirled and the band struck up once more. The Moulin Rouge, Concert Bal – that's what the posters called it. And the Moulin Rouge was where Mata Hari said she'd be that night.

Wiggins signalled to the waiter for another. He sat alone at a small round table in the corner of the vast, pulsating music hall. Young couples swamped the dance floor as the professionals disappeared for a break. He brought the last of the red wine to his lips just as the waiter – a marvel of speed, elegance and awe-inspiring disdain – whipped his coins away and placed down a second bottle. He was not blind drunk. That was just a story he liked to tell Kell and his superiors, to keep them from feeling threatened.

He hadn't gone back to the hotel since leaving it that morning. He assumed the Élysée Palace was being watched – or rather, that Mata Hari was being watched. Large hotels were never safe places to stay. The staff knew everything that went on in a hotel, and a large hotel was full of people paid peanuts who happened to know where you were when you slept. You only had to buy off one of the staff, be it the bellhop or the maid, the concierge or the manager, and you could effectively have them all. Hotel staff gossip was wilder than a forest fire in August. Wiggins knew – he'd done enough surveillance jobs as a kid for Sherlock Holmes, from tailing a cattle baron in Claridge's to watching an heiress at the Savoy. A shilling for a chambermaid would get you all the gen in half an hour.

Consequently, he'd left the hotel by the servants' stairs and strolled out of the back entrance into the Parisian streets. It would have been pointless to try to work out who might have been watching Margaretha anyway. It could have been any one of the staff, or even Claudette the maid. It meant that anyone who knew where Margaretha was knew where he'd been for the last few nights and that needed to stop. And it was easy to follow Margaretha. As Mata Hari she was probably the most visible woman alive. She was a walking advertisement for herself. She commanded everybody's attention wherever she went. He'd seen that at the station in Brussels, and he could see it again here, in the great heaving concert hall of the Moulin Rouge.

She sat in one of the boxes that lined the first floor of the hall. Wiggins sat on the other side of the hall, with the stage off to his left. Above the stage, the band played on an elevated platform. Lined up beneath the boxes opposite, top-hatted drinkers ordered at a long bar, while the electric lights cast a golden glow. He could see Mata Hari easily, for she sat right on the tip of the box, looking both down at the swirling sea of dancers and back into the box at her companions. They were all men, Wiggins noted, at least one of whom was in military uniform. He couldn't make out their faces well enough to see if he recognised any of them, Ladoux for example. He'd yet to see the Man in the Blue Jacket who'd been on the train from Brussels, either, but that didn't mean he wasn't there.

A big man sat down at the table opposite him, spiriting a chair from nowhere. He nodded at Wiggins and placed an enormous, calloused hand on the table. Wiggins waited. The Big Man did not look at him to start with, but gazed out onto the dance floor. When he finally turned his head, Wiggins saw that his left eye drooped slightly and was probably sightless. Ex-boxer, country boy once, came from nothing but doing alright now, running the door no doubt, Wiggins deduced.

The waiter approached with Wiggins's refill, but the Big Man raised a single warning finger and the waiter disappeared. Suddenly, a second man sat down, this time next to Wiggins. Then a third, on his other side. Each of the three men now at his table did not have drinks in front of them. These were men at work.

'*Qui es-tu?*' the Big Man said.

Wiggins shook his head. 'English,' he said.

The Big Man sighed theatrically. He opened his mouth to speak, but just then a commotion broke out at the foot of the main stairs. He got up and pointed. He and his two companions began running towards the noise.

Wiggins turned to see a phalanx of twenty or thirty younger men storming into the crowd. They shouted slogans and began grabbing at the women, pulling their skirts; or dashing drinks from hands of the men. Someone threw a chair at the bar, cracking the mirror behind.

The Big Man and his two helpers – the concert hall's muscle no doubt – tried to deal with the rioters. But it was pandemonium now, with drinkers rushing here and there, women screaming, and scuffles breaking out between the young rowdies and the pluckier of the dancers. The only people in the place who seemed to keep calm were those in the band who, rather than continuing to play the dancing music, instead struck up a tune that reminded Wiggins of the music the clowns came out to at the circus.

Wiggins saw that the Big Man was in trouble, with four rioters now raining blows upon him, and made a decision. He pushed his way through the throng and landed a straight right on one of the rowdies, then a left cross on the next one. The young men were no match for Wiggins, and now that the Big Man was free, the two of them began to get the upper hand.

When the kitchen crew suddenly burst into the hall like relieving cavalry, bristling with knives and frying pans and rolling pins, the rioters knew their time was up. They scrambled to the exits, leaving hats and coats and drops of blood on the floor as they fled.

Within moments, the hall emptied of the rioting young men. A big-bellied, moustachioed manager type strode into the middle of the floor and spread his hands out wide, gesturing for the band to strike up once more and calling to the cowed customers. He clapped his hands theatrically, and a troupe of the professional dancers streamed back into the middle of the floor and began their extraordinary act once more.

'Come,' the Big Man slapped Wiggins on the back and beckoned him to follow.

They walked through one of the side doors of the main dance hall and along a corridor. From there, the Big Man signalled to a shelf that ran along the wall below a curtain. He pulled out a bottle from underneath and two glasses. 'This is a real drink,' he said. 'Not like your warm flat English beer.'

Wiggins grinned and downed the thick green liquid the man offered. 'Christ,' he roared, as the spirit scorched the back of his throat. 'Ain't that the shits.'

The Big Man laughed. 'I am Gilles.'

'Wiggins,' he rasped.

'You are a warrior. An artist with the fists?'

Wiggins shrugged. Now the adrenaline was wearing off, he felt a tiredness creep over him, a feeling of despair and disgust. Was he really the kind of man who enjoyed fighting? He wasn't sure he wanted to be, but he wasn't sure he wasn't either. 'Who were they?' he asked.

Gilles spat and regarded Wiggins with his good eye. 'Camelots du Roi. Creatures of *Action Française*. Ah, but you know nothing of France. They are people who hate. They hate us because we let in Jews, black people. They hate us because we are not good Catholics. They hate us because, because, the people love us!' He gave a bitter chuckle.

'You speak good English,' Wiggins said. 'Better than mine anyroad.'

'I boxed in London, Soho, Old Kent Road, you know, for money. You fight like this too, no? You are a prize fighter I think.'

'Never for money.'

'But for drink, yes?' They smiled, and Gilles pushed another glass of the green liquid across the shelf towards him. They knocked back another glass, and scowled as the muddy-tasting spirit scorched their throats. An elderly cleaning woman bustled past them, carrying a mop and bucket, while at the far end, Wiggins noticed an open doorway beyond which he could see the mirrors and draped clothes of a large dressing room. After a moment, when the fire of the drink – absinthe Gilles called it – had subsided, he turned to his new French friend and asked, 'Why were you on my case – earlier, why were you going to toss me?'

Gilles shrugged again, looked him up and down, and then drew back the curtain that hung above the shelf. Behind it, a large grill – and behind that, the fabulous ballroom itself, the bal du Moulin Rouge. West End clobber and then some: the men in tails, gleaming white shirts, deep black silks; the women in bright finery of every kind; the golden fizzle of the lights; the zinc bar, the smiling, whirling twirl of beautiful people, in beautiful things, dancing beautiful dances to beautiful music, in the most magnificent ballroom of the most beautiful age. Wiggins drank it in.

'Look at them, Wiggins, look out there – you do not belong on that side of the grill, no? You are from this side, with us.' He gestured around him, at the cleaner, and the dressing room. Wiggins looked down again at the floor, lit by one dim bulb. Sawdust scattered here and there. He peered further, into the dressing room, as the cleaner wrung out a bloody mop. 'The feet, of the dancers,' Gilles said before he asked. 'The cancan is not easy, huh. Like boxing.'

A busboy slithered past them. The music built to a crescendo, and out on the dance floor the dancers flung their heads to their knees. The crowd roared and clapped and cheered, as the cancan dancers streamed off the floor all smiles and grace. Wiggins waited and watched as they came through the doors into the dressing room, where they staggered and bent and slumped onto the stools, the smiles wiped from their faces like make-up. 'Not easy is right,' he muttered to Gilles. 'It ain't ever easy.'

Gilles grunted. 'I go back to work now, *Anglais*. Do you want a job? You're one of the best I've ever seen, with the fist, *le puncheur extraordinaire*. We will teach you French, you will keep us straight.'

'I ain't the man for straight.'

'*Comme ci comme ça*. If you change your mind, the Moulin Rouge is always here. I owe you one, *mon frère*. You fight together, and together you fight.' He held out his hand as he said this, and put his left hand up to Wiggins's shoulder. They shook.

'There is one thing,' Wiggins said as he released the handshake. He bent forward to the viewing grill and gestured out towards the line of boxes on the opposite side of the dance hall. 'I need to speak to a woman in the box over there, without her guests knowing.'

'Who?'

Wiggins pointed again. 'Second left from the pillar,' he said.

'Mata Hari! Oh, *mon ami*. This cannot work.'

Wiggins shook his head slightly, smiling. 'It ain't what you think.'

'It is always what you think. It is Mata Hari!'

'I just need a word. And I need to know who else is in there with her. Can you do that for me? It ain't bent, honest.'

Gilles studied him for a moment. 'I believe you. At least, I believe you are honest. Except about why you want to see Mata Hari,' he said with a laugh.

'He's me dad, ain't he?'

'Gawn, get out of it.'

'But you know him?' Jax pressed. She stood at the public bar of the Blind Beggar in the 'chapel, acutely aware that she was the only woman in the room, other than a stooping old girl who shuffled in and out behind the bar. The drunk beside her, an old lag with yellowing eyes and two missing teeth, looked askance. It wasn't the kind of place to ask questions. Bulldog Wallace had taken a man's eye out with an umbrella ten years earlier, and the pub still lived on the legend.

'I don't know no Archie,' the drunk leered. 'And he's not your dad.' He burst out laughing, then quick as a flash reached out and squeezed her arse. 'Gis a kiss,' he growled as he leaned in, hand still on her.

She drove her straightened knuckles into his throat, just like Wiggins had taught her, then swept the stool from under him.

The drunk fell back, coughing and gurgling, and Jax strode out of the pub. Fast but not rushing. She kicked out into the street and carried on down Whitechapel as quick as she could without running. She did not want him to see her running.

Her face was hot with shame. Tears pricked her eyes, which made her angrier still. Why should she cry? Why was she upset? Why was she ashamed? The other men in the pub had laughed when she walked out, leaving the drunk gasping for air. But her cheeks burned hot still.

It wasn't until she reached New Oxford Street, and saw the other ELFS getting ready for the latest march, that the sense of shame and disgust left her. They were women too, they all knew this shame, and they were all fighting for a better life, not just a vote. And later still, as she thought again about this encounter at the Blind Beggar, as she marched shoulder to shoulder down Drury Lane with these active and defiant women, she remembered there was one person at the pub who would be able to help her in her search. She should have known it all along.

Kell waited for his wife, Constance, outside the foyer at Drury Lane Theatre, clutching his hard-won tickets for the Diaghilev jamboree, jostled and harried by excited fans. If truth be told, Kell was not an enthusiast of the ballet. But he'd felt the need to apologise to Constance in deed, if not with words, for the simply ghastly Wimbledon conversation. He'd barely seen her since, given the political situation, but he had the brainwave to secure the sought-after tickets as an olive branch.

And now, she was late. A commotion started outside, and the crowd around the doors began to surge. He could hear shouting, chanting and an outcry. Without thinking, he pushed out into the warm bright evening to see what all the fuss was about. A wedge of very loud women marched down the street, about twenty or so, holding suffragette banners and chanting their slogans. The onlookers, both men and women, shouted back at them in derision and a scuffle broke out to his left.

'Oh god,' Kell muttered to himself. 'Please say it's not her.'

'Good evening, Vernon,' Constance said from behind him. 'What's all this then, are you joining the cause?'

'Thank heavens,' he said. 'You're here. We should go in, dear, or we'll be late.'

'Who are they?' Constance stepped forward, intrigued. 'I don't recognise the banners. Does it say ELF?'

The shrill peel of police whistles broke in upon the hub-bub, and Kell could see policemen massing at the end of the street. A loud and haughty voice cried, 'They're trying to ruin the ballet now, dash it all. Nothing more feminine than that – carry them off, constables!'

Kell touched Constance's arm. 'Shall we . . .?'

'Look,' Constance pointed. 'Isn't that Wiggins's young friend, Jane or Jill – no, Jax!'

'I don't recall,' Kell lied. He wanted his wife as far away from those onrushing policemen as possible, and he did not want her fraternising with the disreputable friends of Wiggins. It could only mean trouble.

'Yes, yes – surely. She looks just like him too. So young, so brave. Here, constable – get your hands off her!' She began pushing into the crowd towards the melee.

'No dear, please,' Kell called after her.

'Enjoy the ballet without me,' she said. 'I'll see you at home.'

'Please,' he hissed. 'Do not get arrested.'

Later, after Kell had gone back to the office – he did not go to the ballet – he went to bed alone. Later still, while he drifted in and out of a troubled, spectre-filled sleep, he felt Constance come in. He listened as she got undressed and got into the bed. He did not acknowledge her, and kept his head still and turned to the wall. She said nothing, and did not make any particularly loud noise or try to speak. But he could feel her excitement, the energy pulsing off her. She positively thrummed.

'I said meet somewhere discreet.'

'This is the most private place I could think of,' Margaretha said, her amusement plain in her voice, a bubble of laughter never far away.

They sat atop a huge model elephant that stood guard in the back garden of the Moulin Rouge. Wiggins had ascended to the glass-covered howdah on Gilles' instruction and waited for Margaretha to appear.

'You don't like it?' she went on, as she sat on a small Benchwood chair on the platform.

'It ain't that,' Wiggins said. 'It's just . . .' He gave up. In fact, now that they were up there, he could see that the revellers down below in the garden party were not actually craning their necks up. With no light on, the meeting spot did have some discretion about it.

'Have you visited the pipe men, down below?' Margaretha bumped her heel lightly on the wooden elephant beneath them. Wiggins couldn't make her face out clearly in the gloom, but he could hear the smile in her voice.

'Nah,' he replied. 'That stuff interferes with the booze.'

Margaretha laughed out loud at that, which made Wiggins wonder for a moment if she herself had visited the pipe men. For the elephant doubled as an opium den and, indeed, two appropriately attired assistants were doling out pipes to discerning customers for a couple of francs a time. 'Ah, you have too much you want to remember to risk forgetting. For sure, this is not me.'

'You smoke it?' Wiggins asked. He wanted to talk to her for a very specific reason, but he found himself again drawn into the conversation. It was like trying to catch and pin down a butterfly, and who wants to pin a butterfly?

'Sometimes, maybe, sometimes it is the only way to forget. Perhaps I have things I want to forget?'

'Like why you're being followed?'

'Are you sure I'm being followed, *mon cher*? The men you spoke of on the train? Were they really there – I wonder.'

'I'm telling you, I'd hardly kick myself in the balls, would I?'

'Hmm, this is not that strange, for a man to lie. Ask your friend Martha.' She laughed and then she spoke again, this time with a less amused edge to her voice. 'Are you sure these men aren't following *you?*'

Wiggins waved away the question. 'Straight up I'm worried about you, the people you're with.' Gilles had given him the names of the men in her box, two German-sounding, one French, one could be anything. At least one of them was army, Gilles said, but they had no more information than that. But he didn't want to let Margaretha know he'd been digging into it. 'It could be dangerous.'

'They are not dangerous to me,' she said. 'I am Mata Hari.'

'Stay away from Ladoux, I'm telling you,' he blurted out. 'Stay away from them all. It's about to get dicey round here. There's going to be a war. I can save you.'

'Save me?' she said wonderingly. 'But you have no money. And your looks will fade.'

Wiggins looked away. The music from the hall drifted over the night, as if for the first time. Sweetish, sickly opium smoke rose up through the floorboards. A burst of laughter came from the outside tables below.

'Will you come back to the hotel tonight?' she asked.

'It's not safe.'

'For a strong man like you? What are you scared of?'

'I don't know,' he said, at last truthful, and almost forgetful of why he was there. A firework suddenly fizzed into the air, and cast bright light across the sky. The drinkers in the garden cooed.

'You are sweet,' she said. 'But I think Martha was right, for sure.'

'About what?'

'About you.' She stood up, as if that closed the conversation. 'I must get back to my box. My public demand it, those men demand it, Wiggins, no matter what my heart wants, they say dance, dance, and they pay for the musicians, no? And so, I must dance.'

Wiggins looked up at her as she struck a pose, silhouetted against the Parisian night sky and the fading embers of the firework. He did not think of himself as a romantic man. Romance was the stuff of cheap novels, or soupy music hall ballads, something for those who didn't have to fight to stay alive. But whether it was the sweet tang of the opium smoke, the spice of Margaretha's perfume or the aftershocks of the absinthe, he had quite forgotten why he was up there with this woman, perched on a giant model elephant in the middle of a foreign country, and staring at a never dreamed-of future.

'Maxim DuPont,' she said suddenly. 'I am going to a festival, how you say, an event, a party tomorrow, I guess he might be there, for sure.'

'Who?'

'DuPont, the man you desperately want to find, no? The reason you are in Paris. Are you sure you didn't take a pipe downstairs, huh?'

'Nah, I hear you,' Wiggins couldn't help but grin. 'What of him?'

'You can drive me, if you like, to this party – you can pretend to be, how the English say, my "man", my butler.'

Wiggins laughed. 'I've played servant before.'

She tilted her chin. 'I saw you, fighting in the hall. You are very good, no? Like a champion boxer. Fast.'

'I get by.'

'You are like a dancer,' she said. 'And we dancers are like boxers. Oh, do not make the mistake of these glamourous clothes, the rich men who watch. Do not let me fool you about that. We bleed too, and when we are too old to dance, no one will pay to watch us, and we will have nothing again.'

Wiggins thought of the cancan dancers back in the hall, the blood on the floor, the rich men clapping and cheering and gurning as they danced.

'Tomorrow, then, for sure,' Margaretha said in a jauntier tone as she set herself to go back down the ladder, into the belly of the beast. 'You will take me to Issy-les-Moulineaux.'

'Issy what?' he said, but she'd already disappeared, like an image from an opium pipe dream.

12

The great sensation in London that night, splashed across both the quality papers and the more sensational penny sheets, was the Ballets Russes, selling out Drury Lane. The great, distant, Diaghilev, the inscrutable Russian mastermind of a choreographer, was fêted to the rafters as his dancers bent, and spun, and leaped to rapturous acclaim. A 'Russian invasion' was declared, though the papers meant a cultural one; they did not seem to know, or care, about Russia's promise to Serbia. If Serbia is invaded, Russia's huge standing army would come to its defence.

One man who knows this is British Foreign Secretary Sir Edward Grey. While he still hasn't taken a meeting with Captain Vernon Kell, on this day, Thursday 9 July 1914, Grey does tell the German ambassador, 'I can only repeat to you that there are no secret arrangements between Britain and France and Russia which would entail obligations on us in case of a European war.' Grey's intention was to illustrate Britain's plain dealing and not to scare Germany into anything rash. But the wisdom of letting Germany know that you do not intend to fight is still to be determined.

Issy-les-Moulineaux wasn't quite as obvious as the Eiffel Tower, which seemed to loom over every step he took in the city, but it ran a close second. For, as Margaretha explained as they drove from her hotel, they were headed to an airfield. And as he pushed and manhandled the heavy Citroën through the Paris streets, he could see the tiny aeroplanes hang and dip and wobble high up in the sky. They were going to an air show.

Other than this information, Margaretha chose not to talk to him. The intimacy of the night before had seeped and disappeared, as sly and evasive as smoke. She looked immaculate, in a dazzlingly white dress with pink trim and a feathered hat. He would have said she looked respectable, except that whatever she wore, she had a way of carrying herself that would make a bishop bark. Nevertheless, on the morning of 9 July 1914, she had no problem pretending Wiggins was nothing more than a servant – she'd even had Claudette kit him out in a chauffer's uniform, right down to the peaked cap, gleaming brass buttons and long boots.

By the time they arrived, the show was in full swing. Stewards waved the car towards a line of similar vehicles parked in one corner of the field, while behind them stood the odd horse and carriage. A gaggle of onlookers congregated by a marquee, while off to one side of the large field, an eccentric array of aeroplanes waited.

Wiggins parked the automobile, got out and went to open Margaretha's door. She raised her gloved hand before he could do so. 'Wait,' she said. 'You must be by my side, until I tell you otherwise.' She said this in a loud and commanding voice, Wiggins realised, in order to be overheard. 'And you must bring my binoculars.'

He nodded. She leaned forward and whispered, 'I am sorry, but this is best I think, no?'

'M'lady,' he muttered, bowing his head as he opened the car door.

She stepped down, and gestured to the huge binoculars. 'Come,' she commanded, and began walking towards the marquee. Wiggins fell into step a pace behind her, head slightly bowed.

The event reminded him of the horse racing, or at least the posh parts of going to the races. He'd been to the Derby down in Epsom a couple of times – once on a job as a child, when Sherlock Holmes had asked them to tail a bent bookie, and once with poor old Bill Tyler for a jolly. Both men dead now.

Up ahead, the quality were out in force. The women wore fine dresses and ridiculous hats, and twirled brightly coloured parasols; many of the men were dressed as for riding. Some tweed, a uniform or two, and lots of loud laughter, and boring monologues about heavier-than-air machines, though Wiggins guessed not one man in twenty knew anything about it. An aeroplane bumped and whirred across the field and then took off in wobbly flight, twenty, thirty, a hundred feet into the air in no time, as impressive and vulnerable as a new-fledged bird. He caught, too, the excitement of the crowd, that extra frisson when danger was in the air, when the threat (or prospect) of watching a death enlivened the show. You could feel it when you went to the jumps with horses, rather than the flat – of the atmosphere when the heavyweights boxed, one moment away from the killing blow.

As he and Margaretha walked towards the watching crowds, she whispered under her breath, 'We have two minutes, yes? The man in the top hat, with the big stomach and the whiskers – that is Jean-Claude I-Don't-Care-Who-The-Hell. This is his show. He will take me on his arm soon, and his bottom lip will drop, for sure, and his tongue

will come out over me, and I will no longer be private. You
understand?'

'I understand.'

'So, quickly now, tell me the truth. Why do you want to
meet Maxim DuPont?'

'I think his real name is Von Bork, I think he is one of the
most senior agents in the German secret service but why I
want to find him is because he killed . . .' He hesitated, unable to get the words out. 'He murdered the man who saved
my childhood, saved my life really.'

Margaretha looked back over her shoulder at him,
pity in her face. Wiggins didn't normally like pity – who
did? – but just then, from her, it helped. 'I understand,
for sure,' she said. 'I will help you find him. Stay close.'
She said this last line as fat Jean-Claude I-Don't-Care-
Who-The-Hell hailed her across the field. As he walked
towards them, Margaretha stopped being Margaretha
and became Mata Hari once more.

'Mademoiselle Hari,' he cried, and then launched into a
stream of fawning, slobbering, lascivious French. Wiggins
didn't understand the words, but he understood everything
else. Margaretha was used to it. She played up to it for a
moment, then indicated the line of aircraft waiting their
turns to take off. After a moment, they set off towards them
–Wiggins with the binoculars in tow. She'd obviously asked
for a closer look at the machines, a royal inspection Wiggins
thought to himself, though he'd bet there'd never been a
queen quite like Mata Hari.

The smell hit them first – hot oil, and engines, and
the wax of the wings, mixed with the petrol and the rank
sweat of the mechanics – a pungent reek impervious to
the stiffening breeze. Margaretha, as usual, played the

celebrated dancer and the beaming pilots stepped forward, excited to have a brief audience with the star. They were mostly mad toffs risking life and limb, Wiggins noted by the cut of their clothes and the familiarity with which they treated Margaretha. Toffs happy to die reaching for the sky. Wiggins was not impressed. The waiting crowd might whoop and wail and gasp at such daredevil heroism, but Wiggins could only think of the servants. The mechanics, the batmen, signed up as drivers perhaps, but now expected to sit in a deathtrap as their masters sought immortality for the glory of France (or the Empire, or Belgium or Germany or any other crackpot death wish).

Still, for all that he disdained the pilots, the machines themselves stirred something in him – the idea of being up there. He'd glimpsed it, up on the Scotsman and the cranes of the city, but to go higher, further, into the great blue would be something else again.

'Binoculars.' Margaretha held out her hand. He hesitated. She called again, but this time turned and whispered to him, 'I think it's the next man. Listen.'

Jean-Claude babbled on as they approached the next machine. A tall, handsome pilot stepped forward to greet them, recognition written across his face. Margaretha brought her hands together in quick claps. 'Herr Von Bork,' she trilled.

He flinched, minutely, then smiled broadly again. '*Non, non*, Madame HARI – *C'est* Maxim. Maxim DuPont.' He carried on in French, and Margaretha laughed and clearly apologised, and they were all smiles and jollity.

Wiggins drifted back from the group, eyes trained still on DuPont. The man's thick brows had dropped for a second, he'd blinked when Margaretha had made the 'mistake', he recognised the name. Margaretha! Wiggins thought again, as she sashayed off back to the crowd with the fawning Jean-Claude. Balls of Sheffield steel, she did it brilliantly, confirming once and for all that DuPont was the right man with only a word. A risky word, for in one swoop she placed herself in the firing line. For him.

He slunk back among the aircraft, hiding under his cap, while keeping watch on DuPont and his well-built bearded mechanic. The airplane in front of them fired up, and began chugging out onto the field. DuPont's craft was obviously the next in line. A young water boy came up to the two men and offered a drink. He obviously startled DuPont, however, for the pilot turned to him sharply and said something. The boy replied, and DuPont knocked him to the ground with the back of his hand. He then turned back to the mechanic and continued his conversation.

Bristling with anger, Wiggins stepped forward. 'Easy, lad,' a northern English voice said. 'It's not our place.'

A red-faced mechanic with a mop of blond hair sat on a box pulling at his laces. Behind him, another aircraft. A toffee-nosed gentleman amateur type, examining the machine, walked around the wings, inspecting connections, tugging at wires like a yachtsman double-checking his knots.

'They always like that?' Wiggins asked angrily, gesturing at DuPont.

The mechanic shrugged.

'How long they up for?' Wiggins asked, calculating the time he'd have to wait to make his move, his blood beginning to boil. He didn't know for sure, but something in the manner of DuPont – the arrogance, the certainty – made him feel instinctively that this was the man he was looking for, that this was Von Bork. The killer of Sherlock Holmes.

'Not long enough, lad,' he rasped.

'Twenty minutes?' Wiggins said while he watched DuPont, twenty or so yards away, who was now being helped into his plane by the strapping mechanic. 'Do they land over the other side of the field?'

'Crash more like,' the northerner replied sourly. 'Though not those Frenchies there,' he gestured at DuPont's plane. 'If they are French. Can't bloody tell – could be from any-where. It's worse than London, this place. All sorts.'

'How long will I have to wait for them?'

He chewed for a moment. 'They's got a Deperdussin. Fastest junk in the air, that one, goes over a hundred so they's reckon. Won the Gordon Bennett last year. But I wouldn't fly in her.'

'Why's that?'

'Clough! Clough!' the English pilot cooed from the other side of the plane. 'Is that Billy on the go?'

Wiggins glanced again at DuPont. The mechanic had started the propeller and the plane was now taxying into position out on the field, back past them to the left. It wheeled round, ready to rush past and take off as close to the specta-tors as possible.

Clough threw down a rag. 'Coming, sir,' he shouted, then glanced at Wiggins. 'None of the planes land back here, lad,' he said. 'If they take off at all, they're heading to Vincennes. East of Paris.'

'But,' Wiggins said, then hesitated. DuPont's plane picked up speed out to his left, soon to pass by where they stood. The man he'd crossed the channel for, the killer, the moment – Margaretha had risked everything to point him out, could he let her down? As these thoughts flashed through his mind he found himself running, running after the plane.

'Here lad, careful!' Clough shouted after him. 'That's an airfield.'

Wiggins sped across the field as the aircraft approached from the left. He didn't know if he'd ever see DuPont, Von Bork, again, but he knew the chance was now.

The plane bobbed and rattled past as he arced his run. It was one of the simpler craft, with a short chassis, one large wing and a smaller wing at the tail. DuPont sat in a cockpit at the wing. Behind, an empty second cockpit. The plane accelerated further, the engine roared and Wiggins strained every muscle, willing himself forward. With a last desperate dive he caught hold of the second cockpit. His feet bounced and skimmed the ground.

DuPont looked around, startled eyes framed by goggles, as the plane sped on.

Wiggins's hand started to shake. Wind rushed in his ears. DuPont shouted, pointed up ahead, wrestled with the controls – and then, in a moment so strange and odd and unworldly, the plane lifted into the air. Wiggins felt the jolt, and then his legs bicycled into nothingness.

The plane jiggled, the wing dipped and rose, wobbling out over the field. It tipped to the side. Wiggins clung on, and his body drifted out into thin air. DuPont corrected the level and Wiggins crashed into the chassis.

With one great heave, like a rider mounting a moving horse, he swung himself into the cockpit.

The airfield was behind and beneath now as the plane accelerated over Paris. Wiggins glanced down, at the snaking river Seine below. DuPont gripped the controls hard, swivelling his head. Wiggins set himself – this was his moment, his heart was thumping, his hair flailing wildly.

DuPont shouted again, and craned around. His eyes were obscured by goggles, but Wiggins could see his anger, and heard him shout out in German again and again, '*Mein Gott. Was machst du?*'

Wiggins dashed the hair from his face and gripped DuPont around the neck. This was his chance, this was the moment, this was the man who plunged a knife deep into Holmes, who threw him off that bridge.

The plane lurched earthwards. Spiralling. DuPont cried out in all sorts of languages. 'You fool, *vous êtes*—' The plane dipped nose first towards the roofs of Paris.

Wiggins released him. The plane screeched along the building tops then accelerated back up into the sky as DuPont struggled for control.

The red mist cleared. Killing DuPont (or Von Bork if it was indeed him) was why he was there at all – and he could do it, there and then. The man's neck was right in front of him. He could throttle the life out of him and be done with it – but then he'd be done with himself too. For they were high up now, with Paris splayed out beneath them, white and grey, split by the river, and he had no idea how to fly a plane or – more importantly – land one. If he really did incapacitate DuPont, he would almost certainly die himself. Fuck. He sat back in the cockpit, stilled by this conundrum.

DuPont clearly had gone through a similar thought process. For once he'd brought the plane under control, he glanced back at Wiggins as if to say, '*What now?*'

Wiggins glanced out of the side of the plane. The engine whirred and clanked, the wind rushed in his ears, but a sense of peace came over him. It really was magnificent up here. Even the shifting, bobbing, creaking machine beneath his feet moved and jolted weightlessly, held aloft as if by magic. The effect was hypnotic, beguiling, and he wondered open-eyed at the otherness of it. He felt like he was in a state of grace, suspended between heaven and earth, unburdened by the worries of the world.

Maxim DuPont had no such airy thoughts. While Wiggins was marvelling at his first ever flight, DuPont checked and double-checked his gear, looked back again at Wiggins – a man who, he now knew, was intent on his destruction – and did the only thing he could do when faced with a man sitting behind him who would kill him the moment the plane touched the ground.

He flipped the aircraft upside down.

Wiggins's stomach lurched into his ribs. His head disappeared out of the plane. He thrust out a hand into the webbing of the cockpit just as his torso slipped out.

The aircraft was totally inverted. Wiggins had wrapped his wrist into the webbing and hung from one arm, his legs twisting and dangling in the roar. His shoulder sang with pain.

DuPont, of course, remained fixed in his seat by the shoulder and leg straps. After a moment the engine began to stutter and whine, and DuPont righted the plane with a lurch. Wiggins's shoulder almost popped from its socket but he held on.

He managed to swing his other arm around into the webbing and hauled himself back into the aircraft. Just then, DuPont tipped the plane up near vertical but Wiggins had wedged his knees into position. He smashed DuPont around the back of the head with his good arm.

The plane lurched down, arced and curled again. It swung left, right and left again, and then to the right. Wiggins punched the pilot again, and screamed out in rage. The nose of the plane dipped and he was flung forward out of the cockpit.

He caught hold of the wing brace just as the plane shifted and rose. DuPont looked down at him, shifted the plane right, left then up and a quick down, trying to shake Wiggins out of the plane for good.

Wiggins knew his wrenched shoulder would give out at any moment. He glanced between his dangling legs at the city below, the beautiful city of light. And death.

Back at DuPont, who grinned down at him, readying the machine for another lurch. Wiggins glanced ahead. A mass of grey reared up in front of the plane, out of nowhere, impossible, in the sky.

He glanced up at DuPont, still grinning down at him, oblivious to the grey mass almost upon them.

DuPont looked up, in horror.

Wiggins let go.

The plane arced left, too late. Its wing caught the side of the grey iron structure just as Wiggins plummeted earthwards. For what he'd realised, a second before the pilot DuPont, was that they were flying directly into the Eiffel Tower.

Wiggins saw the iron, then the white. In a second he ripped through a canvas awning and skidded onto a long table. His landing, broken by canvas, was unexpectedly soft on the table. He'd landed on the viewing platform of the tower.

Chaos all about him. His heart leaped and thudded in his chest. He gasped for air. Around him, women screamed. Men shouted. Men screamed. A grey old woman shouted. He sat on a long thin table, lined with astonished diners. Shouting and screaming and all sorts. An older man with ornate facial hair pointed at him in outrage. Other guests, all equally finely turned out – tailcoats, silk hats, flowing gowns, began to point too and exclaim in French.

Wiggins reached down and felt his trousers, covered with a white, creamy substance. He glanced back. The remnants of a huge but now utterly ruined cake lay splattered across the table. The older man with the fancy beard, Wiggins realised, also wore a large gold chain around his neck. He gesticulated wildly at Wiggins, at the cake, at the ruined canvas ripped and loose around them. Wiggins shrugged. 'Sorry,' he said. 'Anglais.'

By this time, half the guests had stood up around the table, and some of them were looking out over the barrier and down at Paris. Wiggins shifted and saw what they were looking at.

DuPont's aeroplane jagged wildly, jerking like a fatally injured fly. One wing destroyed, ragged and about to drop. Wiggins shifted off the table and joined the others at the rail of the observation deck.

The plane had gone into a death spiral over the pale city and, with a hideous and sudden speeding up – as if up high in the sky it moved in a slowed kind of motion, the speed only evident when it neared objects on the ground – it hurtled, uncontrolled, into one of the bridges on the river, dissolving into a brief fireball and then nothing. Within seconds, the plane subsided into the river, a burst of furious energy and light snuffed out into silence. Any evidence that DuPont or the plane existed had disappeared, leaving only the whistling wind on the top of that magnificent structure.

Wiggins had just witnessed the death of Maxim DuPont, but did that mean the death of Von Bork and the end of his mission? Had he slain the monster in his mind?

The whistles of the gendarmes broke in over and above the howling wind and he turned to see the old man with the gold chain pointing and urging the policemen towards him.

'*C'est lui,*' the old man cried out in fury. More police appeared. A mass of blue uniforms. Gendarmes, running, whistles. The guests started shouting once more, all pointing at Wiggins – as if he, indeed, had driven the airplane into the Seine, as if he was a murderer, and destroyer of their celebration. In fact, they accused him of something far worse.

'*Voilà,*' the old man cried out, triumphant. '*L'Anglais.*'

13

'We've found Sherlock Holmes's murderer,' the voice said. 'This is a matter most important, pressing and I must say urgent. I must speak to Wiggins at once.'

Kell heard these words as he tapped down the stairs at Watergate House. He reached the hallway and called out, 'Let him in, Maddox,' and then addressed the silver-haired, four-square gentleman in front of him. 'Doctor Watson, I presume?'

He brought the old buffer into his office, gave him a whisky and listened as best as he could. 'I have found Sherlock Holmes's murderer,' Watson announced. 'I know the very man. Yet Wiggins does not return my letters or my cables. We must act.'

'Who is it?' Kell asked distractedly. He was not in the mood for dealing with the elderly, but simple manners forbade him from turning out Watson there and then. The doctor must have his say.

'It's to do with the case of the Red-Headed League. Here, it's all in my notes.' Watson produced a battered leather notebook, together with a dog-eared copy of the *Strand Magazine*. 'I've been through all the cases, and I am convinced that the man responsible is an old associate of Jonathan Clay.'

'Is that so?' Kell said.

'Indeed it is,' Watson went on. He launched into an impassioned retelling of some long-forgotten Holmesian triumph. Kell couldn't concentrate. He admired the old man – who couldn't? – but he could see the desperation on his face, the deep irretrievable loss etched into him, the casting about for direction and meaning. Holmes had been a victim of high-level espionage, international intrigue – a new world – and his death had nothing to do with such tales of revenge from the Victorian age.

This, however, was not the reason Kell couldn't concentrate. He couldn't concentrate because Constance had disappeared.

Or rather, she left the house the day before (the morning after their aborted visit to the ballet) and hadn't come home since, nor had she left any kind of word either at the house or at his office. This was unlike her. The children were due back any day from their various boarding schools – the nanny would handle them, of course, but they would at least ask after their mother at mealtimes.

He told the servants to telephone him at the office as soon as she returned home, but they had not rung. He rang home himself just before Watson arrived and still nothing, as of two o'clock in the afternoon. On the one hand, Constance was a powerful woman, with means, perfectly capable of looking after herself. On the other hand, Kell couldn't shake from his mind what Wiggins had said less than two weeks earlier: *you're probably being followed*. And if he, Kell, were being followed would that make Constance herself a target? He'd lost Holmes already – would Von Bork stoop so low as to attack his family?

'You see,' Watson said, banging the desk with his hand. 'All we need is a troop of policemen, and we can apprehend the men responsible for this heinous, despicable deed.'

'Policemen, you say? Do you have an address?' Kell stood up, eager for the interview to be at an end. 'Simpkins,' he called to his secretary in the outer room. 'Please call up Mrs Jepson immediately.'

'Well, no, not as yet. No address, no idea about their whereabouts. This is why I wanted Wiggins. We've . . . I've been . . .' The old doctor became hesitant for a moment, but then pushed on. 'The trail has run dry, or rather, I don't know where she is. That's why . . .' His voice trailed off once more.

The man's babbling, now, Kell thought. He's in a worse state than I am. 'Here,' Kell said, moved by the depth of the old man's emotion. 'Give me the names, and I will see if we can find them. And when Wiggins returns, I will tell him to go to you directly.'

'Captain Kell.' Mrs Jepson appeared at the doorway. 'You called?'

'Excellent, excellent. Can you run these names through the registry?' He handed her the paper with Watson's two names on it. 'See if you can get us an address at least, or police reports.' He then stepped even closer to her, so that only she could hear what he said. 'Could you also call the London hospitals, to see if my wife – Constance Kell – has been admitted?'

Mrs Jepson looked at him in alarm. Kell went on. 'Please keep this to yourself, of course, a precaution.'

'Of course, sir,' she said, pushing her glasses back up her nose reflexively.

'Captain Kell,' Simpkins called out. 'The telephone for you.'

'One moment,' Mrs Jepson said quietly, and then hesitated.

'Well?' Kell asked.

'Should I also check the arrest sheets, sir,' she said nervously. 'It's just, well, I understand your wife is sympathetic to the suffragette cause?'

'Well, I . . .' Kell gasped in indignation before breaking off. He nodded. She nodded in return and scuttled off.

'Sir?' Simpkins called again.

'One moment, please. Doctor Watson, as you can see, I am rather busy. But we will do our best for you.'

'For Holmes,' Watson said gravely.

'Yes, of course, for Mr Holmes.'

'Sir,' Simpkins insisted. 'It's the Foreign Office.'

Finally, Kell had his audience with Sir Edward Grey. The bumptious Carruthers ushered Kell into the inner sanctum of the Foreign Office, past the gorgeous works of art, the gilt frames, the statuary, through Grey's outer office and into the huge corner office, with a rack of large windows opening onto the dazzling green of St James's Park. Grey stood at one of these windows, and turned towards Kell on his entrance.

'Good afternoon, Captain Kell,' a gravelly voice echoed from behind him.

Kell groaned inwardly and turned to the source of the voice, who stood by the door, until that moment unseen, smoking a small cigar. The First Lord of the Admiralty. 'Good day, Winsto— Churchill,' Kell said, and corrected himself. 'My lord.'

Churchill nodded, and then pretended to cede the floor to Grey – although everyone in the room knew that he'd be talking again soon enough. You could never shut the man up. He couldn't keep his fat fingers out of anything and everything, he consumed information like it was free caviar, and he drank up all the gossip of Whitehall like it was his first champagne of the day.

Grey coughed. 'Captain Kell, thank you so much for coming. I apologise for the apparent urgency but one of my under-secretaries . . .'

'Carruthers,' Carruthers muttered under his breath.

'. . . suggested to me that you, as one of the snoo, er snea, er . . .' Grey hesitated, trying not to say the wrong words. Kell knew what he meant to say, that the whole bureau were little more than snoopers or sneaks, but he had just enough tact not to say it out loud. He was the head of the diplomatic, after all. Grey found the words he was looking for 'You, as a *secret service* man, believe that we are heading for all-out European war. Do you have any specific intelligence?'

'I have intelligence,' is what Kell wanted to say. 'Isn't that enough?' Instead, he bowed his head slightly, inclined his chin. 'As you may know, sir, my remit encompasses threats to domestic security from, primarily, Germany. Our most senior agent was recently murdered, we believe, by a German spy. We are making enquiries to ascertain whether this is indeed the case. But yes, I believe we are under attack already, as a preparation for wider invasion. And I am very worried.'

'So you do have specific intelligence? This is very important. I spoke to the German ambassador only yesterday to assure him we have no intention of going to war. Is there some cast-iron proof of their hostile intentions?'

'Agent W must have something from the continent by now.' Churchill couldn't contain himself. He strode into the centre of the room, glowering at Kell as he did so. 'Isn't that right?'

'How . . .?'

'I invited, ah yes, here he is.' Churchill turned to the door as Mansfield Cumming was announced. 'Mansfield Cumming, head of the foreign arm.'

Kell wondered how this meeting might get worse. The older man came in stiffly, but with his chest puffed out all the same. Grey sighed wearily. 'It is so nice of you, Winston, to arrange your meetings in my office. It saves me the bother.'

Churchill ignored him. 'Tell us, Commander Cumming, you are in charge of the early warning system in Europe, you have agents in the field, what intelligence do you have?'

None, Kell managed not to say miraculously. He held his tongue long enough for Cumming to parade his ignorance. 'There's nothing to worry about – certainly, in terms of Germany invading. My many agents, brave men all, have reported nothing on that front.'

'W has reported to you?' Churchill asked.

'All clear,' Cumming chimed, like a foghorn. 'In Brussels anyway.'

He's not in bloody Brussels, though, is he? Kell continued his internal dialogue. Millfield Browne's report from Paris, though cryptic and almost entirely unhelpful, did at least place Wiggins in Paris two days ago. The content of this message was mostly a complaint about Wiggins's ungentlemanly conduct, although it did mention the name of an exotic dancer, one Mata Hari.

'It seems, Churchill, that your nervousness is misplaced,' Grey said after a moment. 'Perhaps now is not the time to use external uncertainty to resolve issues of internal hierarchy.' He let the slight hang in the air for a moment. Cumming stayed oblivious but Kell discerned the meaning clearly enough: Churchill was using the European situation to try to advance his position in the cabinet. Or at least, that's what Grey implied. It was an open secret in Whitehall and Parliament that Churchill yearned to be prime minister. Of course, political ambition was a given for most of them, but Churchill's burned so bright it was almost indecent. He had already switched from being a Tory to a Liberal once so far in his young career, and Kell didn't doubt that he'd switch back if the prospects of a Downing Street address looked better on the other side of the floor. What had never been clear to anyone, however, was what Churchill would *do* were he to ascend to the highest office. It seemed to be a goal in itself.

This was particularly frustrating for Kell. On the rare occasions Churchill was right – for example, at that very moment, with war approaching – his cabinet colleagues were wont to put down any arguments he might make as purely a manoeuvre in his own advancement.

Regardless of their own infighting, Kell knew any further argument was pointless. He felt like Wiggins, looking on as those above him decide on his fate, without any sway or levers to change their minds. His Majesty's Government was like a huge Atlantic liner: changing the direction would take time and be next to impossible, especially when the sailors on the bridge were more intent on deciding who held the wheel rather than in which direction it pointed.

Kell sped back to Watergate House. Despite the impending doom he felt about the situation in Europe, he was far more concerned about Constance.

He arrived back to find that she had not rung. Again, no word at home. He summoned Mrs Jepson to report. She'd found no mention of Constance in the hospital lists, nor had there been any record of her arrest – though she'd not had a chance to go through them all. It was a constant struggle to get information out of the police, and Mrs Jepson had to ring every single police station in London to ascertain who had been arrested the day before. And that was only London. God knows where Constance might have gone, where she might be.

Kell took his cigarettes to the roof. He looked out across the Thames, the great pall of yellow smoke rolling down from Battersea, the impressive cranes of the building site where Wiggins once rose, and pondered the question of Constance's whereabouts. This led him to ponder another, more familiar question: where the hell was Wiggins?

'Where am I?' Wiggins said again.

He'd asked this question repeatedly since the police carted him away from the Eiffel Tower the day before. They'd bundled him into a motorised van and driven through the streets of Paris and subsequently into the side entrance of some police station or other. He hadn't recognised any landmarks through the small window in the back of the van, except to notice that they'd crossed the river once.

Two gendarmes had hauled him out of the back of the van, then hustled him through a narrow corridor until he'd been thrown into a cell. He'd then been visited by two separate plain clothes men he assumed were police, but couldn't be sure because neither of them spoke English. All he could really say in return was 'Anglais?' He decided not to give them his name but he hoped that, sooner or later, someone from the embassy would turn up. In the meantime, it seemed that they didn't know what to do with him.

He guessed it was about lunchtime when a burly, low-browed guard opened the door and tossed a stick of bread at him. It was a new man, and so Wiggins tried again. 'Where am I?' he asked, gesturing about him.

The guard grunted. '*Trente-six.*'

'Eh? Anglais?'

'*Trente-six Quai des Orfèvres,*' the guard said with a hint of pride in his voice.

Wiggins shook his head, indicating the words meant nothing to him. The guard hesitated, then a grin spread across his otherwise forbidding face. '*C'est Scotland Yard de Paris,*' he said triumphantly.

'Ha!' Wiggins said, and saluted. Wiggins had deduced the guard's military background as soon as he handed him the bread. He'd known one or two legionnaires in South Africa ten years or more back and they always carried themselves in the same way; hair cut too short at the back, so that the bristles raged red, the pinched frown and half-closed eyes, forever squinting, and the way he held his thumbs in his fists, as if physically holding himself back.

The guard saluted back. '*Êtes-vous militaire?*'

'Gunner,' Wiggins replied. He mimed the action of priming and firing a cannon.

The guard gurned slightly, then slapped his chest. '*La Légion,*' he said. '*Infanterie.*' This was why Wiggins saluted, to make obvious the connection between them. An ally is always worth making, wherever you are, and military men the world over gravitated to their own kind (when they weren't trying to kill them). They normally had more respect for the men they fought, than for the men they fought *for*.

'Algeria?' Wiggins asked.

'*Oui. Et Dahomey, Mandingo, Madagascar. Vous?*'

'Boer.'

'*Ach,*' the guard spat. '*Les Boers sont des cons.*'

Wiggins knew what that meant. He laughed. 'You're not wrong.'

The guard patted his chest '*Nom est Xavier.*'

'Wiggins.'

Later, after Wiggins had dozed and tossed and turned the afternoon away, wondering still the fate of Von Bork (Did he die in that plane? Or rather, was he Maxim DuPont? For whoever was DuPont, was dead), he heard the rattle and hubbub of someone being escorted down the corridor.

A heavy key turned in the lock and then a tall young man was ushered into the cell. 'Thank you, er . . . merci,' he said with an English accent. The last time Wiggins had seen him, his arse had been going fifteen to the dozen in between the legs of the Parisian 'little sister'. They stared at each other, open-mouthed. Wiggins chuckled.

'Well, I, er, how do you do?' the young diplomat said. 'Nice to see you again. I, er, as you know, um – I'm from the British embassy and, well, you know that of course – yes, this is a bit awkward, really. Should I introduce myself again, perhaps, best foot forward and all that, play up. Yes. I'm Netherfield.'

'Wotcha. You here to get me out?'

'Ah, no, not exactly. I'm here in an official capacity, consular support, given the police here believe you to be a British subject. Are they treating you well, are they?' he asked, glancing around the cell absently.

'What are they charging me with?'

'Right, yes, no. I'm not really sure. Neither are they at the moment. It seems you're a bit of a puzzle, which I must say I can understand. It seems a man died, although they don't quite know who it was. I believe – so the desk sergeant tells me – they are waiting for someone called Ladoux to interview you.'

'That's not a good idea,' Wiggins said. Getting entangled in the French security services was the last thing he needed. 'Look mate, if you can't get me out will you send someone who can?'

'I . . . well, er . . .'

'Get Millfield Browne down here.'

'Er, yes, perhaps Browne might have more success – who shall I say is asking for him?'

'Tell him it's the bloke who stopped you being ripped off by them tarts.'

Netherfield's pale, freckled face reddened. 'Ah, yes, quite so. Quite so. I will return to the embassy at once and ask him to intercede on your behalf.' He knocked on the cell door and waited while the guard slowly unlocked the door. 'I know that he is out this evening, so he may not be able to come until tomorrow. So wait here, will you?'

'I'm hardly likely to pop out, am I?' Wiggins said, gesturing around him.

The door swung open and Netherfield stepped out into the corridor. Just before the door shut again, he thrust his head back in. 'I really did go there for language lessons.'

Saturday 11 July 1914. The British papers are full of the growing crisis in Ireland. In the north of that island Sir Edward Carson solidifies opposition to home rule, or 'Rome Rule' as he and his Ulster Unionists call it. His 'provisional government' meet for the first time, and vow to keep Ulster in trust for the King. The other rumour circulating around the newsrooms of Fleet Street is that the Prime Minister, Herbert Asquith, is suffering from a nervous breakdown. The swell of martial feeling in Vienna is rarely remarked upon, nor indeed is the death of the Russian minister Hartwig, who dies suddenly after a visit to the Austrian legation in Belgrade.

Wiggins woke with a start. The cell was coffin dark. He heard slow footsteps coming down the corridor. A faint glimmer began to appear around the edges of the door. Wiggins already knew he was in a quiet, neglected part of the police station, a special wing or some such. Normally they echoed to the sounds of drunkenness or the screams of insanity, even in the middle of the night. But these cells in Paris were quieter than the dead.

A fan of light spread across the floor as the door creaked open. The guard Xavier held up a lantern. 'Wiggins? *Venez.*' He gestured.

Wiggins came into the corridor and Xavier put down the lantern. '*Pardon,*' he said, as he brought out a pair of handcuffs and bound Wiggins's hands in front of him. '*Allez.*'

Xavier held him by the elbow with one hand, lantern in the other, then turned one dark corner, then another. Wiggins tried to speak but Xavier shushed him, as they turned down a small staircase which led to a side door.

The big policeman opened the door, then ushered Wiggins outside onto a quiet street. In the dim street lights, he could make out a couple of police vehicles and a plain automobile. He turned to Xavier.

'*Pardon, mon ami*,' Xavier said. '*Honneur et fidélité.*'

Unseen hands thrust a hood over Wiggins's head. Strong arms gripped him on either side. He felt two big men. Hamstrung by the cuffs, Wiggins tried to dodge but Xavier punched him in the stomach.

He tried to shout out, but received a blow on the mouth. 'SHUSSH,' a voice hissed in his ear. There was no way he was winning a fight against these men. In a second, they pulled him to his feet and bundled him into the car. It smelled of new leather and fresh polish, mixed with the dusty scratching of the hessian sack on his head.

The car cranked into gear and sped off. So much for the honour of military men, Wiggins thought as he tasted the blood on his lip: Xavier had done the dirty on him.

They had the courtesy not to knock him about, which he appreciated. His split lip was necessary to make the point, but once in the motor the men either side of him relaxed. 'No need for the hood,' Wiggins said as the car rattled over cobbles. The men did not reply. Wiggins found this reassuring, somehow. He'd been kidnapped before and it was normally a frightening experience. In Dublin, he worried they were going to kill him – Rijkard's men too. But these two kidnappers didn't exude that kind of fatal energy. They seemed too professional, too correct, they made sure he didn't bang his head getting into the car, they weren't panicking, there was no rush. If a man was intent on killing you, the nerves would normally show somehow. It wasn't easy to kill a man, even on the battlefield in the heat and fury of the fight; no, these men weren't going to kill him. Yet.

The journey ended abruptly and he was hustled out of the car again, still hooded. This time, the men held onto him at each side – as if helping a drunken friend. Wiggins felt cobbles under his feet, and then a sudden airy cool. Smooth flags underfoot, an echoing tread: they were in a station, and a big one. Once he'd realised this, Wiggins could place every sound and smell and clink. Far off loading of a carriage. The whistles of a night sweeper, the coal dust hanging in the air; and the echo of the high roof.

They arrived at a train. His kidnappers guided him up the steps, one in front, one behind. Once inside, they forced him into a small room – probably the toilet cubicle, Wiggins reasoned – and cuffed him to a pipe running down one wall. '*Auf Wiedersehen*,' one of them said, then locked the door shut.

Silence. He waited a few minutes, then bent his head down to his bound hands and managed to pull the hood free. He was in a train toilet cubicle. The window was shuttered with metal, and he could only just pick out the fixtures and fittings using the glow of the platform lights. Next to the toilet pan was a basin, with water too. As he suspected by the way they'd treated him in the car, these were respectable kidnappers. The cubicle even smelled of disinfectant. It had everything he might need, except something to eat.

Not long after, the train shunted and groaned into action and soon picked up tremendous speed, rattling and moving like no express he'd been on before. They were travelling light. It was daylight outside by the time the key turned, and a whiskerless young man in a clean white shirt opened the door. He bent down silently and detached the cuffs from the pipe, then pulled Wiggins up to follow.

'Breakfast time, is it?' Wiggins asked.

The young man stared at him for a moment without comment, then pushed Wiggins forwards down a corridor.

Pale green countryside rushed by, though he noted that metal shutters were affixed to all the windows. He could only just make out the world beyond.

Wiggins glanced around at the young man. 'Mind what you do with that,' he said. For the young man now had a revolver pointed at him.

The young man said nothing, but pointed the gun into a compartment. Wiggins simply held his cuffed hands up. 'Do the honours then, mate.'

'*Ach*,' the young man exclaimed. He gestured forward with the gun, then stepped in himself and yanked open the compartment door.

'Ta very much,' Wiggins said, and entered.

At the window, dressed in an impeccable cream linen suit and a crisp shirt, patent leather shoes glistening, cigarette smoke curling up from the half-finished Turkish in his hand, sat Maxim DuPont's bearded mechanic. He looked like a different person, from another class entirely. 'Ah Mr Wiggins, good morning,' he said in absolutely unaccented English. 'Please, won't you take a seat?'

14

Wiggins took a seat on the hurtling train and regarded the man opposite. Dressed as a gentleman, legs crossed like a gentleman, speaking like an English gentleman.

'Pay no attention to good old Hans there, he likes to wave it around, as young men do.'

Wiggins glanced back at Hans, who now stood in the corridor with the revolver. 'He don't look like he knows how to use it,' he said.

'Ah, now that would be a mistake. You're perfectly at liberty to find out, of course. But let us get down to business, yes? Do you mind if I shave while we do this?' He pointed to a sloshing bowl of water on the floor. 'I hate beards.'

Wiggins nodded and the man, shaving brush in hand, began to lather up. He said, 'I believe you know who I am?'

'You mean, apart from being DuPont's flight mechanic?'

'Poor Max,' he said. 'That really was most unfortunate.' He sloshed his chin with the soapy foam, as if to dash away the memory of the dead with the fresh smell of a close shave.

Wiggins did not reply. He waited and watched the man shave; took in the finely manicured fingernails (not those of a mechanic, certainly), the razor-sharp creases in his collar and cuffs, the St James's shoes (Lobb, Wiggins could tell by the marks on the sole of the one shoe presented towards him by the elegantly crossed legs).

The man brought the razor up to his chin and, despite the jolts and jangles of the train, shaved with swift, precise movements. He flicked the foam of his razor impatiently and without ceremony. The whole show was a means to an end, not an enjoyable task to be savoured.

Wiggins couldn't help but watch, for a new man's face began to appear from behind the beard. And the single most remarkable feature of this face was the two-inch scar that ran from his left ear diagonally down to his chin. A pale white streak, stark against the clean shave.

The man finished, dried his face with a flannel, then tossed it into the soapy bowl. He lit a cigarette, took a drag and then looked carefully at Wiggins. 'It is called a Mensur scar, from duelling,' he said at last. 'At university, us young chaps you know, young gentlemen. It is a sign of bravery among the upper classes here – or rather, in Germany.'

'I ain't ever heard your first name,' Wiggins said.

'Apologies, I should introduce myself – although you know who I *am*, of course. My full name is Gustav Phillip Justinian Graf Von Bork – you will forgive the Justinian, my father adored his classics professor. Fathers, eh?' He pulled out another cigarette and lit it without offering one to Wiggins. Von Bork took his time with the match, then drew deeply before going on. 'It's a bit of a mouthful though – as a name I mean – and so these days I prefer to work under different aliases, depending on where I am. But I believe you first became aware of me as Von Bork, and so here I am – Von Bork! And now, may I ask your name in return?'

'You know I don't smoke, but you don't know my name?'

'Oh come on, the jolly English humour. We've been fighting since, what was it 1910?'

''09'

'Yes, yes of course. Those crazy Russians. They didn't really need any provoking, but it made my name in the service. Then you and Captain Kell managed to close the Belgravia operation.'

'The knocking shop you mean?'

'As you say. I presume you were also involved in the scuppering of the guns to Howth, back in '12? Yes, I can see from your eyes that you were. Come now, Wiggins, will you tell me your first name?'

'Wiggins'll do,' he grunted. Then he pointed with his hand towards Von Bork's white scar. 'What's that called again?' he asked. Something was chiming in his head, a word but then it's meaning too – from the old days, when he knew a few German mercenaries out in South Africa – that, and what Sherlock Holmes said to him when he was dying.

'Mensur,' Von Bork answered helpfully. 'It's a fairly normal practice in Germany's elite universities. It's made with a duelling sword, a schläger.'

Schläger.

Wiggins dropped his head slightly. He didn't want Von Bork to see the stab of recognition. Holmes had known what the scar was, Holmes had told him as he lay dying what to look for, what was the quickest clue. Schläger. Poor dead Holmes. And here in front of him, for sure, was his killer, with the scar that marked him so.

He shot a glance into the corridor, Hans still there with the gun; down at his own wrists, still cuffed. Finally he looked back up at Von Bork, who sat like a man who's just called seven no trumps and seen the winning dummy.

'The English are often put off by this.' Von Bork touched his scar as he spoke. His accent was so perfect,

so landed gentry, his mention of 'the English' discon-
certed Wiggins again. Von Bork went on. 'It's a squeam-
ishness, I think, an unwillingness to face up to the cruelty
of the world, of nature. Mostly, when I travel under an
English alias, I wear a beard and whiskers. But I am sure
you don't wish to know all this.' He fixed Wiggins with an
empty glare. For a man who exuded so much intelligence
and energy, Von Bork's eyes had a deadening greyness
that chilled Wiggins's heart. This man was a killer, no
question.

Von Bork tutted, crossed his legs again. 'I must say, I am
very impressed that you found me so quickly. A very smart
piece of work, very smart indeed. Kell must pay you well.'

'He don't wave guns at me, if that's what you mean.'

'Ha, yes yes. But even so, I assume you must be recom-
pensed appropriately. I know if I had an agent as good as
you, I would be prepared to pay the world.'

'And yet.' Wiggins held his cuffed hands aloft. 'Here I
am.'

'Here you are: on the way to Germany as a guest of a
German nobleman.'

'What'll you do about me at the border? Kidnapping
ain't legal in France, is it?'

'We shall not stop at the border. This is a sealed train.
You see the shutters? This train will not stop at all, in fact,
except to refuel. I am needed in Berlin, and I thought I
would take the opportunity to bring certain valuable items
back with me. Documents from the embassy, of course;
wine, in particular cases of claret, as the English say. It's
hard to get in Berlin and, I fear, I won't be welcome in
Paris very soon. And of course, there is you – super cargo.
I believe you have some value to me as well.'

'And you can't legally torture me in France either, can you?'

'I can't *legally* torture you in Germany either. But come now, Wiggins, we are not as barbarous as all that. Really. There will be no need for such methods. But you are right, insofar as if one of our people wanted to do such a vile thing, then they would have to do it in Germany.'

'If I'm so valuable, why did you try to have me killed?'

Von Bork raised an eyebrow at that. 'No, old boy, not my style at all. Not me.'

'Not your fucking style?' Wiggins growled.

'Please, no need for the Anglo-Saxon. I merely meant that you are far more valuable to me alive than dead.'

'Just like Mr Holmes?'

'Exactly unlike Mr Holmes. I admit, I was flattered to discover he was on my tail – oh yes, we Germans have the utmost respect for the man, we even enjoy Doctor Watson's stories. But this is a man you don't want as an enemy, a man never to be suppressed. I was this close to giving him my crown jewels, he – or rather Altamont – was to be my number two in England, and then I discovered the truth. There could never be an accommodation with such a man. I paid him the honour of doing the deed myself at least. But you saw that.'

At that moment a steward appeared. He squeezed past the gunman Hans and bowed smartly to Von Bork. The buttons on his white coat gleamed. He didn't so much as look at Wiggins. Von Bork barked some instructions at him in fluent, almost violent German. The difference between the diffident, affable-sounding Englishman and this German gentleman was stark and startling. It was as if he became a different person. From DuPont's bearded mechanic, to the English squire and now this severe German military man, the transformations were swift and discombobulating. Wiggins wondered if such changes came naturally to those with many languages, if having different words meant seeing the world differently. He'd noticed it with Margaretha, with Martha too – whenever they spoke in another language their whole demeanour altered.

When Von Bork had finished, the steward clipped his heels together, collected the shaving tackle and exited the compartment without a sound.

'Who are you when you're English then?' Wiggins asked once the steward had gone. Hans, and his gun, remained in the corridor.

'Now, now, I am not so foolish as that.' Von Bork settled back into his English persona. 'Let me just say that I have managed to travel up and down your country unmolested. Indeed, I've been welcomed with open arms. I have taken tourist tours, guided tours of some of your great ports and factories, the marvellous sewage system of London. The British – the complacent, arrogant British – think I'm a hearty squire, of course, and not the duplicitous German spy of Mr Le Queux's imagination. I don't suppose you read?'

Wiggins had trained himself not to react to such remarks. He'd had a lifetime of training, dealing with supposed gentlemen. Von Bork, like most gentlemen, remained oblivious to the idea that a working man might have education or interests beyond his hands and heart.

'What struck me about Great Britain – ha, that little 'great' is so quaint, is it not? – when touring the country, was seeing the slums of Dublin, Liverpool, Glasgow. Seeing the miners and those desperate, dark factories where even the children work. We are told – by the British themselves of course – that they and their Empire are the richest in the history of the world. It may be true, it probably is true – but . . . you would not know this from walking its streets, from talking to its people, from seeing how they live.'

Wiggins remained silent. He'd taken the same tour himself, been to the docks of Newcastle, Glasgow and Belfast, the pit towns of South Wales, the factories of Birmingham, the mills of the north. Kell and Churchill between them years earlier had sent him off to suss out dissent, to see what the working men and women think, and to whip up trouble if they needed a barney. He'd seen all that Von Bork described and more. The country was not a happy place, not for the poor, and never had been since he could remember.

'Have you been to the colonies, by the way? The way they treat the natives is even worse. But let's not argue over this. This is your Empire, this is what you fight for. I respect that.'

'I lost someone,' Wiggins said quietly.

'Yes, yes. I also lost someone. You flew his aircraft into the Seine, didn't you? Schmidt, his real name was. But we are soldiers, this is what happens in war. It's evened out, I think.' He began to remove invisible specks of dust from the trouser of his crossed leg.

'And what makes the German Empire so much better than the British one?' Wiggins asked carefully.

'Oh, I don't know if it is really. It's poorer certainly. But at least we pay our soldiers well. And we pay the talented ones *exceptionally*.'

'So,' Wiggins said at last. 'What is it you want me to do?'

* * *

'Simpkins.' Kell shouted for his secretary. 'Anything?'

'Nothing, sir,' the man called out from the anteroom, not even daring to come into the office.

Kell's search for Constance had drawn a blank. She'd been missing three days now. In the end, he'd been honest with the police. He had a private interview with Sir Edward Henry, the head of Scotland Yard, where he'd reported her missing, and intimated that foreign powers may be at work. He could see that Sir Edward didn't really believe him about the foreign powers, but nevertheless he put Constance's name at the top of the missing list. Every constabulary in the country was on the lookout.

He had also enlisted the help of his own department, in particular Mrs Jepson. She had been through the arrest lists of every police station in the South East for the last three days; she'd been going through the newspapers just as assiduously. She'd been in constant contact with the major hospitals of London. Still, nothing. He'd even taken it upon himself to investigate a railway accident in Croydon (three dead), and a boating accident at Southend pleasure pier. But none of the corpses were Constance.

A double rap at the door. Simpkins and Mrs Jepson. 'Sir,' she said firmly. 'I have an idea. May I come in?'

'Sir,' Simpkins said, annoyed that a woman had spoken before him. 'I have Doctor Watson on the line.'

'Again?'

'He is most insistent.'

'Tell him I'm busy . . . no, tell him I'll send the household cavalry, Special Branch and the light infantry, tell him anything just so long as he stops telephoning.' Kell paused, took a breath. 'Say I'll call him back directly. Mrs Jepson, come in please.'

She slipped in past the affronted Simpkins and took a seat opposite Kell without being asked. Then she looked back at the secretary and waited for him to close the door.

'We must have missed your wife, sir. She can't just have disappeared off the face of the earth.'

'Of course we've missed her. We've all missed her.'

'I didn't mean, I don't mean . . . look, why don't you tell me something about her, sir.'

'I beg your pardon?'

Mrs Jepson shifted in her seat, and tapped the notebook in her hand. 'It might help us to find her, sir, if we know *who* we're looking for and not simply her name?'

Kell gazed at her in astonishment and dismay. 'I . . .' he began to protest, but the words died on his lips. No one had ever asked him such a question. Not his friend Soapy, nor the chaps in the club, nor even his mother when he first announced he was interested in marrying her. The only question that had mattered to anyone was who her parents were. But that wasn't what Mrs Jepson was asking at all.

'She is a remarkable woman,' he said at last. 'Braver than any soldier I know, sturdier of purpose. She is far cleverer than me, sharp you might say – quick – like Wiggins. She is a wonderful mother, a perfect wife. She is proficient in ju-jitsu – it's a martial art, from the East – she is all a person should be, and all they can be too.'

'Friends, other family, have you . . .'

'I've checked, yes. Nothing.'

'And she's an active suffragette?'

'She was, once – perhaps she still is. Certainly, in her heart she is committed to the cause. She was involved with some radicals a few years ago – a splinter off the Pankhurst crowd, right out on the edge. She stepped back from that but, who knows?'

Who knows indeed, Kell thought as he looked at Mrs Jepson – she was looking less and less like a maiden aunt and more and more like a Pinkerton detective or a daredevil aviatrix.

Mrs Jepson tapped her notebook again quickly, smiled tightly to herself, took a deep breath and said, 'May I ask, sir, does she love you?'

'I don't know what you mean?' Kell gasped.

'Does your wife love you?'

The telephone jangled on the desk in between them, breaking the moment and allowing Kell to evade the question. 'Simpkins,' Kell cried. 'I told you not to put him through.'

Simpkins appeared at the door. 'I didn't, sir, it's just ringing by itself. Honestly, what's wrong with a telegram?'

Kell snatched the telephone from the desk. 'Listen Doctor Watson, I understand you're perturbed but really, I must insist, please let me do my job.'

'Captain Kell, is that you?' A gravelly, crackling, unmistakable voice came through the horn.

'Churchill? Yes, this is Captain Kell.'

'Is this line secure?'

'What do you mean?'

'Is anyone else listening to us?'

Kell glanced up at Simpkins, then at Mrs Jepson. He waved Simpkins away. 'No.'

'You need to get me the intelligence.'

'Which intelligence?'

'The intelligence identifying the imminence of a European war, in particular, the plans of the German imperial army to mobilise aggressively.'

'But I have none.'

'Then invent it, man. Isn't that what you're there for?'

'Sir, I'm not sure . . .'

'I thought you said this line was secure?' He then rang off without another word.

Kell stared at the receiver for a moment. Then he looked up slowly at Mrs Jepson. 'I think she does, yes. I think she loves me.'

She pushed over a piece of paper. 'Then write down all the names you can think of — family, friends, enemies, heroines. I think I've got an idea.'

On Saturday 18 July 1914, Foreign Secretary Sir Edward Grey resigned himself to the inevitability of a small, local war in Europe. The Austrians have become convinced the Serbian government sponsored the assassination of their Archduke, and have been constructing a pretext for invasion. The French newspapers are more concerned with the trial of Henriette Caillaux, wife of former Prime Minister Joseph Caillaux, who is on trial for the murder of a newspaper editor. In Fleet Street they still fear war in Ireland, they fear industrial strikes and, most of all, they fear women who fight for their right to vote. Annie Bell is foiled in her attempt to blow up the Metropolitan Tabernacle and goes to police court unrepentant. Up and down the country, in Winson Green, in Strangeways, in HMP Holloway, suffragette women refuse to eat. Prison doctors ram hard rubber tubing down their throats, in fear.

Kell rushed out onto the street without his hat on. Mrs Jepson came tumbling out of Watergate House behind him, holding the hat, into the yellow-dark London night. They rushed up to the Strand, flapping and whistling, until a motor cab swung to the kerb.

The taxi wheeled northwards as Kell urged the driver on: round the Aldwych bend, up past Drury Lane (he'd missed the ballet there last week – it seemed an age), on through King's Cross and Barnsbury.

'There's no need to panic, sir,' Mrs Jepson said quietly.

'I'm not panicking,' he cried.

The cab slewed around the corner to a halt. It was there in front of them, lit by small fluttering lights, a dark gothic horror show, like something out of a lurid novel. A medieval-style gateway, dwarfed by a castle turret disappearing into the darkness, ramparts, and the hollow echo of a great unknown beyond. His Majesty's Prison Holloway.

Kell skittered out of the cab, across the scattered gravel and up to the great wooden door. He banged with his fists, and shouted for entry.

'There, sir.' Mrs Jepson touched his arm lightly, and pointed to a small door within the huge wooden gate. He looked around, eyes awry, so she stepped forward and rang the bell herself.

Within minutes, they were in the guardhouse waiting for the arrival of the deputy prison governor – the governor was 'dining out', the warden said, to which Kell replied, 'Were they shoving tubes down his throat at White's?'

'What's all this?' A clean-shaven man of thirty-five stepped into the guardhouse, oozing petty authority. He examined them through very small, round glasses. He wore his hair in a sharp crease down the middle, and his markless skin spoke of a man who hadn't smiled a genuine smile since he was a babe in arms.

'This,' said Kell, 'is a demand from the highest levels of government to hand over custody to me, instantly, of one of your inmates. Her name is Georgina Allcard.'

'Is it?' the Deputy said. 'May I see the paperwork?'

Kell glared at him, his gorge rising. 'How dare you? I'll . . .'

'If I may,' Mrs Jepson interrupted. She stepped past Kell and presented the Deputy with a piece of paper. As he began to read the letter, with exaggerated care, Kell motioned to the guard and pushed past the Deputy into the prison proper.

The Deputy let out a token mew of resistance, but he was cowed by the combined power of Mrs Jepson and Kell's all-purpose authorisation of action (signed by the Home Secretary, the Minister of War and the First Lord of the Admiralty, it essentially gave him carte blanche to command any employee of the Crown to do his bidding). He nodded tamely at the guard.

'Allcard,' Kell repeated through gritted teeth as the iron gates swung open and he marched into the prison.

Kell, who had been in male prisons once or twice in his life, both in England and in China, had always assumed that a ladies' prison would somehow be different – kinder, gentler, perhaps even less foreboding. Stepping onto a wing in Holloway, though, felt like stepping into a circle of hell.

The noise was terrific. Even though the wing was shut up – he could see no prisoners on the floor, just rows of cells with walkways to the sky – he could hear everything. Screaming, crying, shouting, banging, clanging, and a horribly high-pitched wail that spoke of profound pain. Kell glanced around at the guard. 'Feeding time, sir,' he said. 'An 'unger striker. For their own good, course, but it ain't pretty.'

'Hurry man.'

'Shut it, Mortimer!' the guard suddenly shouted as they passed a cell. He smashed the door with his stick, as if words alone were not enough to make the point.

Finally, they reached a cell at the end of the block and the guard thrust a key into the lock. 'Allcard,' he cried. 'Stand to.'

The door swung open and there she was, standing by the high cell window, hands on hips, a look of fierce determination etched across her beautiful face. Georgina Allcard, otherwise known as Mrs Constance Kell. 'You took your time,' she said.

Georgina Allcard. The alias was simplicity itself, in the end, and so typically Constance. Kell loved his wife and, though he rarely admitted it, he loved her cleverness. And he loved her irreverence too, her disregard for convention and the way she would tease him – prick his bubble of pomposity – when it was most necessary. She had the sensitivity to his position, she knew not to be arrested under her own name, and yet still she had the flair to ruffle his feathers – even in such a moment.

It was Mrs Jepson who realised Constance would never give her real name, were her arrest certain, and that she hadn't run off to be with someone else. That's why she asked Kell if Constance still loved him: to confirm that she hadn't deserted, and to confirm that she would not deliberately embarrass her husband.

Instead, Mrs Jepson had made him write down all the significant names in Constance's life he could think of – mother, sisters, children and the like. He even included members of his own family, even his mother's maiden name. Mrs Jepson scoured the arrest list connected with suffragette protests but found none.

Finally she came back to him, exhausted. 'There is nothing here,' she said. 'The only names that vaguely match are definitely not Mrs Kell.'

Kell squeezed the bridge of his nose. 'Are there any half-matches?' he asked. 'Christian, surnames that kind of thing?'

'None that leap out. I mean there is a Georgina arrested about the right time, but according to your notes your mother's maiden name is Konarska and this woman's name was something different entirely.'

'What was it?'

'Sir?'

'The name, for heaven's sake. Georgina who?'

Mrs Jepson scrabbled through the notes. 'Here it is,' she said at last. 'Placed in Holloway Prison. Allcard. Georgina Allcard.'

'It's her,' Kell said, getting up.

'But, how?'

Kell grabbed his coat. 'It's her,' he repeated. It was his mother's name – not her maiden name, nor her name when she became his mother. It was her name once she remarried after divorcing his father in 1892. Kell never spoke of this divorce – who would? – and it was a source of great embarrassment and secrecy. Constance, of course, knew but few other people did. What better name for an alias – and yet, too, pricking his own vanity, for why should he be ashamed?

'Allcard?' he said, as he embraced her in that cell, squeezing her tightly.

'I knew you'd get there eventually,' she said. 'Have you come to take me away?'

'I was struck with fear, my darling. I thought . . . I thought . . .'

'Good god, Vernon, I was never going to stop eating,' Constance gasped. But then she hugged him close again, and did not make light of the moment. 'Let's go. This is a terrible place. We must get the others out, too, we must.'

'It's all I can do to get you out,' he said quietly. 'Any more and it will become official, and official means questions and it won't wash. I might lose my job, and you'll be right back in here.'

'One more, then? Just a girl. It's for Wiggins.'

15

'Let's get down to business,' Von Bork said. 'Holiday camp is over.'

'I don't much like the sound of your holidays,' Wiggins said.

'English humour.' Von Bork nodded without smiling. 'It will be the death of your country. Come, time to earn your money.'

The 'holiday camp' Von Bork referred to was a barracks of some sort. Wiggins had been taken off the train in Berlin – he could see the signs on the platform – and driven for twenty minutes to a set of low brick buildings surrounding a parade ground. There had been no signatures, no official imprisonment or incarceration, no hint of a judge or a legal process. He remembered back to '10, when those disastrous toffs Brandon and Trench had been arrested on the German coast – despite his and Kell's best efforts to save them. The Germans had tried them as spies, and imprisoned them – all very proper and by the book, sticklers for the correct procedure. He wasn't in that boat. He wasn't a toff for one thing, nor officially an army officer. And he wasn't taken in Germany, either, which itself was an act of war if it became official. All this would be raising eyebrows if he ever went to court.

But of course, as Von Bork kept insisting whenever he visited over the following week, Wiggins wasn't in prison

– he was a guest. Only a guest whose door remained locked, who could only exercise on the deserted parade ground in the presence of an armed guard, and whose only visitor was Von Bork.

On the train to Berlin Von Bork had made his pitch to Wiggins, promises of high pay, criticisms of Britain, of the Empire. Smooth, persuasive, inevitable. 'But what do you want me to do?' Wiggins said at last.

'Why, be my agent of course,' Von Bork replied.

'Is that why you've got Hans here, waving his thingy about at me?'

Von Bork smiled. 'Come on, old boy, I'm not stupid,' he said in his disconcertingly perfect English accent. 'Hans's revolver is insurance. You are a resourceful man. Which is why, in the end, I think you'll agree that working for us – for very, very good pay – will be your best option.'

'I don't speak the lingo,' Wiggins said.

'You misunderstand. I want you to go back to London, go back to Kell, and continue to work for him. And me.'

'You mean, double up?'

'Yes! Exactly, you will become a *double* agent – I like that, play both sides. Of course, you will be loyal to the man who pays the most. That is the way of things.'

'What about my honour?'

'Honour? Where is the honour in spying? Besides, shouldn't we leave honour to all those grown-up public school boys – Kell and Cumming and the like? They can keep their honour, while we take the spoils.'

Wiggins let that settle. He peered through the gap in the metal shutters, out at the browns, yellows and greens of the French landscape – a green and pleasant land, not so different from his own. Would Von Bork really send him back to London, just like that?

Von Bork uncrossed his legs and hunched forward. 'Look, I don't expect you to agree to this straight away, not at all. That wouldn't be decent in any case, I understand – wouldn't be cricket and all that.'

'You don't look like no cricketer to me.'

'No?'

'Following folk around, in their own country – that's hardly fair, is it?'

'Ah.' Von Bork nodded slightly. 'You are upset naturally, about your tail in London. But think of it this way around – how else do you suppose I found out about Altamont, if not by following you and Kell? And before you protest, remember that Altamont had been lying to me for years – I almost gave him everything. It's not as if anyone else is playing cricket here.'

The steward came in with a steaming cup of coffee and handed it to Von Bork. He didn't offer Wiggins a drink, but sipped his own for a minute or so. 'I fear the old rules are gone now, don't you?'

'Were there ever any?'

'Oh yes indeed, between gentlemen of honour. Rules of engagement, that type of thing. Very much so. But machines don't have a sense of honour, do they? And the next war, and the next and forever more will be wars wielded with machines. Honour will be out of place.'

'Folk'll still die though, won't they? That won't change.'

'Just so. Which is why we must strive to make good decisions for ourselves and our futures. Once we get to Berlin, once you're convinced of Germany's superiority in every way – *then*, then I think you'll come around to my view.'

'But how would you trust me? If you sent me back to London, what's to say I wouldn't spill everything to Kell, and play you at your own game?'

'A *triple* cross-over?' he chuckled. 'Wouldn't that be a thing indeed, for the history books. But no, I don't think this would happen. Kell would never pay you what I can pay you, would never offer you the life you could lead under me.' He let that hang there for a moment, the bald offer itself – not the figure, but the idea of the figure. 'Besides,' he went on at last. 'I do have another lever. But enough of this to and fro. You will work for me in the end, gladly I'm sure.'

'You seem sure of a lot.'

'I like gambling. Your English gentlemen like it too, don't they? A flutter? Most often they flutter with their soldiers' lives, ha ha. But in any case, we do not have to decide this now. First of all, you will be my guest in Berlin – the world's most modern city, by the way. It is fully electrified, elektropolis we call it now. So unlike the dark and dingy streets of London, you'll see. There are no dark corners there. It is the city of the twentieth century!' It was the first time Wiggins saw Von Bork out of his English gentleman persona, the zeal. 'You'll see,' he went on. 'Hans will take you back now.'

'To the khazi?'

'Um, yes, as you say. Once the journey is over, you'll stay in Berlin – as my guest – until you realise the truth of the situation. That working for me is your only good option. Come, Wiggins, it will be exciting. The game is afoot, is it not? I will come for you soon, when the time is right.'

Which was why Wiggins found himself staring at a barrack wall for more than a week. Von Bork visited him once every day or so, and interrogated him about Kell's operation. It was the usual stuff – working practices, personnel, weak spots. All the information any traitor would be expected to hand over before becoming trusted as a double agent. Wiggins didn't mind, for the money Von Bork proposed to pay him – in marks, not pounds, and into a German bank only accessible in Germany – was truly extraordinary. Enough money, in fact, to make a new life abroad.

Von Bork's plan, as he outlined on the second day in Berlin, was for Wiggins to pretend he'd been detained but escaped. He would work for Kell in London, while all the time feeding information back to Von Bork. He would be paid in marks, in Germany only, and other than expenses, he would be unable to access this cash unless he came back into the country. Wiggins would be given German citizen-ship – once he proved his worth – and come the end of any war he would be made for life. Von Bork was talking thou-sands, not hundreds.

In addition to this, and to prove his fidelity to the cause, Von Bork required him to hand over any and all informa-tion on Kell and the Secret Intelligence Bureau that he already possessed. Hence the long period of debriefing in the barracks.

On day nine of this process, Von Bork had come in with a new energy and zeal – as if he'd made the decision, counted now on Wiggins's loyalty, and they were going to move to the next stage. He'd never been in Wiggins's presence with-out an armed escort but today, as Von Bork sat down and talked of holiday camps, Wiggins noted that the door had been left open and the guard did not have his gun drawn.

'Training day,' Von Bork said, and gestured for Wiggins to stand.

'What do I need to learn?'

'Not you.'

Von Bork led him out into the corridor then onto the parade ground. The guard followed close behind and, though the revolver that he always carried was now holstered, Wiggins knew it was still there.

A dozen or so men came to attention as Von Bork strode out into the dust and heat and blazing sunshine. Wiggins shielded his eyes.

Von Bork gestured to the men. They were all dressed in civilian clothing but their military training stood out a mile – not just military, naval; and not just naval, officer corps. 'Teach them, will you?'

'Teach 'em what?'

'What it is you do. Surveillance, street craft, how to follow, how to evade being followed. My men could not follow you – one of them died in the process, did they not? – and yet you found Max and I in Paris. You are the best we have ever encountered, and so you'll teach these men to be the best.'

'I don't mean to be funny . . .'

'You're English, you always mean to be funny.'

'But,' Wiggins went on, 'this lot aren't street. I can see the silver spoons stuck up their arses from here.'

Von Bork pursed his lips. He obviously had the same problem as Kell, that most of his potential agents were officer class, posh as fish knives. 'I know, old man, but that's where we are with N division. This is who we have, and this is why you'll teach them. Lothar here,' he gestured to the armed guard. 'He'll supervise and translate where necessary. Carry on.'

'You're leaving?'

'Listen, Wiggins, you will be a very important agent for me – perhaps my most important. But we are on the verge of war, my masters are on at me every hour, the preparations for invasion are almost complete. I'm a busy man.' He couldn't keep the pride out of his voice.

'I can't teach 'em nothing here,' Wiggins said. 'You want street? I need to show 'em the street.'

Von Bork looked at him carefully, calculating. Ever since that first conversation on the train, Wiggins had become accustomed to this gaze – and he knew exactly what Von Bork was weighing up. *Has his rhetoric worked, has Wiggins taken the shilling (or the pfennig more like)?*

Certainly, Von Bork was right about one thing – Wiggins had no burning desire to fight for Britain, or to save the Empire. All that Von Bork had said about the poor in England, about the colonies, was true at least as far as Wiggins knew. He didn't care for the government, the King, or the toffs that got rich off the working man. So why not work for Germany rather than Great Britain, why not take that coin? Why would a man of Wiggins's class – the put-upon poor – wish to fight for a country that put him in the gutter? That was Von Bork's pitch, and it made sense.

Once Wiggins had agreed – to the debrief, the training, the whole lavishly paid bagatelle – the only process that remained was this building of trust, of Von Bork's trust in him. Wiggins thought for a moment, as Von Bork surveyed him still in the dust and sunlight of the Berlin parade ground, of his old mentor, Sherlock Holmes. He remembered the V. R. pockmarked into the wall of Holmes's room in Baker Street. The detective had used a revolver to mark his respect and fealty to the old Queen, startling Mrs Hudson in the process. A patriot and royalist, Holmes would have been horrified at the thought of Wiggins here, now, in Berlin.

Wiggins was no patriot, though, and no royalist. He was too rational for that, too hard-headed. It was one of the few realms where the detective's rationalism deserted him.

Von Bork clicked his tongue, glanced at the line of eager naval officers, then back at Wiggins. 'You're right,' he said at last. 'The street it is. Lothar will collect you tomorrow morning. I trust you can plan a training exercise.'

'Mind if I go for a stroll?' Wiggins nodded at the parade ground gates. 'Seeing as you trust me an' all.'

'Your time will come.'

Sunday 19 July 1914. The British Naval review at Portsmouth, the most powerful navy the world has ever seen: 60 battleships, 4 battlecruisers, 26 armoured cruisers, destroyers, submarines, minesweepers and more. All who see it, and especially the gentlemen of Fleet Street, are awestruck. In Saint Petersburg, Tsar Nicholas reads a secret memo from his ambassador in Vienna. Austria-Hungary is drafting a set of draconian demands on Serbia, including reparations for the death of Archduke Franz Ferdinand and the right for its police to work in Belgrade unmolested.

Lothar came for Wiggins the next morning. Over the preceding few days, Wiggins had the chance to observe his host-cum-gaoler. He was a shade older than Wiggins, but fit for all that and built like a rugby football forward with short-cropped hair, greying at the temples, and pale blue, lively eyes. He refused to speak to Wiggins at all, other than to give terse orders to do with when he should eat, move, get up, go to sleep and even go to the toilet. A barrel of Bavarian laughs.

'We go,' Lothar indicated from the door.

'No need for the shooter,' Wiggins said.

Lothar shrugged and holstered the piece. 'Transport. Training is now.'

They walked out onto the parade ground. A military lorry idled by the gate, and Lothar pointed Wiggins towards the back. As he lifted himself over the tailboard, he saw the young naval officers of the day before, all lined up in their civvie bests. 'Morning all,' he said as he sat down.

Lothar followed him in and grunted his translation. '*Guten Tag!*' the officers chimed as one, as the lorry trundled into life.

Wiggins grinned. 'That's right, lads, street craft is all about improvisation.'

Lothar coughed and began haltingly to speak to the others in German. 'Nah, don't bother,' Wiggins said. 'It's a joke. Where we going?'

'Site number one,' Lothar said as he rubbed his fingers together gently. He sat squeezed between the tailboard and Wiggins on one of the benches in the lorry, massive frame squeezing down on him. Wiggins could smell the man's odour, sour meat sweat and badly dried clothes. 'Potsdamer Platz, square. For the tailing . . . trial. Now, tell them – what to do.' Lothar pointed.

Von Bork had not specified a role for Wiggins in training new agents while they were negotiating his fee. But Wiggins could hardly complain given that the money on offer was into the thousands. As the van rattled into the centre of Berlin, he outlined a training drill for the officers – translated by the huge Lothar. It was similar to the one he'd tried to teach to Brandon and Trench, but those two hadn't listened to a word he said. He wondered if these German

Hooray Heinrichs would be any better at following each other across town.

Eventually, the lorry pulled up and Lothar ordered everyone out. Lothar himself kept a light hold of Wiggins's arm as they reached the pavement. They'd parked on a wide and busy street that led into a huge open plaza with at least five roads leading off it in different directions. Before he could complain, Wiggins caught sight of Von Bork.

'*Guten Tag*,' Von Bork said, striding towards them. He tossed a half-smoked cigarette into the gutter. 'I have one minute,' he said to Wiggins, and then addressed the officers in swift, barked German.

He finished, nodded, then addressed Wiggins. 'You've made the right choice, you know, joining us. I shall be most interested to see the outcome of this little jaunt.' Then, quite deliberately, he looked at Lothar without saying another word.

Lothar, massive form cramping Wiggins still, slipped a cuff around Wiggins's left wrist and then fixed the other one to his own.

'Eh? What?' Wiggins asked. 'I thought . . .?'

'Oh, I do trust you, Wiggins. I would trust any working man to do as I asked for two thousands pounds. But you must stay with Lothar today.' Von Bork stepped in closer, so that only the two of them could hear. 'You're a foreign national on the streets, soon to be an enemy national. It's not safe for you. And it's not safe for me, either, if you were discovered. Stay close to Lothar, or you might be killed.' As if to emphasise the point, Wiggins noted Von Bork's accent had changed – he sounded more German, and even though he spoke in English, there was no trace of the country squire now.

Von Bork stepped back and gestured to the trainees. '*Auf Wiedersehen.*' He waved his hand in an expansive gesture, then strode off to a waiting motorcar.

Wiggins felt the cuff on his wrist, glanced up at Lothar. 'Alright then, son,' he said, 'let's tell 'em how it's done.'

Potsdamer Platz opened out in front of them, a wide expanse of criss-crossed tramlines, horse and motor traffic, telegraph wires, and hundreds and hundreds of people rushing to and fro amid the newsstands and hawkers and long-booted policemen. It was like a cross between Piccadilly Circus and Trafalgar Square, with the grand and the squalid, the posh and the poor, jostling together in one high velocity mass. Wiggins saw a street band starting to tune up on a far corner.

The trainees were divided into groups, followers and the followed, and Wiggins told them to scatter. 'Come on, Lothar,' he said when he'd finished. 'Let's get in the thick of it.'

As the officers went into the crowd, Wiggins led Lothar towards the band. He stumbled as they stepped over the kerb and crashed into a very small woman in a blue satin dress. 'Sorry, sorry,' he said as he helped her to her feet. With his one free (uncuffed) hand, he picked up her hat, a dazzling affair with peacock feathers and pins and a tasselled veil.

Lothar muttered a gruff apology to the woman and pulled Wiggins away. 'Street craft?' he glared. 'Huh!'

They found a spot on the kerbside by the band. Wiggins pointed out the different pairs of 'followed' to Lothar. 'There,' he said. But by this time, Lothar's attention had begun to wander.

The band was magnificent. It was set up outside a large cafe, but rather than the usual decorous pitter-pattering of a tea dance ensemble, this lot jumped. A five-piece, arrayed around a small piano, it sounded to Wiggins more like the music he heard in Manhattan two years earlier, or like the fast dance sets of the band at the Moulin Rouge. He could feel the rhythm pulsing through Lothar. His foot tapped the beat. His fingers minutely imitated the actions of the musician on the double bass. He was entranced. As Wiggins knew he would be.

As the music spiralled to a crescendo, Wiggins calmy inserted the hatpin he'd stolen from the small lady into the handcuff lock. In a second his hand was free and he stepped off the pavement into the road.

'Hey!' Lothar cried out, just as Wiggins caught hold of the tram rattling past. The force almost ripped his shoulder off, but he clung on and got his foot on the plate.

The tram hurtled around the corner. As it did so, Wiggins glanced back to see Lothar staring after him, roaring.

Lothar's chief mistake was to cuff his left hand. Always put the cuff on the hostage's strongest hand – which likewise means it's probably on your weakest. As it was, Wiggins had his right hand free to first steal the hatpin and second to pick the lock. Lothar's second, perhaps unavoidable, mistake was to so plainly advertise his obsessions. Wiggins deduced he was an avid player of stringed instruments from the indentations in his fingers. Every time they heard the bugles or stray music in the barracks, Wiggins also noted the flickering in Lothar's eyes, the alertness at the sound of anything melodic. Hence his two moves on Potsdamer Platz – first to lift the hatpin, and second to stand by the band.

The bungles of Lothar, however, were nothing compared to Von Bork's missteps. Wiggins jumped off the tram as it slowed to its next stop and melted into the crowd. This wasn't a training drill – this escape was for real.

He would never work for Von Bork, he would never make a deal. Not because of King and country, not because of Kell, not even because he wanted to stride down Piccadilly a free man. Von Bork had been right about that. He didn't owe England anything, and owed the King even less. To him the German Empire was no worse than the British one, and the pay was certainly much better. Von Bork trusted him to follow his self-interest, and the reasoning was sound. Sound and wrong.

He would never make a deal with Von Bork because Von Bork had killed Holmes. It was this simple fact that trumped everything, would trump everything for ever. Wiggins did not believe in country, did not believe in royalty but he did believe in Sherlock Holmes. He felt it in his bones. He felt it in every inch of his frame whenever Von Bork spoke, he felt it in his hot cheeks at the very thought of that knife plunging into the great detective. He had come to the continent to kill Von Bork, and kill him he would.

Monday 20 July 1914. A small article appears in a
German newspaper, placed there by official sources,
suggesting that maybe Austria-Hungary are best
left to have a 'little war' with Serbia, without
the need for the Great Powers to intervene.

Hector Charles Bywater, naval correspondent of the *New York Herald*, finished his last *kaffee* of the evening at his local cafe and crossed the Kreuzberg street to his apartment block. He felt bloated from the large dinner he'd had in town, carousing with a couple of officers from the

German navy, and he greeted the dozing caretaker with a muted *Gute Nacht*. 'Any visitors?' he joked.

'*Nein*,' the old man replied without smiling. Bywater never had any visitors.

He walked up the stairs to the third floor, electric lights still blazing in the halls – as they seemed to everywhere in Berlin – and casually checked the 'tell' in his front door. A small shard of packing-case wood, jammed into the crack of the door a foot or so above the ground. It would fall were anyone to open his door without him being there. No one had.

Once in his own small hallway he hung up his hat and coat, took off his shoes, and pattered into the sitting room at the front of the apartment, where he turned to switch on the light.

'Never take your shoes off until you're sure you don't have to run,' a voice said from the armchair. 'It makes you vulnerable.'

Bywater gasped. 'You!' he cried.

'Me,' said Wiggins.

16

Tuesday 21 July 1914. In London, a conference
begins in Buckingham Palace about the fate of
the northern counties of Ireland, now that the
Home Rule Bill is progressing through Parliament. In Vienna, officials think it unlikely that
Russia will mobilise its army in support of Serbia.
They finalise the details of their ultimatum.

'I see you've found the brandy, old sport,' Bywater said
after he'd recovered from the shock of seeing Wiggins. 'And
my stash of international newspapers.' He gestured at the
newspapers strewn around Wiggins's chair. 'I'll let you into
a secret – the best source of stories for a journalist is other
newspapers.' He poured himself a glass, and took a seat on
the sofa opposite. 'How long has it been, four years?'

Wiggins eyed the American. He'd aged a lot in the time.
His hair was thinning and the deep creases in his forehead
were more noticeable, as was the extra inch on his waistline.
'Like yesterday,' Wiggins replied.

The two had met in Bremen, the year Wiggins and Kell
(and Constance) tried to save the arrested British agents
Brandon and Trench. Bywater worked part time for Mansfield Cumming, reporting back on German naval matters.
As far as Wiggins was concerned, Bywater – or H2O as
Cumming had codenamed him – was the one reliable agent
working in Europe for British intelligence. Long-limbed,

elegant and obviously American, he spoke German like a native, had street smarts in spades and was loyal to the old country by virtue of his parents. America was staunchly neutral in European affairs and so – presumably – Bywater could stay in Berlin unperturbed.

'Did C send you?' Bywater asked, still rattled. 'I mean, old sport, if you don't mind me putting it like this – what the hell are you doing here?'

'I've been looking for someone,' Wiggins said levelly. 'Von Bork he goes by, one of their top spies. *The* top spy. He's got something we want.' Bywater was a cool hand, for sure, but Wiggins thought it best not to mention why he wanted Von Bork so badly – what his real mission was. Instead, he decided to concentrate on the book. 'A list,' he went on. 'Of all the German agents in England. It's my job to get it back.'

'Are you mad? I hear nothing from C for weeks and then you turn up on a suicide mission. Do you have any idea what's happening in Berlin? In Germany?'

'You've heard nothing for weeks?' Wiggins said sharply. 'How do you send your information?'

'Via a cut-out in Brussels.'

'Stop sending anything, immediately. It's probably blown.'

Bywater grimaced, as if he knew the truth of this but didn't want to acknowledge it. He took out a cigarette, went to offer one to Wiggins and then said, 'You don't, do you? Maybe it's time to start.' He lit the smoke and sat for a while admiring the rings he sent towards the ceiling. 'It's reassuring, in a way. I've been trying to tell London of the danger here, but I see nothing to show they've taken any notice.' He gestured to the newspapers strewn around

Wiggins's chair. 'But it's good at least you're here – you can go back, you can tell them.'

'I've got a job to do,' Wiggins persisted.

'What, dying? You're a dead man if you stay in Berlin anyhow, that's for sure. You've got to get out in the morning, as fast as possible.'

Despite the offhand arrogance, Wiggins liked him. He always liked smart people, and he liked toffs who offered him a cigarette, rather waiting for him to light theirs. He'd been hanging around his 'betters' for over twenty years, and most of them never even saw you – not in the way Bywater had just done, not as an equal. Maybe it was an American thing, he thought, remembering New York.

He took another sip of his brandy. 'You're sure it's war?'

Bywater stared at him. 'You betcha. The only question is when, and who.'

'Go on then, Yankee, show me how clever you are.'

'Alright, Agent W,' he said with a grin.

'I'm all ears – H2O.'

'Germany *will* go to war. And they'll almost go to war before anyone realises it; and when they do realise it, there'll be nothing anyone can do about it – even the Germans themselves. You want the full schoolboy explanation. Scratch that, you're gonna get it – you'll need to explain to London, so it better be simple.'

'Imagine I'm Mansfield Cumming.'

'Do I have to?' Bywater groaned. He put down his drink and stood up. 'Russia and France are allies, right? So if Germany were to fight one of them, they'd have to fight both – you follow? But picture the map – Germany is squeezed between the two of them, give or take a minor territory here or there. They're in a natural pincer.'

'Between the Rooskies and a hard place.'

'Exactly. Now, if we assume Germany is to go to war with one, it has to assume it will go to war with the other as well. It's an almost impossible task. Russia is enormous, France is a developed military power. Therefore, so the old German chief of staff von Schlieffen argued, the only way Germany can win is by fighting them one at time. To do that, they must beat France first, then turn everything on Russia. They don't want war on two fronts.'

'I get you – knock out France lightning style, then turn east. But why do they have to go to war at all?'

'Come on, old sport, you're smarter than that.'

'Teach me.'

'They have to go to war with someone, right? They've been building up their navy for years, they're after a bigger piece of Empire pie – just like the British, by the way, and the French, but the Germans are starting from further back – and the Kaiser? The Kaiser's going a little crazy – he's been called chicken once before and he's damned if anyone will call him chicken again.'

'So they're up for fighting someone, and if Russia's involved, that means they'll have a pop at France an' all?'

'And quickly, remember – they'll have to invade France before they invade Russia, and they'll probably have to do it by surprise too.'

'And why is this going to happen *now*?'

'It's already happening!' Bywater cried, slapping his hands together. 'Serbia won't accept Austria-Hungary's demands, Austria will declare against Serbia, Russia will come in on Serbia's side, and Germany will back Austria – they've *already* promised to do that, so I'm told. And that's that. The only thing at stake – the last chance – is whether Great Britain comes in or not. Which is why you've got to get out of Berlin, *yesterday*, and tell London, *yesterday*, to read my goddamn reports! They could be facing a German superpower in a couple of weeks, they could be facing ruin and you've got to stop it.'

Wiggins bit his lip, more in disappointment than annoyance. Bywater's case made complete sense – it even chimed with what Kell was saying when he was back in London. Judging by the preparations Von Bork had clearly made when leaving Paris, Bywater's analysis was correct. The disappointment was purely a personal one. He was disappointed in Bywater, a man he respected – for Bywater's chief concern was the possibility that Great Britain might be severely disadvantaged by the advent of war. That it might lose its position in the world. His first thought hadn't been for all the poor fuckers likely to die in European ditches for nothing; it wasn't war he was trying to prevent, merely a bad one for Britain.

Britain hadn't had a real war since the Boers, and all its children wanted blood once more. It wasn't just the Germans. Wiggins knew this from the streets of London. He knew it from the papers, from having his nose to the wind: the press, the toffs, the government, were ready for a war back home as well. They thought it would be with the Irish, or the workers, or the women – they were ready for a fight, just not this fight.

Then Wiggins remembered why he was in Berlin himself. On a mission of bloodletting, of personal violence. Was he no better than these warmongers? Was that the only language he understood, like those raging pressmen? And what of this mission, if war broke out? He'd never get to Von Bork then. Should he give up on his chance of justice, to save a country he didn't believe in?

He knocked back the last of his brandy and said, 'If London doesn't believe you, they won't believe me.'

'Then you've got to take proof.'

'Constance, I beg you – please not now.' Kell stood in the middle of the vast Persian carpet that filled his Hampstead drawing room, pleading with his wife.

She pulled her gloves on. 'Don't worry, Vernon, I shall not get arrested again. Though you must allow me to support those women who are – it's barbaric, what is going on. We're only going to Bow Street, to cheer Annie Bell.'

'The church bomber?' Kell asked.

'Catherine H an' all,' Jax said. Kell looked at the young woman. Ever since they'd got back from Holloway, Constance had taken the girl under her wing. A lower-class friend of Wiggins, all mouth and bones, she never left a word unsaid. She was now ensconced in one of the spare rooms, acting as Constance's 'assistant'.

'Thank you, er, Jax – I'm not sure your contribution is entirely welcome just now.'

'That's the point, ain't it! The contribution of women is never welcome, 'cept when we're doing something you don't want to do, like cooking and cleaning and having babies.' She pushed her hand out in a theatrical gesture.

'Listen to me, a war is coming – a big war – and . . .'

'You mean in Ireland?' Constance countered. 'Surely that is more of a local difficulty.'

'Believe me. No one else does, but you must,' Kell said quietly. 'It'll be a big war and the suffragettes will have to stop.'

'Never!' cried Jax.

'They will. Remember the Boer War? It will be that a hundredfold. The patriotism, the flags in the street – no one, not even the most reasonable of people, will have time for anything else but war and a war effort. It will hurt your cause if you do not desist.'

Constance stared at him evenly. 'I believe you,' she said. 'But until that time . . .'

At that moment, the doorbell rang. While Jax rooted around in the sofa for her gloves, the maid came in. 'Sir,' she said to Kell. 'It's a Doctor Watson, most urgent he said.'

Kell groaned. 'Will that old fool never leave me alone?'

'Vernon! Is that any way to talk about *the* Doctor Watson?' Constance said.

Kell reddened. 'Send him in.'

'Got 'em!' Jax cried in triumph, holding up a pair of Constance's old gloves.

'Doctor,' Kell said, as Watson appeared in the doorway. 'Please come in.'

'Thank you, Captain Kell, good morning.'

'I'm surprised you've come here, perhaps the office would be a better place. You see—'

'It's not—' Watson tried to interrupt but Kell carried on.

'We really are very busy at the Bureau and my time is short.'

'Captain.' Watson finally got him to stop. 'It's not you I've come to see.'

'I . . .' Kell stepped back, astonished.

Watson shifted around and pointed at Jax. 'It's her.'

'Berlin's hot, and getting hotter by the day.'

Wiggins watched young boaters mess about on the small lake. Flies flitted lazily to and fro, interested in the rim of his beer glass. He felt the sweat on his neck, then pressed the half-empty but still cool glass to his forehead.

Wind fluttered in the trees above him as he sat at the Café am Neuen See, an idyllic spot in the Tiergarten, and waited. Bywater told him that Berlin was hot and he wasn't wrong.

The city was sweltering, but that's not what he meant. On the way over from Bywater's apartment, he must have seen more uniforms than plain clothes. Soldiers, police-men, sailors – even a troop of schoolchildren in semi-military get-up. 'Speak to no one,' Bywater warned him. 'Say nothing. You're a danger to me and to yourself here. I'll be at the cafe by lunch. And remember, the cops can ask for your papers here – and if you don't have them . . .'

It was now gone one, and still Wiggins waited. The tables around him were full of jolly Germans, clinking glasses, eating huge plates of food and laughing in the shade of the linden trees. Wiggins eyed his beer and considered a chaser when, across the terrace, he finally saw Bywater appear with the mark.

Bruno, Bywater called him, a desk-bound Navy man ensconced in a huge new office complex on the edge of the Tiergarten, the Bendlerblock. Bywater pulled his chair out for him, and the two men fell into conversation over the menu. Bruno was Bywater's best contact in the German Admiralty, and he was going to try everything to get a paper proof out of him. Wiggins watched and waited.

'It's no use,' Bywater whispered to Wiggins, as the two men pissed together at the cafe urinals. 'He admits he's had the order to prepare for mobilisation, but he refuses to give it to me.'

Wiggins, who'd followed Bywater into the toilet at the signal, glanced around to the empty stall. 'Get him to show you the order. Say you need it for your editor.'

'But what good will that do with London?'

'Just get him to meet you somewhere later, and all he has to do is show you the written order. I'll do the rest.'

'What if he won't?'

'Tell him you know all about the brothel. And you know his wife.'

'But I don't.'

'Yeah you do.'

Later, after Bruno had gone back to his office, Bywater and Wiggins met on a bench in the Tiergarten, the Bendler-block in view across the road. They used the old dodge; arriving at the bench separately. Wiggins pretended to read a paper while Bywater smoked. 'He went for it, about the brothel I mean. How did you know?' he said.

Wiggins turned a page of the paper. 'Where're you meeting?'

'Beer house, two streets that way, can't miss it.'

'Is it busy?'

'Will be by six, heaving, old sport. What are you going to do?'

'Just get him there, with the document. And leave the rest to me.' Wiggins tossed the paper to one side and walked away from the bench without another word.

Wiggins spent the rest of the afternoon doing his best not to be noticed, which meant travelling on the city's transport system. You had to move with purpose in a city like Berlin otherwise you stood out. He went from tram to bus and back again, and paced quickly through working men's streets, through the factory district – lit up by electricity even in the day – down linden-lined avenues, and among the crowds at the gigantic Wertheim department store, always moving too quickly to be stopped. And Bywater was right – it was a city ready for war, he could feel it in his bones.

The English were always up for a scrap, but not like this, he realised. It was the uniforms, the deference to the uniforms, even something about the architecture that screamed martial intent. The monuments, the simmering excitement, and excess of national flags, it was bubbling over almost and that energy, that lust, had to go somewhere.

As his tram rattled past the Reichstag and the other official-looking buildings, flags drooping in the windless heat, Wiggins wondered about Von Bork – was he in there? He had no way of knowing where he was – and wasn't Bywater right? Didn't he owe it to back home to do everything he could to alert Kell and the rest? Not to save the Empire embarrassment but possibly to stop a bastard war. He wondered on, about Bywater's failing communication lines back to London, about that cut-out in Brussels, about his own unanswered questions lying in that city and, most of all, he wondered about his own blood lust. He could feel his anger simmering still as he looked out at the wealthy, pompous, overbearing Berlin architecture; the sourness at the root of all these violent urges, those that understood violence anyway; and the sourness that must lie in his own heart, to want to follow a man halfway across a continent simply to end that man's life.

He approached the beer house, the one Bywater had pointed out, at just gone half past five. A young lad was playing with a hoop and stick in the street, probably waiting for his mother working in one of the buildings. They were close to the Tiergarten, and it was a wealthy business and embassy district, while the boy looked poor. A couple of young men walked past, kicked the hoop into the gutter and laughed. The boy retrieved it without a word and carried on his game.

Wiggins went into the boozer and placed himself at the bar. He spotted Bywater off to his left. The American had chosen his table well, in a secluded corner by a screen but still visible enough that Wiggins could see him. The place was filling up, with workers and with a 'first drink after work' energy. Smoke bloomed. Glasses clinked. Laughter barked out here and there, loud and jaunty. It was an office worker's boozer, not a labouring man's hangout, but that didn't stop it getting more and more boisterous. Bywater read a German newspaper at his table, while Wiggins pretended to fix his watch.

Bruno arrived late, pink-faced and sweating. He hurried into the bar, dabbing his head with a handkerchief and breathing hard. He spotted Bywater and pulled up a chair. Bywater signalled for a drink. Wiggins observed all this from his spot on a high stool. He took another huge gulp of beer himself, but this time he took care to spill some down his chin and shirt.

Bywater began the process of getting his mark drunk. Bruno was nervous and obviously reticent, but Bywater pulled him over to his seat – on a bench with their backs to the wall – and gave him another draught of a clear spirit. The drink loosened Bruno and, eventually, he pulled a document from his inside breast pocket. He opened it, but shielded the document with his coat so Bywater had to peer over him, his head held close.

Bruno swiftly replaced the document. As he did so, Bywater locked eyes with Wiggins and moved his head minutely. It was on.

Wiggins waited until Bruno readied himself to go. Wiggins stood up too, swayed and missed his step slightly.

No one cared. The bar was full of men who'd had one too many. Bruno got to his feet, rounded his table and headed to the door. Wiggins stumbled towards him, travelling in the other direction to the toilets (Bywater and Wiggins had choreographed it exactly between them, so that Bruno must walk past Wiggins to exit).

As they passed each other, Wiggins swayed slightly and squeezed next to the naval man. It was all he needed. He'd been dipping since he was a nipper, and Bruno was so distracted that he could have taken his underpants and he wouldn't have noticed. Instead, he filched the document and his wallet for good measure. Bruno hurried out of the bar, oblivious.

Wiggins stumbled some more and, like a good drunk, pulled up the spare chair at Bywater's table. He put his hand up in faked apology, but did not speak. Instead, he slipped the document into his pocket, stripped the marks from the wallet, then tossed it underneath Bywater's chair. He nodded almost imperceptibly at the American and stood up abruptly, the spies' goodbye. Wiggins had been drunk so many times, seen it so many more in others, that playing the role was hardly a performance at all. No one in the bar gave him a second glance.

Out on the street, he headed back towards the Tiergarten. He reckoned he had at least fifteen minutes before Bruno would return to the bar, twenty at the outside. Once he got back to his office and tried to replace the order, only to find it – and his wallet – gone, he would retrace his steps immediately.

The small boy with the hoop and stick was still there, Wiggins noticed, but this time a larger group of bigger kids were hassling him. A portly devil in tight shorts picked up the hoop and began to bend it almost to cracking point.

Wiggins snatched it off him and gestured angrily at the gang of bullies. They ran off, shouting, and he returned the hoop without a word. He fumbled in his pocket for a coin and gave it to the boy, who still said nothing.

A hubbub broke out behind him and Wiggins turned to see the gang of bullies, the portly devil at their head, leading a huge uniformed policeman towards him. They pointed at Wiggins and the policeman marched up.

He barked at him, in words Wiggins did not understand though he got the gist. He shrugged.

'*Wer bist du? Wer bist du?*' the policeman demanded. And then, he held out his hand. '*Papiere. PAPIERE!*'

Wiggins hesitated, then pulled out a banknote. He didn't like bribery as a rule – too risky, except with children who at least had a sense of honour when it came to money – but in that instance, it would be the easier way out.

The policeman stared down at the note, then back up at Wiggins. His face reddened, his neck quivered and he roared out in anger.

Wiggins ran. The copper's whistle screeched. He knew if he got to the park, he could disappear. More shouts and whistles now. He glanced back, expecting to find the policeman in hot pursuit. But the policeman was on the ground, his legs tangled in the small boy's hoop. Good lad, Wiggins thought as he hared around the corner and across the road into the safety of the trees and bushes of the Tiergarten.

Wednesday 22 July 1914. Serbia awaits word from Austria-Hungary. Representatives from all over Ireland meet in Buckingham Palace to search for a way out of the crisis over home rule, and the special case of Ulster. No one mentions Serbia.

Whistling. A high-pitched, childlike whistle. Wiggins knew that tune, it was one of Marie Lloyd's favourites – 'The Boy I Love is Up in the Gallery'. He'd heard her sing it often, when he himself stood in that gallery as a boy and man as she warbled up to the gods, and every man and boy in that gallery gazed down wishing the song was for them.

A young man shuffled past him on the concourse of Stuttgart station, shambling almost, and clearly – painfully clearly – an Englishman. The whistling gave it away as much as anything, a music hall staple to boot. Wiggins fell into step just behind him. 'You English,' he hissed.

The young man turned, startled, wide-eyed fear written across his face. The whistling wasn't jaunty, it was nerves. 'Yes, I am rather.'

'Shush!' Wiggins hushed him. 'Quiet like, let's keep walking.'

'Foley,' he said. 'I'm a student. I'm trying to get home.'

'Me an' all.' They strode across the station concourse together, finding a path through the commuters.

Wiggins had made it halfway home, which was why he found himself in Stuttgart. Although the set-to with the policeman in Berlin had been unexpected, the route out of the city had gone much as he and Bywater planned.

The best and fastest way across Germany to the border was on the train, and Bywater told him to jump one of the goods trains leaving south in the night. He was unable to tell exactly where they were going beyond either Hanover or Dortmund – if they went west – or south to Munich. Either way, Bywater said, he would find it difficult to get over the border without proper documents. Bywater did not have to detail what would happen to Wiggins were the police to find Bruno's navy order.

One of the benefits of Von Bork's 'holiday camp' – the nine days Wiggins had spent in the barracks – was that he'd recovered somewhat from the battering he'd taken in Paris. His head no longer hurt, his shoulders – so wrenched on DuPont's airplane – felt loose and able once more.

He hid among the dormant rolling stock outside Berlin central station until darkness fell, and waited for the sound of the drivers taking up their positions. When a pair of chatterbox drivers walked past, Wiggins found it surprisingly easy to follow them to their train, and then squeeze into one of the carriages at the back. He even managed to get some sleep.

With the dawn light breaking behind the train, he knew he was going in the right direction. He slipped off as it approached a goods yard – Stuttgart he later found out – and subsequently decided that, in order to get any closer to the border, he'd need to risk taking a local passenger train. It was too hard to work out where the goods trains connected to on his own, and he was running out of time.

Which was why he found himself in Stuttgart station, walking behind an English student who liked to whistle nostalgic music hall laments.

'Do you speak German?' Wiggins asked him as they pretended to look at the menu of the station cafe.

'Oh yes, really quite well. I've been studying here. But the atmosphere is not good now, not good at all,' Foley replied.

'I'll say,' Wiggins whispered. 'How are you getting out? The border might be a bit hot.'

'You think, ah – um, I don't really – I was in the middle of my third semester. This has really played havoc with my thesis.'

Wiggins gripped him gently by the elbow, and they began walking again. 'Do you know the south? The border with Switzerland?'

'Yes, well, I've been on walking holidays around about there in the past.'

'Do it. Get a train down there, walk over the border – you'll be golden. The Swiss border will be the least protected. Just don't tell anyone where you come from.'

'Somerset?' Foley said, alarmed.

'England,' Wiggins hissed. He pressed his eyes shut for a moment. 'Go to the ticket office over there – here, take the money – buy yourself a ticket on the first train south. First class. Don't whistle. Don't fold your arms. Don't put your hands in your pockets. Think like you're on parade the whole time.'

'Like in the scouts?'

'Sort of. Speak only German. Once you get to Switzerland, get back to England as soon as – cos an army'll be coming after any moment.'

'Gosh.'

'Gosh indeed. Now. Buy another ticket while you're at it – third class, to Aachen. If the clerk gives you the eye, say you're going south but you're sending your manservant back to see his dying ma. Got it?'

'Got it.'

'Once you're done, I'll meet you in the pisser over there,' he gestured at the gents.

'Ah, yes I see.'

And to be fair to the lad, he did see. Fifteen minutes later, he handed Wiggins his ticket to Aachen, the platform number and a railway timetable. They shared the toilet stall, while Wiggins watched out for anyone else who might enter.

'You ain't bad at this malarkey, are you?' Wiggins muttered in approval.

'Malarkey?'

'You're smart enough to guess who I work for. I reckon they'd give you a job one day. I know I would.'

'I think I see.'

'I'll put in a word.'

Foley nodded then refocussed. 'The trains are pretty good,' he whispered. 'You have a watch, I see, so you'll know where you are at all times. I assume you will try to cross on foot into Belgium or Holland?'

'That's the plan.'

Thursday 23 July 1914. An ultimatum. At 6 p.m. the Austro-Hungarian government delivers a series of demands on Serbia, couched in the language of reason and persuasion, but intended to provoke war. Compliance with the demands would be impossible for any sovereign nation. The Serbian government is given forty-eight hours to respond, otherwise Austria will declare war. Earlier that day Grey has asked if Russia and Germany, together with Great Britain, will convene a conference to mediate between the two sides. Russian Foreign Minister Sergey Sazonov agrees. The Kaiser rejects the offer as 'condescending'.

Wiggins did indeed cross on foot into Belgium. He arrived at Aachen, took a bus, posed as a railwayman and, ultimately, went for a walk in the woods. Beautiful, dark green undulating woodland. He skulked his way across when actually there proved no need. There was no fence. No border patrols tried to stop him, no one checked his papers. It was as easy as going from England to Wales.

Which meant an army would have no trouble either, Wiggins thought sourly as he approached a town called Kelmis in the golden hours before sunset. He thought again of that document in his pocket, an order of impending mobilisation, and remembered what Bywater said: mobilisation meant war. And the Schlieffen Plan meant coming through Belgium. This town would be awash with German soldiers in days, if those fears were founded.

He vowed again to get back as soon as he could, to carry out any small act to stop a war, to try to persuade Kell and Churchill and whoever else to act, to threaten, to gesture, to do whatever it took to avert catastrophe. But he would not give up on his own, personal fight. For he'd worked out how to get Von Bork – all he needed was a little more time; more time and a helping hand from a traitor.

17

Friday 24 July 1914. News reaches the British government of the Austria-Hungary ultimatum. Grey is
outraged. Prime Minister Asquith writes to his
young, unmarried confidante Venetia Stanley.
'Serbia cannot possibly comply. This means almost
inevitably that Russia will come on the scene to
defend Serbia and it will be difficult for Germany
and France not to lend a hand on one side or the
other. We're in distance of a real Armageddon.
Happily there is no reason to think we shall be
anything more than spectators but it is a blood-
curdling prospect.'

Wiggins went through the front door of the beautiful Brussels townhouse this time. He strode into the hallway just as
Paul, Martha's ineffectual heavy, came towards him. Wiggins held up his hand and nodded, but did not break stride.
Boy stood at the foot of the stairs, open-mouthed. Wiggins
barely gave him a glance as he took the steps two at a time.

The brothel was in full swing. He could hear the phoney
laughs and moans of the girls, the grunts and cries of
(hollow) triumph from the men, as well as a lively piano
number. News of impending doom had not reached the
clientele. Or maybe it had, and it just made their *amour-
propre* all the harder to deny. He did not stop at the second
landing or the third.

Finally, he reached Martha's secluded hideaway on the top floor and flung open the door. '*Mon dieu!*' a small, round man cried, startled. He sat at the desk, his eye pinned to one of the peepholes.

Wiggins barely glanced at him as he slumped onto the chaise longue in exhaustion. The small, round man gaped at him, but could utter no words. He wore a ridiculously ornate moustache, which he now touched and fiddled with nervously. 'Ummm . . .' He tried to speak but Wiggins glared at him, then leaned back and shut his eyes.

Martha came hurrying in. 'What the hell are you doing here?'

'Who's the peeper?' Wiggins asked.

'I . . . I am no peeper,' the man said indignantly, in heavily accented English. 'I am the Chief of Police. I am Monsieur Her—'

'Hop it,' Wiggins interrupted. Then to Martha: 'We need to talk.'

'Madame, this is, this is . . .'

'A moment please, monsieur.' She said something else in French, all honey and milk. After a moment, he got up and she shuffled the short, fat policeman out of the door. She closed it carefully, composed herself and then said, 'Well done there. First you bring down the wrath of Block on me and now the Chief of Police. What are you doing, running for office?'

Wiggins swung around to a sitting position opposite her. 'Why are you still here? There's going to be an invasion.'

'You think Germans don't fuck?' she said simply, and sat down on her office chair.

Wiggins shook his head. It was a reply that confirmed his suspicions. Martha misinterpreted his reaction, and went on annoyed. 'You think you've come to save me, to save us? Swinging your big dick around, like any fucking man. Without men there'd be no bloody wars.'

'No syphilis either,' he muttered.

'So no, Mr Wiggins, you are not my saviour. If anything it's me saving your bloody skin. First Block and now the chief there – he's probably getting a couple of cops right now to pick you up, and I'll have to protect you again.'

'Oh, so you protected me from Block, did you?'

'I told you he was the most dangerous criminal in Brussels. If it wasn't for me, you wouldn't have got out of the city alive.'

'Then why did one of his men try to kill me on the train to Paris, eh? Is that what you call protection?'

She opened her mouth to object but then thought better of it. 'I bought you enough time to get out.'

'By telling him I was with Margaretha?'

'Like I said, he had the power to close me down completely. He has the power to kill me too for that matter. I did what I could for you. In the circumstances.'

Wiggins chewed on that for a moment. 'Have you seen her by the way?'

'Ah . . .' Martha leaned back in her chair and shook her head slightly. 'I knew you'd fall a little bit in love with her. Every man does, she's Mata Hari.'

'I worry about her, she's getting in pretty deep.'

Martha shook her head and smiled.

'It ain't like that.'

The telephone jangled. She picked it up wearily. '*Oui? Merde!*' She turned to Wiggins. 'I told you, that's the chief coming up the stairs to arrest you. Looks like *I* need to save *you*. Again.'

Wiggins got up from the chaise and locked the door. 'No sauce now, Martha, I need you to do something for me.'

'Don't worry, we'll talk him round, I'll—'

'Nah, not him. I need you to send a message to Berlin. A telegram. To Von Bork.'

'Who?'

'Don't give me that,' he rasped. He drew himself up to his full height and suddenly felt large and dangerous, he could see it in her eyes.

'I . . . really . . . don't . . .' The lie died on her lips. She couldn't pretend to keep it up. It was one thing to sell him out to Block the local criminal – he'd half expected that. He'd cocked up the situation, she probably didn't have any choice, those are the risks you take in the business. But Von Bork.

'He killed . . . he killed . . .' Wiggins hesitated. 'He's a killer, and I know you're working for him.'

'How?' She barely whispered it.

They could hear the protests from below as the police approached. 'You ain't bothered about the Germans invading for one thing,' he said.

'I told you, they like to fuck as much as the next army.'

'Nah, you're in with them. Have to be, to keep going. To be so cool about it anyhows. But that's not how I knew, that just confirmed it.'

'So?'

'Don't worry, you didn't make many mistakes. It was him, Von Bork. He told me he had another lever to get me to do what he wanted. You're that lever.'

'I never wanted you to come to any harm.'

'You're also Cumming's Brussels cut-out. Agent in Berlin tells me nothing's getting through. That you an' all? Yeah, thought so. You put Boy off the scent at the post office too, didn't you? It had to be you.'

'The British are so much better than the Germans, are they? Is that what you're saying, that your money's so much better than his?' She jutted her chin out. Now she was rumbled, she'd obviously decided to stick it out unashamed.

'Did you know DuPont was one of Von Bork's?' he asked suddenly.

She opened her eyes wide at that. 'No . . . I . . . He didn't tell me anything.'

'Makes sense. You wouldn't have given me DuPont otherwise.'

'I just wanted you out of town. You're a danger to me, and I might add, to yourself.'

'Good of you, yeah, thanks for your concern. I had two men following on that bloody train. I thought they was after Margaretha but no, they were following *me* – thanks to your oh so considerate concern. Block's man tried to kill him.'

She looked questioningly at that.

'Oh, he's dead. And Von Bork must have had someone on me too. You did tell him about me, didn't you?'

'Like I said, it's not as if one side's any better than the other.'

A banging started on the door. Wiggins looked down at her, waiting.

'What, you want me to apologise?' she said. 'Come on – anyway, look at you, you're fine. Now I'm really gonna have to open that door.'

'You were good at it,' he said at last.

'Good at what?'

'Lying. But I guess that's the training.'

It was as if he'd slapped her across the face. She reddened, took a breath and stood up. 'Get the fuck out of my house. Is that honest enough for you?'

'One thing,' Wiggins said. 'And I'll keep things sweet with Cumming. I'll never bother you again.'

'Is that so? Now, open the door.'

'Martha. You nearly got me killed, you've been doing the dirty on the British Secret Service, your business is in a city that's about to explode. You do this one thing, and two of those problems disappear.'

'You, and Cumming.'

'Exactly.'

The banging continued, now accompanied by the rather camp voice of the Chief of Police. 'Madame, madame!'

'What about him?' Martha pointed at the door behind which the chief cried plaintively.

'I know exactly what he wants,' Wiggins said. 'I'll deal with him. But first. Von Bork. Send him an urgent message.' He pressed on quietly. 'And say this.'

```
Saturday 25 July. Huge peace protests in Berlin
appear to fall on deaf ears. By lunchtime the
Serbian government gets confirmation that Russia
will support it. It begins to mobilise, as do sections
of the Russian army. The Serbian ministers scram-
ble to get a response to the ultimatum typed up by
6 p.m. but the machine does not work. At 5.45 p.m.
they deliver their handwritten reply - they will
comply with some of Austria-Hungary's demands, but
not all.
```

The gulls swept over Dover, like flakes of fog detaching out to sea, then swirled back over the hidden town. Wiggins stood at the rail and watched the birds over the wet port as his ship steamed into harbour. The horns blew loud and he turned to go back inside, ready for the arrival. He didn't have much time, and he had one shot at each part of his plan.

Martha's voyeur, the now ex-Chief of the Brussels Police, waited for him. The policeman had wanted to get out of Belgium as soon as possible. He was smart, he knew the Germans were coming – unlike the rest of the country it seemed. He wanted to beat any refugee crisis and – credit to him – he'd realised that Wiggins could help get him into England.

'I know some things,' he said to Wiggins as they left Brussels. 'Madame Martha's operation is, how you say, a *front* for foreign intelligence. This I did not mind. Madame Martha is an exceptional woman.' He fingered his moustache gently. 'And when I see you come into her office, with your English ways and your English confidence, I know that she is in the pay of British intelligence. So, I use my little grey cells, and deduce that you are the man to get me to England.'

They walked down the gangplank together, amongst a scrum of returning passengers. A rowing squad, towering over them, all hurrahs and dropped boaters, two or three families hurrying to Terra Firma, and a steady stream of what looked like commercial travellers, cardboard suitcases and all. Wiggins took the chief's arm and steered him along the quay to the customs house.

Having the portly policeman had been useful in getting them out of Brussels and onto the ferry, and now Wiggins returned the favour. He shepherded him away from the normal customs line of 'Alien' and 'Home', and towards the security desks. The chief cut a faintly ridiculous figure, small-ish and round with jet black (too black?) hair, and ludicrously curlicued moustaches pointing out either side of his face. He even wore white gloves. Despite this, he carried himself with lashings of self-regard and arrogance. Still, he was smart.

The customs hall was busy, with people rushing to catch the London train, customs officers poking through suitcases, children crying, and the wet damp mist smell that brought home to Wiggins that he was, really, home. He strode straight up to a closed door behind the desks. 'Oi, you – sir!' one of the customs men shouted, but Wiggins pushed on unconcerned.

He opened the door. A pale-faced official looked up from his desk, pencil in hand. 'Watch out there, my man. No public allowed in here. Please leave, immediately.'

'I ain't public,' Wiggins said as he strode to the telephone. 'Clear out, I need to speak to the boss.'

'Constables,' the pale face cried, incredulous. 'Really, I must insist. Constable!' he shouted through the door.

'Get me Whitehall, 412,' Wiggins said into the horn as a large policeman appeared at the doorway.

'I don't care if he's with the Household Cavalry, get out of my office at once. Constable, there – take him away!'

Wiggins glanced unconcerned at the policeman, then handed the telephone back to pale face. The man listened for a moment, and then began to nod and nod again. 'But . . .' he tried, but was silenced into nodding once more. If anything his pale face paled even further. After a moment, he handed the telephone back to Wiggins. 'That's quite alright, constable, leave us now.'

'You an' all,' Wiggins shifted his head at the clerk. 'Oh, and see that little bloke there, with the moustache – let him through control, will you?'

'I . . . well, I'm not sure.'

Wiggins pointed at the telephone, and the pale-faced man nodded and went to leave. The Belgian, meanwhile, had witnessed this all from the doorway. He strode in, smiling, and offered a small, precise bow. '*Merci, Monsieur Wiggins, merci beaucoup.*'

Wiggins nodded, keen to get back to the telephone call.

'My plan is to be a, how you say, private detective?' the little man said. 'I would be honoured if, after this silly little war, you would come to work for me?'

'Nah mate,' Wiggins said, turning back to his call. 'There'll only ever be one great detective.'

Kell transferred his original Whitehall telephone number with him wherever he went. It was one of his first acts when he set up the Bureau, much to the annoyance of the operators at the telephone exchange. They'd insisted that he had a new office number if he changed addresses – the geographical anomaly too much to stomach for the engineers apparently – but he in turn had insisted that his Whitehall number be retained and any call to it be rerouted to Watergate House. Not that anyone was calling that Sunday. The situation on the continent was as dire as dire could be, and yet on that particular Sunday most of Whitehall had been enjoying the good weather in the countryside or on the golf course. Even Sir Edward Grey, the Foreign Secretary, was 'birdwatching and fishing' at his country abode, according to Carruthers, who seemed to be one of the only people at work that day at all in government, other than Kell and Simpkins, and a lowly clerk in each ministry dealing with the streams of telegrams coming off the wires.

Whitehall may have been taking an unearned break, but Reuters and the AFP were running red hot.

'It's him!' Simpkins cried just as Kell stared forlornly at an empty police report. The secretary ran in, pointing. 'On the telephone, sir, Agent W.'

'Where the hell have you been?' Kell cried, trying to hide the relief in his voice.

'Listen,' Wiggins crackled down the line. 'We don't have much time.'

'I know, I know. Have you got the book? Did you find Von Bork?'

'He's coming to London, tomorrow I reckon.'

'How do you know?'

'I invited him, of course.'

'Be serious, man. Are you on the drink again? You need to get back here at once, we need you – sober!'

'Nah, listen. I got one of his agents to send him a message – telling him that Karl Gustav Ernst and his post office have been discovered by British intelligence, that they've been monitoring him for months and that he needs to get back to rescue Ernst and close down the operation without poisoning the whole UK set-up.'

'You did what!' Kell exploded. 'Have you gone stark raving mad?'

'Keep your hair on, we don't have much time.'

'I can't believe it, I can't believe it,' Kell intoned to himself as he held the speaking horn away from his mouth for a moment. This is what it must feel like when your career collapses, he thought. 'You're worse than that bally doctor. Insanity, the pair of you.'

'What about the doctor?'

Jax liked the doctor. He was respectful, careful in how he spoke and, best of all, he paid on time. She hadn't seen

Wiggins in dust, and if it weren't for Watson she would have given the game up total.

Wiggins had paid her up front to help Watson follow up his names. That was why she'd been to the Blind Beggar, and that's why she had to go back. It was the only lead that smelled right. Trouble was, she got lifted – along with Constance – by the rozzers outside Bow Street and she spent a week in stir.

She wouldn't tell Wiggins if she saw him, but she kind of gave up on him a bit there. In Holloway, full of screams and misery, full of women on the fat end of the male world, with nothing left to chew. Constance got her out, and gave her a bed, and that seemed like best of all, especially since all she wanted to do was fight the fight. Then the doctor turned up to remind her she had a job, and she couldn't deny him.

This time, she didn't make the mistake of asking any of the men in the Blind Beggar the whereabouts of Archie Moreton. She waited outside in the breeze, and watched for her only ally in the pub. The old lady, the char who'd been cleaning and carrying out the back, the one seeming to do most of the work while the barman and his cronies drank and swore. The old lady had inclined her head just so when Jax had mentioned Archie's name, and that he was her dad.

The very same old lady exited the pub now, and began walking east down the 'chapel, towards the market. Jax quickened after her.

'Hello, ma,' she said at her elbow. 'Give you a hand with that.'

'Get off, you!' the old lady cried, pulling her basket away before taking a second look at Jax.

'Leave off, ma. I'm just giving you a helping is all. A help for a hand.'

The old lady squinted up at her, suspicious. The reason for the squint, Jax realised, was she only had one good eye. She must have come up on her blind side. 'You was in the other day,' the old lady said at last.

'I was so,' Jax said, taking the basket gently.

'You didn't buy no drink,' she barked, but began to walk on with Jax at her side.

'I didn't want no drink. I wanted Archie Moreton.'

'He really your father?'

'What, you think he's got *me* in the family way?'

The old lady hesitated, then burst into cackling laughter, like rifle fire.

'Listen, ma.' Jax leaned in to the old lady as they approached the hubbub of the market, with its smell of burning chestnuts, and the barrow boy cries. 'I don't know if he is or he isn't. All I know is my old dear – departed – told me she thought it might be him, 'fore he went inside.'

'Might be?'

'Well, that says more about my old dear than him, rest her soul. I ain't sure, either way, but I fancy to meet him, look into his eyes you know? Touch him for a bob or two.'

She'd felt bad, lying to the old woman like that. She also felt bad for lying about her own mother. Sal wasn't dead for one thing, she was still running a caff for cabbies out by Waterloo, empress of her domain. That's what the cabbies called her behind her back – the Empress of Waterloo. For all that, Sal had never told Jax who her father was. She'd only been about fifteen or sixteen when Jax was born, so it probably wasn't a very happy subject.

The old lady hadn't known where Archie Moreton lived, but she did know where he drank regularly – which was the same thing, really, certainly for that class of person. Jax had run the ex-con to ground at the Old Number 9 in Hoxton, a rough old boozer but one that had theatrical pretentions, as it was opposite the theatre.

She checked her facts – he was in there two days running – but she did not approach him. Moreton was a tall, wiry man who drank often but who never got drunk. He had leathery brown skin that hung loose around his neck, and small shifting eyes. Each time he left the Old Number 9 he would look about him carefully and then lope off into the night, always with an eye over his shoulder. Following him was not a job Jax relished. Down Hoxton everyone thought you were a whore, even if you dressed posh – especially if you dressed posh – and she didn't like sticking around. It was job done, as far as she was concerned – find a man's local and you've found the man.

'But where does he live, miss, where do we find him?' Doctor Watson had urged, when she reported all this back. 'Did you follow him anywhere else?'

'Once,' Jax said, and began to tell him the story of when she followed Archie north from the Old Number 9.

It was a story Doctor Watson then told enthusiastically to Captain Vernon Kell. A story that Kell found himself, rather less enthusiastically, having to regurgitate over the telephone to Wiggins in Dover.

'Does it really matter what Watson said?' Kell asked, irritated. 'If you must know, he's been peddling some cock-and-bull story about Holmes's supposed assassin.'

'What did he say?'

'Nonsense, all nonsense. He had this nobody followed – an ex-con who Holmes convicted.'

'By Jax, yeah? I asked her to help.'

'You! Is everyone working for you? Watson, Jax – my wife, by god?' He was sick, utterly sick of people acting as if they were cleverer than him. Wiggins, Constance, Mrs Jepson and even bloody Doctor Watson. And now it seemed Wiggins was operating a shadow service, under his very nose.

'It works best if everyone does as they're told.' Wiggins's voice sounded even and calm over the telephone, but he got to the point quickly. 'What did Doctor Watson say?'

'The girl, Jax, followed this man into a barber's shop and he came out again without getting a haircut. That's it, the sum total of this supposed vital intelligence. You know, I really might laugh about it if it wasn't all the end of my blasted career. They'll probably send me off to head a platoon of native troops in Bechuanaland or some such. I can't believe you gave up Ernst,' he almost wailed.

There was a slight pause on the line, a crackle and shift. 'Which barber's shop was it?' Wiggins asked.

'I didn't ask. You're not seriously suggesting . . .'

'It's a curious incident,' Wiggins said. 'Of a haircut.'

'There was no haircut.'

'That's the curious incident.'

'I don't follow.'

'Luckily Jax did. I'd bet your pension that barbershop is Ernst's. Set a twenty-four-hour tail on the bloke as soon as – get Jax to do it if you can, at least the daytime shift.'

'Oh righto, yes of course. Is there anything else you'd like me to do?'

'We're gonna get Von Bork, sir.' Wiggins added the sir almost sarcastically. 'But you have to do exactly as I say.'

As Wiggins travelled northward to London from Dover, Sunday 26 July 1914 drew to a close. Sir Edward Grey had indeed spent the day birdwatching, but he did nevertheless send messages to his counterparts in the governments of those 'Great Powers' not yet fully involved in the Balkan crisis: Germany, France and Italy. Can we not, he asked, mediate between Austria-Hungary and Serbia? Can we not stop them fighting? In Vienna, meanwhile, Foreign Minister Leopold Berchtold is ready to declare war. The chief of the general staff, von Hötzendorf, stills his hand a moment, for the Empire's army is not quite ready.

18

Monday 27 July 1914. The London press is full of the dramatic news in Dublin. British soldiers fired on a 'rioting' crowd of nationalists, killing four and maiming many more. Foreign Secretary Grey is increasingly exasperated about the situation in Europe. He tells the German ambassador that any move by Austria-Hungary on Serbia will cast it as a clear aggressor. The ambassador reports back to Berlin: 'If we should have a war, Great Britain is against us.' Berlin thinks this response is just 'for show'.

'This is pointless,' Kell said, for the third time that night. 'He's not doing anything.'

'He will,' Wiggins said.

The two men sat in the back of a plain police car, watching Karl Ernst's barber's shop on the Caledonian Road. They'd been there over two hours, and night had fallen. Warm rain lashed the windscreen, and the gutters ran full. It sheeted down.

'Won't Von Bork have warned him by now?'

'How? He thinks he's blown. No, Von Bork's coming for him. What's the opposite of infiltration?'

'Exfiltration, I'd say, if you were following the rules of the language, though it's—'

'That's it,' Wiggins interrupted. 'Exfiltration. He's doing an ex-fil. They'll 'ave some protocol, some plan, won't they? Von Bork's too smart not to 'ave a plan.'

'And you're sure Von Bork will come himself?'

'I know he will. Moment he puts on that accent, them clothes, he's as English as you and me, and he knows it. Loves himself for it too, thinks he can stroll around anywhere he pleases. I'm the only one who knows what he looks like – me and Mr Holmes, and Archibald Moreton.'

'You're sure Doctor Watson was right about that?'

'He went into *this* barber's shop, without getting a cut? Do me a favour. You've got people on him now, right?'

'Yes. Jax led us straight to him. Remarkable girl, her, actually. My wife has taken her under her wing.'

'Sign her up.'

'I tried. She said she'd only take orders from you. Or Constance.'

'Where is he now?' Wiggins asked, back on Archie.

'He's been out twice today, at the last report. Once to a garage in Hammersmith, and once to an unremarkable side street just north of Aldwych.'

'Did he do anything there?'

'No. He strolled around the area for five or ten minutes, then left to go back home.'

'Curious, you reckon?'

'I think he's done nothing out of the ordinary. And neither has Ernst by the look of it. Now, I don't like repeating myself but you said you had proof of the German intent to mobilise. I need to get that to the cabinet at once.'

'We get Von Bork, or you get nothing.'

'But we may never get Von Bork!'

'Look. It's two hours after closing time, ain't you noticed? The lights are still on, he ain't gone home, his lad's still there. Believe me. . .'

At that moment, Ernst's lad – the assistant Wiggins had sent out to get him his lunch less than a month ago – came out into the street, into the squall. He wore a great overcoat, despite the warm evening, and held in his hand a large cloth bundle, clearly visible from the light in the shop window. He stood on the pavement, waiting for a cab. Wiggins noticed he also had something bulky in one of the great coat pockets.

'Start her up,' Wiggins growled to the police driver.

The lad finally hailed a motor cab. He got in, but left the door open. A moment later, Ernst himself came out and hurriedly got in. He left the lights on in his shop. As the cab pulled away from the kerb Wiggins said, 'This is it.'

They trailed the cab south towards King's Cross. At the bottom of the Caledonian Road it turned right towards the station, pushing through the tangle of motor, horse and foot traffic that congregated around the great terminus, day or night. Wiggins instinctively opened the car door on his side, and held onto it. If Ernst were ever going to evade a tail, he would do it in such a place.

The cab suddenly swung round in a traffic-stopping U-turn in the middle of the street. It pulled up alongside the head of the taxi rank outside the station. A form in a great coat with a bundle got out of the cab and flitted into another one. Almost instantly, both cabs accelerated away, the original cab veering right and the new one going straight on.

'The assistant's changed cars,' Kell cried. 'Follow the original car.'

'No he ain't,' Wiggins yelled, jumping out of the police car as it started to turn right. He hailed a cab going past.

'I'm with Waterloo Sal,' he shouted at the cabby as he climbed onto the running board. 'Follow that cab.' He dashed the rain from his brow, his hat already gone. He only had a trench coat for protection now.

The cabby nodded and crunched though the gears. As he did so, Kell leaped onto the board behind Wiggins. Wiggins shouted back to him as the car picked up speed. 'The lad didn't change cars, he changed clothes. Ernst's in the big coat now.'

'The car's following the assistant,' Kell said. 'Just in case.'

Tap tap tap. 'Excuse me,' a voice piped up from inside the taxi. 'This taxicab is taken, don't you know?'

Kell peered through the glass. A young dandy, in top hat, tails and white gloves, stared back at him.

'This is most inconvenient. I'm due at the Cave of the Golden Calf at ten thirty. Nancy will be most put out if I'm late, I won't hear the end of it.'

'You won't hear the end of it if you end up in a police cell, will you?' Kell snapped.

Ernst's taxi went down Pentonville Road, then right at the Angel, then right again, almost back in on itself, into the small roads, hidden squares and alleyways of Clerken-well. 'Alright, cocker,' Wiggins said to the driver through the window. 'Kill your lights, we're almost there.'

Sure enough, Ernst's cab pulled up. He got out and watched as the cab drove off, rain pooling at his feet. He looked around, then took a right down a pedestrian alleyway.

Wiggins tapped the roof of the cab and leaned into the window. 'Ta for that. Tell Sal to give you a free sarnie, on Wiggins.'

'No need,' the cabby said. 'A friend of the Empress is a friend of mine.'

'Are we ever going to get to the Cave?' a plaintive voice called from the back.

'Charge him the full fare,' Kell said to the driver and glared at the foppish passenger.

He and Wiggins paced down the street after Ernst. 'I'll find the beat policeman,' Kell whispered. 'Every bobby in London's been told to expect a word from me or you.'

Wiggins nodded and turned down the alleyway. He could just make out the barber's pot-bellied form, made massive in shadow by a softly burning gas lamp at the far end. Wiggins knew this part of London – he'd even chased a Latvian revolutionary through these very streets five years earlier. Ernst headed into a small square at the end, no bigger than a courtyard really, with a solitary lamp post, two alleys leading off it and not much else. The office buildings were dark and clearly closed up.

'Karl.' Wiggins heard the voice coming out of the distance. 'Good of you to make it. Were you followed?' It was Von Bork, using the English squire persona once more.

'No,' the barber said, as Wiggins crept down the alleyway, approaching the now stationary Ernst from behind. 'Can't we speak German? I long to speak German.'

'A few hours more, my friend, just . . . hey!' Von Bork cried, for Wiggins grabbed hold of Ernst from behind. He held him by the neck, and thrust a cosh into his side to imitate a gun. Wiggins never carried a gun.

'How do, cocker?' Wiggins called across the square. 'Game's up, I think. Don't you?'

'Ah good evening, old boy.' Von Bork grinned almost, a ghastly sight under that pale gas lamp. 'I see you must have got to Martha. A clever message. Stupid whore, she'll die for that.' He saw Wiggins flinch at the mention of her, and went on. 'But I think I've got the advantage of you. You see?' He held out a revolver. 'I know you have no gun.'

Wiggins glanced back. At the far end of the alley, Kell appeared with two policemen in tow, their torchlights jagging in the wet. They started running, and the whistles blew.

'Karl will tell you nothing,' Von Bork said flatly, then fired the gun. The first shot missed but the second caught Ernst full on, he slumped back into Wiggins's arms.

Wiggins cushioned the big barber to the floor as blood pumped from his shoulder. He looked up, just as Kell and one of the coppers sped past – after Von Bork. 'Far corner,' Wiggins cried as he laid down the bleeding Ernst. 'Stay here,' he said to the other policeman. 'Press on the wound, like this.' He then ran after Kell.

Wiggins dashed down the far alley, then rounded a corner to find Kell and the policeman standing, facing each other in bemusement. The constable held up his torch to Wiggins as if to say, what do you make of it?

'He came down here,' Kell said. 'I swear it. But now, he's disappeared.' And he had. The mysterious thing was, the alleyway they were in led to a dead end. Or rather, the back of a building, with buildings on either side, and no doorways or windows. It was one of those anomalies of the old city, a pointless by-blow of expansion. The policeman cast his light high, to show Wiggins that there was no way Von Bork could have climbed his way to freedom.

But Wiggins wasn't looking up – he was looking down beneath Kell's feet. 'Off,' he cried, pushing his boss aside. He knelt down to the circular manhole in the middle of the alley. 'Penknife,' he said, thrusting his hand out to Kell, and, 'Torch,' to the copper.

In seconds, Wiggins had pulled up the cover and was preparing to go down the ladder. 'What are you doing?' Kell asked, as Wiggins gestured for the policeman to hand over the torch.

'This was his plan,' Wiggins replied. 'It's the ex-fil. He was meant to take Ernst down here – check his pockets, I bet he's got a torch on him. They'll pop up somewhere else, probably with a lift waiting for them, and off.'

'But, how?' Kell coughed, suddenly aware of the smell.

'It's a brilliant way to get out, so it is – now, you coming?'

'Er, I'll wait here and coordinate.'

'Keep a man here, and make sure the others stay on Archie.' And with that, Wiggins was gone, down into the dark, mephitic underbelly of the city, one of Victorian Britain's greatest achievements: the London sewage system.

It wasn't just the smell that got you down there, the deep nose-numbing stench of shit and piss, old and new, and rotting rats and live ones, and food, and rubbish and all sorts; it was the wet and the dark, and the enclosed space. Wiggins dropped down into the first tunnel, up to his knees in foul water. He cast the torch left and right, and looked as far as he could down the long, brick circular tunnel that was just above his height in the middle.

'It's the sounds,' his friend, the sewage sweeper Tosher, told him once over a pint at the Kings Arms. 'It's different down there. Travels further, down them pipes, with the water an' all. You can never be quiet neither, not if someone's listening close. You can hear *everything*, for miles.'

And so Wiggins listened close, listened over the drip, drip, drip from the ceiling, over the running water of a distant storm drain, over the thudding of his heart. And there it was – *swish, swash, swish, swash* – the sound of a man wading through water.

He set off at a jog. Twice more, he had to stop – at splits in the tunnels – wait, and listen again. He went through two small tunnels and as he went deeper, darker, downwards into that wet hell, he knew he was getting nearer. The sounds of the swishing became louder and louder. Wiggins came into a big underground chamber, with three different levels. It was almost like a religious building, the scale, the magnificent arched brickwork. As he raked his torch around, he saw a sewer up high, dropping down into a large storm drain. It rushed thick and fast with rainwater that night and for a moment Wiggins lost his bearings. With the sound of the drain, and two possible tunnels to follow, he found he could hear Von Bork no longer.

Then, at the last, as he peered down one of his options, he saw the flash of a torch, a long way off. It jiggled and veered, but didn't move forward. Von Bork was at his exit. Wiggins turned off his own torch, and inched towards the jagging of the light.

'Archie!' Von Bork's voice echoed down the tunnel, followed by a loud metallic banging. 'Archie, are you there, old boy?'

Wiggins reached the corner and looked up. A long shallow staircase disappeared upwards towards a landing. On the landing a ladder rose, presumably to the street, though Wiggins could barely make it out. Von Bork must have attached the torch to his side, for the light swung and jiggled as he rose. Wiggins hurried up the stairs.

He could see Von Bork tugging at the manhole cover from below, his arms stretched up above him. A loud scraping noise followed, then he heard, 'Archie, I – what! *Mein Gott!*'

Von Bork pulled something from his pocket.

BANG! BANG!

The muzzle flash lit up Von Bork like a camera. The sounds of the shots cascaded down the stairway towards Wiggins.

Von Bork clattered down to the foot of the ladder and stumbled, his hand still clutching the gun. Kell's men had obviously stepped in when they saw Archie open the manhole. And now Von Bork was barrelling down the stairs in headlong panic – the torch clipped to his belt sending a flashing crazy light along the walls. He barely saw Wiggins before the two collided.

They fell, rolling down that staircase, clinging together like farewelling lovers. Wiggins landed on his back in the water, while Von Bork was thrown clear. In a second he was up and running. The torch continued to cast strange, jumping shapes.

Wiggins gave chase. 'It's no good,' he cried. 'It's over.' His voice rolled down the tunnel towards Von Bork.

Suddenly, the jumping light stopped. Von Bork hesitated. Wiggins peered along the tunnel. He'd kept his own torch dark, and as he stepped forward he saw Von Bork turn back towards him. For he stood on the edge of some precipice, the sewage at his feet dropping down presumably into a bigger flow.

'It's Wiggins,' he shouted. 'You hear, you German bastard. There with your fucking torch. I'm Wiggins,' he shouted again, and squatted down. 'I don't need that shit.'

'What are you talking about?' Von Bork replied. 'Come into the light, like a man.'

BOOM, BOOM – the bullets pinged off the brick tunnel, over Wiggins's head, then a last BOOM – that rang and crashed and echoed around his ears.

Wiggins stood up and walked towards the light, towards Von Bork. 'That's your lot,' he said. 'You ain't nothing without your pop gun.'

Von Bork squeezed the trigger again, to an empty click, to make the point. 'There's still time, old boy. If you help me escape, you know I'll pay you well. The whore Martha, I'll spare her – Mata Hari too, for that matter, I know—'

Wiggins charged, roaring. He caught Von Bork about the midriff and they crashed to the floor. The sewage was a foot deep around them as they tussled. Von Bork struggled to hit him with the butt of the gun, but Wiggins wrenched it clear.

He was a big man, though – bigger and stronger than Wiggins, and in better shape. Wiggins was tired. Von Bork flipped over, and pinned him down by his main weight. 'Wiggins, *mein Gott*. You will die if you don't help me.'

Wiggins brought his knee up into Von Bork's balls with a vicious squelch, and heaved him over his head with a grunt. The torch flashed and fizzled, Von Bork countered with an elbow to the head, but Wiggins managed to haul him up in a bartitsu hold, like a half nelson in wrestling.

By this time, they'd reached back to the end of the tunnel, where Von Bork had first stopped and turned, and where the small tunnel's sewage fell into the big drain many yards below.

They tottered together upon the brink of the fall. 'We'll both die,' Von Bork croaked, as Wiggins squeezed the life out of him.

'I'm tired,' Wiggins grunted.

Von Bork made one last massive heave and, together, they fell into the abyss.

WHOOSH – into the rushing whirl they went – deep down. The impact was terrific. Von Bork took the full brunt as they twisted and turned in the air.

Now they struggled under the roaring tide. They were in the main storm drain. Von Bork tried to push Wiggins's head under, but his weight mattered less now. Wiggins pulled him down – 'keep your mouth shut, keep your mouth shut!' Tosher's warning in his ears – as they writhed and twisted.

The current increased as they went eastwards and downwards, in the dark shit stream. But Von Bork was injured. Wiggins felt the weakness in him, heard him gulp in the liquid death, the life spluttering out of him as they swayed and dashed the sides of the tunnel in the pitch black.

Suddenly, the stream dropped over a cliff edge and they careered down in the waterfall of dark nothingness. Von Bork's head crunched off the side of the tunnel as they landed back in the drink, and Wiggins felt the big man sag.

Finally, Von Bork spluttered no more. Wiggins held onto him still, as they were carried forward by the current. He held on and closed his eyes, and waited for his own end.

'Watch out there!' a voice cried. 'Plunder!'

Wiggins jerked his eyes open. Up ahead, a light in the tunnel. The current was still strong, but he found he could put his feet to the floor. Von Bork's body was sagging by his side.

'Wiggins,' Tosher shouted. 'Is that you?'

'Course it is,' he croaked. 'You diddycoy fuck!'

In seconds, Tosher waded into the soup and dragged Wiggins onto a platform that opened out to the side of the drain. A lantern swung this way and that off a nail, and a dark staircase opened upwards from the platform. 'Get that body!' Wiggins rasped.

'Did you keep your mouth shut?' Tosher cried.

Wiggins nodded. He got out onto the platform and lay flat, breathing heavily. The lantern cast a golden glow. He listened as Tosher hauled Von Bork's body out of the drain and onto the platform. This was Tosher's domain, and he moved steady and deft, with the strength of ten men. 'Thank you,' Wiggins said at last. 'How did you know I'd be here?'

'When ya told me to watch out for you, you said if it happened it would probably be north of the river, right? Well, all the shit in north London eventually comes to Abbey Mills, this way – gravity, ain't it, like Isaac Newton and his apple? – so I started along here and worked up. This is where it ends. This is where it always ends. Then I heard you screaming, something rotten so it was. Why did you shout your name like that?'

'So you knew it was me, you div.'

'Who's the cadaver?'

'A nasty fucking bastard, that's who. Here roll him, will ya, I'm knackered. He should have decent dosh on him, and a notebook.'

It didn't take long for Tosher to pick Von Bork clean. Glasses, tobacco pouch, wallet – stuffed with notes – a cigarette case and lighter, a tortoiseshell comb. A treasure trove. 'Blimey,' Tosher said. 'I can live off this for weeks.'

'It's all yours,' Wiggins said. 'Just give me that notebook, and take me to the streets. I ain't ever coming back down here again.'

Wiggins stood up, and looked down at Von Bork's bedraggled body. He didn't look like an English squire now, nor a German spy, nor even the murderer he was. He looked like dead men always do. 'There ain't nothing to celebrate here,' Wiggins muttered, as Tosher pitched the corpse back into the water.

'You stink, I can't – ugh.' Kell gagged. 'Might you change first?'

'Let's do it now,' Wiggins said, sitting in the back of the car next to Kell as the car sped down the Strand. His clothes were sodden with sewage, his hair a shitty tangle, and his body crying out with exhaustion. 'They need to see what it takes, what it is. He needs to know what a spy is.'

The car rolled through a near-deserted Trafalgar Square – St Martin-in-the-Fields had just struck 2 a.m. – and slewed to a halt at Admiralty Arch. 'Take it straight to the depot,' Kell told the driver through his handkerchief as they got out. 'And for heaven's sake get it cleaned, will you, otherwise I'll never hear the end of it.'

They entered through a small door in the side of the great arch – which was more like three arches strung together – holding up a huge double-storey building that operated as the offices and private apartments of the First Lord of the Admiralty.

'Good god, Kell, what the devil are you doing here at this time?' Churchill said, once the footman had woken him up.

Kell stood, drinking down a whisky from the cabinet in Churchill's huge office. It overlooked Trafalgar Square on one side and the Mall on the other. As the First Sea Lord came in, Kell was in the act of passing a tumbler to Wiggins. 'It's war,' Kell said simply.

'Here, pour me one of those, will you,' Churchill said. 'What in heaven's name is that smell?'

'That would be me,' Wiggins said, turning to look at the famous politician for the first time.

'And you are?'

'Agent W, you know me as, I reckon. And I'm here to tell you Germany is going to war.' He drew from his pocket Von Bork's notebook and gave it to Kell, who took it in his handkerchief. 'That's a list of all the major German agents working in Britain – over twenty, think of that, twenty! And this one's for you, personal like. Captain Kell tells me that none of you bigwigs think there's any danger of all-out war – well, look at that. That came from the German Admiralty in Berlin less than a week ago – check the date – they're on for it.'

Churchill grasped the order that Bywater and Wiggins between them had stolen from Bruno. He read it quickly and immediately began bawling at his staff members to get Number 10 on the line. 'It's the proof, Kell, the evidence!'

Wiggins turned and looked out of the window, back over the south side of Trafalgar Square and up the Strand past Charing Cross. 'Fleet Street beyond,' Kell muttered by his side. 'Winston always likes to have an eye on Fleet Street.'

Churchill cried out in exhalation as he put the telephone back down on his desk. 'The PM agrees. I have ordered the Fleet to Scapa Flow, to battle stations. Everything tends towards catastrophe and collapse.'

'And yet,' Kell said, turning to him, 'you seem interested, geared up and happy.'

'Is it not horrible to be built like that?' Churchill replied, unabashed.

Wiggins looked from one man to the other and back again, then down at his own hands. Horrible indeed.

19

Tuesday 28 July 1914: Austria-Hungary declares war on Serbia at 11 a.m. The declaration is delivered by telegram, a first in the history of warfare.

Captain Vernon Kell of the Secret Intelligence Bureau in London sends out to police around the country the arrest list of German agents, to be actioned on the eve of war.

Wednesday 29 July 1914: The Austrian SMS Bodrog bombards Belgrade. The first shots of the war.

The German ambassador issues a warning in Saint Petersburg. If Russia continues her military preparations, then Germany will be forced to mobilise. At 9 p.m. Tsar Nicholas calls a halt to full mobilisation, at the request of his cousin Willy, the Kaiser.

Thursday 30 July 1914: Faced with advice that his dynasty could fall if Russia doesn't act like a Great Power, the Tsar orders full mobilisation. The British press finally decides to cover the growing crisis in Europe, although there is no suggestion that Britain will become involved.

Friday 31 July 1914: The Kaiser discovers his cousin 'Nicky' has in fact mobilised the Russian military. He suspects Britain of plotting against Germany. Germany orders full mobilisation and issues ultimatums to France and Russia, warning them to desist in war preparations. In Paris, Socialist leader Jean Jaurès, who has called for a worldwide general strike to stop the threat of war, is shot dead. Stock exchanges around the world are in freefall. Trading is suspended in London for the first time since 1773.

Saturday 1 August 1914: The French ambassador in London waits in vain for assurances from Sir Edward Grey that Britain will support France in the event of war. France mobilises its army. At 5 p.m. Germany declares war on Russia – a legal prerequisite for mobilisation.

Sunday 2 August 1914: In Brussels, the German ambassador delivers an ultimatum to the Belgian government: let our troops travel through the country, to prevent a French attack, or else consider yourselves our enemy. They have twenty-four hours to comply. The British government is split between those who wish to go to war to guarantee Belgian neutrality and those who do not. Sometime after midnight, Belgium delivers its reply: we resist.

Monday 3 August 1914: In Britain, a clear parliamentary majority is now in place to go to war, given the imminent invasion of Belgium. Only the small Labour Party and some Liberals disagree. In Paris, the German ambassador delivers Germany's declaration of war to the French PM. German military plans depend on defeating France so it can't help Russia, despite the fact that France has done nothing to provoke Germany. As he leaves, the ambassador hands the PM a private note: 'This is the suicide of Europe.' That night, Sir Edward Grey tells a colleague, 'The lamps are going out all over Europe, we shall not see them lit again in our lifetime.'

Tuesday 4 August 1914: At 11 a.m. the British cabinet sends an ultimatum to Germany – respect Belgian neutrality, or face war with Britain. The Kaiser fumes –

'neutrality is just a piece of paper' – but it is too
late. German troops have already invaded Belgium.

Under Kell's direction, police arrest twenty-one
of the twenty-two German spies in the UK. Only
one escapes.

At 11 p.m. Great Britain declares war on Germany.

Wiggins looked up at the cranes of County Hall. He looked
across at the Houses of Parliament and he waited by the rail
of the police steam launch for Doctor Watson. They drifted
mid-stream in the Thames on a grey windswept late morning. The river was at full tide, and it tossed and pitched, the
smoke whirling above them in flowery plumes.

'You remember,' Wiggins said, as the doctor came by his
side, an urn in his hands. 'The *Aurora*, was it? Mr Holmes
had us looking at every boat on the river, so he did.'

'The Sign of the Four,' Watson muttered. 'I called the
case. The Agra Treasure is still down there, somewhere in
the dark ooze of the river bed.'

They fell silent for moment, as a coal barge eased by in
the crowded riverway. Ahead and above them the clanging, whistling bustle of Charing Cross railway bridge, and
the station's pier just beyond. The doctor held up the urn
and placed it on the side of the boat. 'He expressly forbade
a marked grave or headstone in his will,' he said sadly.

'It's as good a place as any,' Wiggins replied. 'This is the
heart of London, and Mr Holmes was London in his heart.'

Watson nodded slightly, a tear appearing in his liquid eyes.
'He often said my stories turned him into an unrealistic, ide-
alised idol. I suppose he didn't want to be an idol in death.
"You build me up so much, Watson," he'd say. "I will forever
be a disappointment."'

'He ain't never been a disappointment,' Wiggins said. 'He was a legend. You and him together, made him a legend. Make sure he stays that way, will ya?'

'What do you mean?'

'Von Bork didn't kill him really, did he? You can't kill a legend. Not when you're here, doctor, not when you can write like you do.'

'I see, yes. Maybe I can think of something, when I am ready.' With that he held up the urn, glanced at Wiggins, and then emptied the ashes into the river.

When Watson was done, Wiggins stepped back away from the prow, to leave the old man his moment. A police sailor was at the wheel. Beside him, keeping a respectful distance from the doctor, Captain Vernon Kell. Wiggins shuffled back towards them.

'Are you ready?' Kell said.

'What, to fight your bastard war?'

'*I* didn't march on Belgium. That was Germany, remember.'

'This time. But you've all been playing the same game. Building warships, ripping off Africans, fighting over deserts, building more guns, preparing for war. You brought it on yourself.'

'That's quite wrong,' Kell bridled.

'You're right, that is wrong. You've brought it on me, you've brought it on half of Whitechapel; you've brought it on millions of poor sods, who'll die in a ditch cos the timetable had to be kept to, because honour must be satisfied, because it was easier to have a war than not.' Wiggins turned his head aside in disgust.

'But you'll stay? Dulce et decorum est pro patria mori, as the Latin has it.'

'I ain't Latin, I'm London. And that still smells like horse-shit to me.'

'But look at what they did.' Kell thrust his hand out, pointing along the launch, to the old man Watson, hunched over, cradling the empty urn, almost shaking with emotion as he looked out over the river. 'If you won't join me in the fight for King and country, surely you'll fight for him? For Holmes?'

Wiggins looked along the launch to Watson, a big man made small, then he looked back at Kell. 'For Holmes.'

Historical Notes

Sherlock Holmes and His Last Bow

It has always been assumed that Sherlock Holmes enjoyed a long, peaceful retirement in Sussex. This assumption stems partly from Doctor Watson's story *His Last Bow*. Published in 1917, it tells the story of how Sherlock Holmes had assumed the character of an Irish Republican, Altamont, how he'd set this up by going to America for two years, and how ultimately he bested the German superspy Von Bork. It is clear that Watson took Wiggins's advice, and created an alternative, more fitting, legacy for his great friend. It may not be factually correct, but who can grudge the good doctor his one deviation from historical accuracy.

Mata Hari

Born Margaretha Zelle in the Netherlands in 1876, by the time she met Wiggins, she'd been married to – and subsequently divorced – a Dutch army captain Rudolph Mac-Leod. She'd established herself in Paris as an exotic dancer and rose in fame, infamy and acclaim. During the First World War, however, with her dancing star beginning to fade, Mata Hari became associated with ever more dangerous rumours about her involvement in espionage, caused in part by the fact that, as a Dutch citizen, she could travel freely about Western Europe.

Whether or not she was a spy, and if so for whom and to what extent, has never been satisfactorily established. As with every story about Mata Hari, the picture is complicated by her own talents for self-invention, exaggeration and theatrics. What is a matter of historical record, however, is as follows: she was arrested in February 1917 (in the Hôtel Elysée Palace) for handing the names of suspected agents to the Germans, a charge formulated by Captain Georges Ladoux among others. At the heavily manipulated trial she was found guilty. She was executed by firing squad on 15 October 1917. She was forty-one years old.

The Baker Street Irregulars

In his own accounts of Sherlock Holmes, Doctor Watson briefly acknowledges the role of the Irregulars on three occasions. Young Wiggins is cited as the leader of the gang working on two cases – *A Study in Scarlet* and *The Sign of the Four* – while in a third case, Wiggins is mistakenly identified as 'Simpson'. Most historical sources are convinced that the Irregulars, and Wiggins in particular, played a far more substantial role in Holmes's work than Watson credits. This would be in keeping with the mores of the time, when it was rare for lower-class people – and street 'Arabs' or urchins in particular – to be given prominence.

Acknowledgements

My thanks to my agent Jemima Hunt, who has championed
Wiggins from the very beginning and who continues with
great expertise and enthusiasm to support him and his cre-
ator. My editors at Hodder, Nick Sayers – especially for his
patience – and Morgan Springett, thank you for believing
in the book and for working so hard to make it the best that
it can be. Thanks to Natalie Chen for the magnificent cover
design, Sadie Robinson for the eagle-eyed copy edit, Helen
Parham for proofreading, and to Kim Nyamhondera,
Olivia Robertshaw, and all the team at Hodder.

Thanks also to the team at Mobius: Amanda Harkness
in particular, but also James Whittaker, Rachael Hum and
Tayla Monturio.

There's a version of these acknowledgements where
I could list every book I read (or stole from) in order to
research this story. But freed from the constraints of a PhD,
I no longer make the kind of notes necessary to adequately
credit such works – and consequently, I fear that I might
insult by exclusion. If I insult everyone, then it hardly counts.
I will, though, tip my hat as ever to Sir Arthur Conan Doyle
who gave us the Great Detective and, of course, his dirty-
faced lieutenant in the first place.

Richard Ford's first piece of writing advice was 'marry
someone you love and who thinks you being a writer's a
good idea.' This is true. His second piece of writing advice

was 'don't have children,' which is baloney, and illustrates the one piece of writing advice I cling onto: don't take writing advice. I had barely published a word before my daughters were born, so I should thank them now. Thank you. The real point here is my partner, Annalise Davis, has always thought my being a writer was a good idea, and she thinks it still, which shows her sense of the absurd. She is my first reader, and the fact that she is very funny and very clever helps too. Thank you.

If you enjoyed *Spy Hunter*, why not try . . .

THE YEAR OF THE GUN

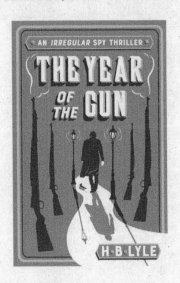

1912.

Released from the Secret Service, Wiggins sets out for New York and his lost lover Bela. But after an altercation on board, he finds himself among the low-life of Britain's poorest city, Dublin.

Wiggins falls in with gangster Patrick O'Connell and is soon driving the boss's girlfriend around town. Molly wants O'Connell to support her Irish nationalist cause - a cause needing guns to defeat the British - and then they go to find them in America.

Finally, Wiggins can solve the mystery of Bela - and meet his old mentor, Sherlock Holmes in a story of escalating intrigue, danger and violence.